LOST & FOUND CAFE

LOST & FOUND CAFE

A Sam Dawson Mystery

By

STEVEN W. HORN

Cheyenne, Wyoming
www.granitepeakpress.com

GRANITE PEAK PRESS^{Cheyenne}

Granite Peak Press
www.granitepeakpress.com

This book is a work of fiction. Names, characters, places, businesses, corporations, organizations, and incidents either are products of the author's imagination or are used fictitiously without any intent to describe their actual conduct. Any resemblance to actual events or locales or persons, living or dead, is entirely coincidental.

First printing 2025

ISBN: 978-0-9991248-6-4
LCCN: 2025937039

ATTENTION CORPORATIONS, UNIVERSITIES, COLLEGES, AND PROFESSIONAL ORGANIZATIONS: Quantity discounts are available on bulk purchases of this book for educational purposes. Special books or book excerpts can also be created to fit specific needs. For information, please contact Granite Peak Press, P.O. Box 2597, Cheyenne, WY 82003, or email: info@granitepeakpress.com.

Printed in the United States of America
10 9 8 7 6 5 4 3 2

For M^2

CHAPTER 1

Noon

Brad Holcomb

Winston Tucker was dead, and Brad Holcomb's left hand began to shake. "Breaking news as we come on the air at midday," the NBC news anchor had said with fabricated concern. "Winston Tucker, the failed presidential hopeful and charismatic CEO of one of the nation's largest trucking and shipping corporations, was found shot to death at his Wyoming ranch today."

Brad glanced around the cafe: three customers, a man and young woman in a booth, and a middle-aged woman with her back to the kitchen. They paid no attention to the dusty, vintage Sylvania portable television that hung above the cash register near the door. "Jessica's Theme" played on the Seeburg Wall-O-Matic jukebox, two plays for a quarter, which sat on the table of each booth. The piano solo from the movie *The Man from Snowy River* was Brad's favorite record on the playlist. The music competed with the noon news. "The eighty-six-year-old—, former secretary of defense—, Nixon insider—, Cambodia, Laos—, POW/MIA—, Republican frontrunner—, disgrace on the campaign trail—" were the soundbites that registered above the din of music and cafe clatter.

"Order up," Joe Dobransky, the weedy-looking owner and short-order cook barked as he turned from the grill toward the counter. He wiped his heavy spatula on a greasy towel that hung from the pocket of his soiled apron and stared up at the TV. "Ever wonder why wicked bastards like that prosper while the rest of us wallow in misery?"

"Is that a question, Joe?" Ida Faye said, picking up the plate with one hand and grabbing the coffee pot with the other. "Or are you just spouting off as usual?" Her Texas Panhandle accent always manifested when she challenged authority. The yellow smiley face button on the lapel of her only waitress uniform contrasted sharply with the stern look she gave her boss, her eyebrows crunched together.

"The Bible says it's fate," Joe said. "Ecclesiastes, I think. 'The race is not to the swift, nor the battle to the strong.' You don't have to be smart to be rich and fat. Just lucky; it's all a matter of chance, simple as that. Given enough time, it could happen to anybody," he said matter-of-factly and then pushed the bill of his Ranchway Feeds cap up with the business end of the spatula in his right hand. Since he had not shaved that morning, his salt-and-pepper beard stubble matched the shocks of hair that stuck out at right angles from beneath his hat.

Ida Faye paused, tipped her head sideways, and squinted at Joe. Her makeup and lipstick crudely masked her blackened eye and swollen, split lip. "That's horse pucky! Fate had nothing to do with his wealth. The man was egotistical, arrogant, a liar, a bully, a womanizer, and a murderer. He was as crooked as they come. He got what he deserved." She turned toward Brad. "Ain't that right, Brad?"

Brad ran misshapen, arthritic fingers through his thinning, gray-white hair. Bulging blue veins coursed across the backs of his hands. He looked down at the floor and softly said, "Not soon enough." He shuffled back into the kitchen, leaning precariously forward as he approached the sink filled with dirty dishes. He thought he might be sick. In the background, the TV news anchor continued to regurgitate and inflame: "Four hundred thousand dead in brutal Syrian civil war—, Surprising Brexit vote—, Racially charged Flint, Michigan water crisis—, Russian hacking of the Democratic National Committee—, Trump's nomination at the Republican Convention."

Outside, a noisy truck loaded with Wyoming cattle rushed east on U.S. Highway 20 into Nebraska. The cafe trembled. *Maybe it was the wind,* Brad thought as he slowly slipped his swollen hands into the hot dishwater. Lately, he had felt as if the earth was quaking, some seismic event that no one else seemed to notice. Maybe it was his body finally sighing with relief that the great Satan was dead. Thirteen years was a long time to plan.

⊶⊷⊷◉✠◉⊶⊷⊷

Ida Faye Mensinger

"Authorities in Lusk, Wyoming, were called to a disturbance at the Lamplighter Motel, where they discovered the body of a Texas man. They have described it as a crime scene and are releasing no details until next of kin has been notified." A young, corpulent, big-eyed brunette read the news from an unseen monitor, her eyes moving slowly right then darting back left like the carriage on a typewriter. She stuttered on words with more than two syllables. KNEP, the NBC affiliate serving Scottsbluff and the Nebraska panhandle, also provided local news for east-central Wyoming.

Joe and the diners had watched the animated discussion between Ida Faye and an officer who had been summoned outside by a man with a uniform and badge. The cook looked up with tired eyes at the grease-streaked TV then casually glanced around the cafe. He absently rubbed the stubble on his chin with his left hand, still holding the spatula in his right. No one was watching the television or him. Joe had told Ida Faye the television and rabbit ears antenna were high-tech investments for a cafe twenty miles from nowhere, where nothing ever happened, and even if something did happen, no one watched.

He had bought the abandoned Standard Oil station seven years earlier and turned it into the easternmost eating establishment in Wyoming. He informed everyone he would name it the State Line Cafe and paint the name in the deserted oval of the Standard Oil sign that loomed over the parking lot. Like so many of his projects, he never got around to it.

"Moving on to local news," the news anchor said with a disturbing smile, "a Scottsbluff City Council member has been arrested for driving a motor vehicle while intoxicated…"

Again, Joe looked out the window at Ida Faye. She stood in the cafe parking lot looking both bewildered and aggressive as a Niobrara County sheriff's pickup truck spun gravel and lurched onto U.S. 20 from the cafe parking lot and headed west toward Lusk.

Ida Faye rushed back into the cafe and made a beeline across the dining room and through the kitchen, her ever-present cowboy boots scuffing across the linoleum floor. She fumbled for the cigarette pack in her dress pocket. She pushed open the back door and flicked the disposable lighter in a fluid movement practiced a thousand times. She inhaled the smoke deeply and then bent over, placed her hands on her knees, and exhaled loudly. She shook her head.

"You all right?" Brad said, holding the door open with one hand and steadying himself against the frame with the other.

"It's finally over." She straightened up, not turning to face Brad. Her bruised eye and swollen lip were clearly visible. "Darrell is dead. Somebody killed the dirty rotten pup." Ida Faye never cursed. "They want me to come by the funeral home and identify him. I told them I never wanted to see him again, dead or alive." She pulled another drag on her cigarette then blew the smoke upward by funneling her lower lip outward. "They found a picture of me in his wallet and my address written on the back of a private investigator's card that was stuffed in his shirt pocket. The sheriff took one look at my face and said he wanted me to come by his office and answer some questions."

Brad said nothing. He maintained a neutral expression as he stared at his friend, his only friend. Ida Faye was a handsome woman, no longer beautiful and too old to be considered pretty. Trim and energetic, she moved quickly, seldom still. Her light brown hair was streaked with gray and cut short. In her early sixties, she was comfortable in her skin and could easily pass for a woman ten years younger. "Estranged" was the word she used in describing her marital status. Too afraid to seek a divorce from Darrell or involve the law, she had disappeared. A neighbor woman from Borger, a boom-and-bust oil town in the Texas Panhandle, had taken her northwest to Dumas, where she caught a bus and headed north through the Oklahoma Panhandle, eastern Colorado, and into Wyoming. That was six years ago.

"We knew he'd find you," Brad said quietly. "It was only a matter of time."

With a trembling hand, she brought her cigarette to her lips. She studied Brad's face as she blew smoke between them. "I'm glad he's dead. He was a monster. I've wished him dead for a third of my life, but—"

"No buts, Ida Faye. It's a good thing. No looking back, no second-guessing. Think about the future. That's what you tried to teach me. You're finally free."

"Is that how you do it, Brad?" she said accusingly. "You're not one to talk. You've been looking back for most of your life. I can't count the times I've told you to bury the past. The future doesn't wait forever. Look at us." She flicked the cigarette in an arc toward the dilapidated single-wide behind the cafe. "We've waited too long. The train has left the station. What are we going to do now?" Her eyes became glassy as tears formed.

"What the hell am I paying you two for?" Joe shouted from the back door. "We've got paying customers in here that need waiting, and dishes are piling up."

Ida Faye extended her middle finger in Joe's direction without looking at him. "Tell me, Brad, what do we do now?"

--=◉=⚓=◉=--

Jessica Martindale

Her father had disappeared. Jessica Martindale wanted answers. She had wanted them for a long time. Shock and disbelief had gradually yielded to frustration and anger. All these years later, she was still tormented. "Annoyed" seemed the perfect word, she thought, to describe her state of mind. She had felt annoyed for more than a decade. Noisy distractions always made her anxious. Jessica looked out the smudged cafe window at the stark reality of eastern Wyoming. She was a long way from home, in unfamiliar surroundings. "Jessica's Theme" had always soothed her. Not today. The competition with the drivel emanating from the television and the confusion of unintelligible conversations and the clatter of dishes put her on edge. "Jessica's Theme" ended on a high note with a plink of a piano key on the right side of the keyboard. There were no high notes in her life. A stalled career, unappreciative children, a messy divorce, and now this: another failed quest to find the truth about her father's disappearance.

"Here you go, hon," the waitress said, suddenly appearing and placing what appeared to be a chef's salad in front of her.

Jessica stared down at the iceberg lettuce, orange on the edges and slightly wilted that lay beneath globs of white dressing of uncertain origin. The waitress smelled of cigarette smoke.

"Can I get you anything else?" the waitress said with the same feigned sincerity as her smiley face button.

Jessica was tempted to say yes, a chef's salad. Instead, she shook her head and attempted a smile. The waitress had already turned away and noisily scuffed toward the kitchen. Jessica picked the cellophane-wrapped saltine crackers from the ooze and set them aside. She was no longer hungry. *Why here?* she thought as she looked around the bleak, wind-swept prairie. It was a hundred and eighty-eight miles out of her way. The drive from Laramie was not scenic. Perpetual drought seemed to be the norm. Most of Wyoming seemed to be a high mountain desert. This area, tucked against the Nebraska Panhandle just below the South Dakota state line, appeared to be more of a rolling prairie of luxurious western wheatgrass, blue grama, rank silver sage, and big sagebrush, where skinny-legged antelope with bulging eyes easily outnumbered people. The man she was supposed to meet here was working on some project nearby and had agreed to see her at this godforsaken cafe with a ceiling leak-stained with orange blotches like marigolds. She glanced at her Rolex. He was late.

Jessica had said goodbye to her boys in Laramie, the small southeastern Wyoming college town. The squalor of their apartment was like fingernails on a blackboard to her. She had raised them better than that. She had long suspected they chose the University of Wyoming to get away from her and Iowa. Valedictorian of her graduating high school class, Iowa State University was good enough for her, even though Business Administration was not the forte of the Land Grant University. An MBA from the Wharton School of Business had made her competitive. Pioneer Hi-Bred International had been good to her. Rising through the ranks, she was now vice president for domestic marketing with stock options and a six-figure salary. DuPont's bitter fight with Monsanto appeared to be over, yet she sensed trouble on the horizon as the public began rejecting genetically modified organisms. A frightened value-added manufacturing sector had begun splashing *No GMOs* over their packaging. Even products with no connection to the food industry had jumped on the no GMO bandwagon. The public, without a clue as to what a GMO was, seemed convinced they did not want it. The panic ran through the retail food industry like a virulent disease. Corn, wheat, and soybeans had been genetically modified since man's knuckle-dragging ancestors had experimented with an agrarian lifestyle. Pioneer's herbicide-resistant grain seeds were now suspect in causing every malady afflicting humankind. The fear had even surpassed the wheat gluten allergy that everyone seemed to have. Jessica no longer had patience for the spoiled public's ignorance. Pioneer had noticed. They wanted fresh ideas. At forty-seven, she was considering retirement. She wondered if she would still be annoyed.

-→⊢◉ ✖ ◉⊣←-

Sidney Dawson

Her mother had died a horrible death, her throat sliced open by a psychopath, the same crazed killer that had twice kidnapped Sidney in an attempt to exact revenge on her father. Three years was not enough time to forget or forgive. She had tried hard not to hold her father's youthful mistakes responsible for her now countless fears and depression. He, too, had been a victim. She looked across the table that divided the booth. Her father, Sam Dawson, was as imperfect as they come. Still, she loved him as only a daughter could. He had struggled financially to put her through college, then law school. All the while, he had picked up the tab for the progressive disease that would eventually render her deaf and blind. It pained her deeply that she was still dependent on him, at least physically. At thirty-two, it was her turn to struggle financially. It was not from lack of money. Her mother's family fortune was now hers. Sidney and her father had never spoken about her multimillionaire status. Her struggle was how to help Sam financially without hurting his pride. She was well aware that pride can be a tricky emotion.

Sidney had been barely six years old when her parents divorced. Her father had made a decent living photographing lost and abandoned cemeteries and scenic mountain vistas. Coffee table books, calendars, and greeting cards were the mainstay, now all victims of technology. Sales had plummeted as smartphones became ubiquitous. The *coup de grâce* was when his publisher canceled his contract and married Sidney's mother, Sam's ex-wife. Sidney now owned the publishing company.

"What brings you folks to the middle of nowhere?" the waitress said somewhat perfunctorily as she sloshed water and ice into their scratched plastic tumblers from the side of the pitcher she was holding. "Don't tell me it's the scenic beauty of this godforsaken country."

Both Sidney and her father stared up at the bruised waitress, their mouths full from the burgers they had ordered earlier. They did not respond. Instead, they turned their heads and looked out the grease-streaked window at the featureless expanse of high-plains desert and short-grass prairie where the horizon met the earth quickly then disappeared.

"Sorry," the waitress said, looking first at the young woman then the man. "It wasn't a trick question." She smiled politely. "I'm afraid your time is up. Let's move on to the bonus question: would you care for dessert?"

"I know the answer to that one," Sidney said quickly. "Nothing for me, thanks. My dad will have a slice of that coconut cream pie that he's been eyeballing since we walked in."

"You win, sir. There's a woman over in Van Tassell, a few miles from here," she pitched her head to the left, "who makes our pies fresh almost every other week."

Sidney could not stifle a laugh at the waitress's gentle humor and lighthearted mood. It had only been minutes earlier when the woman stormed into the cafe from the parking lot and disappeared into the kitchen. "There's a town near here?"

"Sort of. Besides me, there are fourteen other people who supposedly live there. I ain't met 'em all yet. I've only been there six years. It's more of a crossroads where 159 heads south off of U.S. 20. We've had us a post office since 1910. Van Tassell has the distinction of being the least populated town in the least populated county in the least populated state in the U.S. Like I said before, it's the middle of nowhere."

Sidney and Sam continued to stare up at her.

"I'll bring that pie right over. Maybe," she added as she turned and walked away, her boots clacking noisily across the floor.

"Is that the place you're looking for, Pop?"

Sam shook his head. "The Historical Society believes I missed a cemetery here in Niobrara County. If you'll remember the convoluted funding scenario, it was Wyoming State Parks and Cultural Resources, using pass-through money from the county commissioners, that actually contracted with me to catalog and take photographs of all the cemeteries in the state. They believed there were a total of approximately one hundred and sixty cemeteries. I said I could do it in three years."

Sidney smiled. She remembered the contract well. "It took you a little longer. I believe there were three contract extensions, if I remember correctly."

"Yes, well, we had some unforeseen situations arise."

"That's the understatement of the century, Pop," Sidney said with a crooked smile, referring to the near-death experiences she and her father had endured.

"Anyway, it's down the road to the west about a dozen miles, just a crossroads really, called Node. The cemetery is supposedly a couple miles south. I've seen it on Google Earth's satellite view. The resolution isn't good. I'm pretty sure there's something there."

"So, you missed one, huh?"

"Sweetie, I've missed dozens, if not hundreds. There are ghost-town cemeteries and family plots all over this state that have been neglected and abandoned. There are no records. Just to the northwest of here are two more cemeteries that very few people know of, Dellview Cemetery south of Manville and Jireh Cemetery toward Keeline to the west. I'll bet you didn't know there was a college out there in the middle of nowhere. The town of Jireh, which no longer exists, had a couple of banks, a post office, several general stores, a hotel, a blacksmith shop, and even a newspaper. All there is now is a historical marker. This area, like the rest of the state, had its booms and busts associated with mining, railroads, ranching, and oil and gas development. There are lost and forgotten cemeteries in every county of the state. My point is that as soon as you try to put out a listing of cemeteries, somebody screams to holy hell that you missed one. It's the nature of the business. State Parks knows it. They've got to respond because the state senator from this county called the director. It's now political. Their budget could be threatened. That's why we're here."

"Well, if anyone can find lost graves, it's you, Pop."

Her father squeezed his chin between his thumb and fore-finger. "I'm glad you decided to come along with me. I know how busy you are. It's nice to have a father-daughter getaway once in a while."

"Here you go," the waitress said as she placed a wedge of coconut cream pie in front of Sam. "I tasted that one, and it's still okay. I had to throw the rest of that one out. There was stuff growin' on it."

Sam looked up at her with wide eyes.

"It's on the house," the waitress said as if he were looking a gift horse in the mouth. "Actually, I jacked up the price of her cheeseburger to cover the cost of the pie," she said, gesturing with her thumb toward Sidney.

Sidney had to cover her mouth in order to avoid laughing out loud.

The waitress grinned from ear to ear. "Sorry. I'm just funnin' ya. I can't help being in such a playful mood. Some Good Samaritan killed my husband last night. Blunt-force trauma, they say. I say it's about time." With that, she turned and danced across the floor.

-*>=•★=•<-

Sam Dawson

Dying was so simple. Because she was a dog, she had no idea how beautiful she was. It was her eyes, amber windows that told you everything you needed to know. When she looked at you, all else blurred in the background, all the flaws. The light behind them disappeared quickly. The honey-colored irises that had sparkled like polished gemstones faded suddenly, dulled by fixed, dilated pupils. L2 was gone. Dying was so simple.

L2 had stopped eating and drinking. She had staggered toward her bed in the living room but flopped down on the cool tile of the kitchen floor instead. A puddle of urine appeared from beneath her. She panted from the effort or from the pain. They were indistinguishable. She was fifteen, old by bloodhound standards. Annie had surprised him with the eight-week-old puppy after the untimely death of her predecessor, Elle. L2 had been Sam's constant companion through all the trials and tribulations of being himself. She had been Sidney's girl friend and confidant in the isolated environment Sam had created. Someone had once asked, how can you love something that doesn't love you back? Sam was convinced that L2 loved both him and Sidney. She would sweep her thick tail back and forth across the floor expectantly and look at them as if they were the only beings left on Earth. It was dog love.

Father and daughter both broke down with emotion as L2's eyes faded. Sidney wrapped L2 in her favorite blanket, the one she covered her with at bedtime in the winter. Sam contributed the knotted sock with a tennis ball inside. It was her go-to toy. He steered the wheelbarrow down the hill from the deck toward the grave he had dug a week earlier. The aspen grove with a tiny seasonal stream was where he wanted his ashes spread. The fall colors were stunning. It was Sam's quiet place. In the summer, Indian paintbrush, columbine, pasque flowers, vetches, brown-eyed Susans, and purple lupines put on a colorful show beneath the quaking aspen that always made Sam smile. In October, he would lie on his back among the trees when their bright yellow leaves would float gently to the ground. In the spring, the stream spirits were plaintive, their sorrowful chatter unintelligible as the icy water trickled over smooth stones. Both L2 and Sam could rest there.

When all was done and the earth tamped tight, the rocks placed in a grave-like pattern complete with a flat-sided headstone, Sam and Sidney stood somberly over the grave, not knowing what to do with their hands. Neither talked; the spasms in their chests would not allow it.

Almost two years had passed since L2's death. Still, in the mornings when the red sky gave way to pink and finally orange, Sam would see her running between the trees, head down, scenting. At night, he heard her toenails on the floor as she padded from room to room, looking for him or Sidney. Her soft brown fur remained embedded in the front seat of the Willys, always a reminder.

"All I'm saying, Pop, is you might consider another dog," Sidney said as she poked a French fry into her mouth. "Maybe something a little smaller than a bloodhound, something that doesn't smell like dirty socks, something that doesn't throw spit clear to the ceiling, something that can actually bark rather than bay."

Sam was watching the local weather report on the television above the cafe's cash register. "Uh-huh," he managed. "Clouds are going to build by late afternoon. We'll need to find the cemetery, get the shots, then hightail it back to Cheyenne."

"Hightail it," Sidney said as she scrunched her eyebrows together. She looked out the cafe window at Sam's pride and joy, a classic Willys station wagon, parked in the gravel lot. "That thing hasn't hightailed it anywhere since 1953. It shakes so bad at speeds over sixty-five that we have to stop and get our kidneys repacked. We should have brought my pickup. It actually has a radio."

Sam ignored her. "They're predicting rain at home tonight."

"Do the windshield wipers work?" Sidney asked, her eyes wide with anticipation.

"They would if I could keep the cable on the pulley under the dash."

Sidney shook her head in disbelief. "Anyway, you might think about it."

"Think about what?"

"Getting another dog," she said.

"Why?"

"To keep you company on these road trips."

"That's what I have you for. You're not enjoying the father-daughter thing? You're not thinking about moving out again, are you?" he said, referring to her ill-fated attempt at independence two years earlier when a slick-talking Colorado Greenie had attempted to con her out of start-up money for a microbrewery he wanted to build in Cheyenne. When she saw through him and turned him down, he called her a dimwitted, four-eyed freak and stuck her with the check as he stormed out of the restaurant at Little America Hotel. She moved back in with Sam the next day.

"No, Pop, you're stuck with me for the time being. I'm just saying that another dog might be nice."

Sam looked out the cafe window. The stark parking lot had the remains of a narrow, crumbling cement island where gas pumps had once stood. Their rusted bolts poked upward, attesting to better times. The Willys and a late-model sedan with fleet tags from Colorado were beside each other. He could see L2 as plain as day sitting in the passenger seat of the Willys, a strand of drool hanging from the corner of her mouth as she waited for Sam to bring her a table scrap. Sam glanced at the only other customer, a woman who looked as wilted as the untouched salad in front of her. She, too, was looking at the Willys.

CHAPTER 2

12:08 p.m.

Brad Holcomb

Resting tremors were recurring reminders that he was not well. At first he had thought it was an earthquake. The world around him shook. The repetitive occurrence told him otherwise. The nightmares were premonitions of the hallucinations. He worried about delusions. From the open doorway to the kitchen, Brad turned his head sideways and stared through the cafe's front window at the Willys. He closed his eyes, counted to five, then opened them. It was still there. It was real. He remembered. Memories tormented him. They were all he had. He did not share them. Sometimes he floated within himself, adrift with the stranger he had become as he assumed different identities across the sparsely populated, forgotten heart of America. With each job, each acquaintance, with each new landscape, he had attempted to escape his ruined world. His only comfort was solitude as he sought equilibrium between the past and his uncertain future.

"Earth to Brad," Ida Faye said as she waved a hand in front of his face. "Are you all right?"

"Of course I'm all right," he snapped with a menacing look.

"Don't bite my head off, Brad. Did you get up on the wrong side of the galaxy this morning?" She cocked her head sideways and looked at him seriously. "Did you sleep okay?"

"How do I know? I was asleep." He attempted a smile. His face seemed paralyzed. He worried about his increased aggression and sudden anger. Ida Faye was his friend, the only person he had truly talked with in thirteen years. She had done what he thought no other woman could do: she had touched his heart. A heart that he was convinced was untouchable. Although he had not reciprocated her confidence, she was the only person he felt close to. It troubled him deeply when his uncontrolled anger flared. Ida Faye knew all about anger. Her battered body was testament to the lessons she bore. He had sought solace from her, and he had deceived her. "Sorry," he said. "I should be the one asking you if you're all right."

Ida Faye studied him for a moment. "Funny," she said, then her voice faltered. "I dreamed of this day for years. Now that it's here, I'm not sure how I feel. There's no grief, at least I don't think there is. Relief is what I feel. Yeah, I'm pretty sure that's what it is. It's hard to tell. My head is like one of those cheap little-kid kaleidoscopes you look through while twisting the thing. Images, lots of images, remembrances, I guess."

She pushed her hair behind her right ear and then shook her head. "He was a monster, you know, a rabid dog that would turn on me without warning." She attempted a laugh by huffing through her nose. "I thought I could change him. I told myself it was the drugs. He was always a mean, no-good SOB, even when he wasn't high or drunk."

She looked at Brad and smiled. "I know what you're thinking. Why'd I marry him? Besides being young and stupid, I was gullible. He filled my head with enough BS that I actually thought it might be true. The man promised me the moon. The only thing he gave me was gonorrhea. He told me he had a degree from Texas Tech in petroleum engineering and that he had invented some process that would revolutionize oil production. I found out later that he was nothing but a roughneck, a roustabout who never even graduated high school. He made his money selling dope. Here I was, the pride of Hutchinson County, Miss Texas Panhandle and the Boomtown Queen that held barrel racing records that stood for twenty-six years, married to a grafter who didn't have two nickels to rub together."

She took a deep breath and shook her head again. "My parents went to their graves disappointed with their only child." Her eyes suddenly filled with tears.

Brad took her hand in his and squeezed it softly. His lips parted, as if he were about to say something. He could not find the words.

"What happened to your hand?" Ida Faye said as she pulled his hand upward to inspect his swollen, red, and cut knuckles.

Brad pulled his hand away. "Nothing," he said, looking down. "The wind caught the door to the trailer last night and slammed it against my hand."

"You're both fired," Joe the cook interrupted, spatula in hand. "Now get the hell out of my cafe."

"Bite me, Joe," Ida Faye said, placing her hands on her hips. "Just who you gonna get to drive all the way out here and work in this sorry excuse for a restaurant and put up with your lip? Answer me that, big man."

Joe tucked his chin and was seemingly at a loss for words. "All right then, you leave me no choice. I'm putting you both on notice with letters of reprimand to be placed in your personnel files. Further, I'll instruct HR to reclassify your job descriptions to entry level and place you on disciplinary probation."

Ida Faye smiled and winked at Brad. "Whew! For a moment there I thought we were in big trouble." She picked up the water pitcher and headed for the lone woman.

"She's a beauty, ain't she," Joe said with a grin.

Brad nodded. "A '53 with a SM420 Chevy transmission, a Dana 44 rear end, a 4.27 gear ratio, and a Muncie overdrive. She's a beauty, all right."

Joe followed Brad's gaze from the kitchen door, out the cafe window at the Willys in the parking lot, then back at Brad. "I was referring to Ida Faye."

Brad turned to Joe and smiled. "So was I."

-->==◉ ✂ ◎==<--

Ida Faye Mensinger

Free at last, free at last. Thank God I'm free at last, Ida Faye thought to herself as she approached the stern woman who appeared uncomfortably wooden, as if hemorrhoidal. "Can I get you anything else?" she said with a smile as she filled the woman's water glass. A pickup truck pulling a flatbed trailer with a backhoe on it sped by on the highway, headed west. Its oversized tires produced an annoying hum that caused both women to look up and out the window. Ida Faye hoped it was headed to Lusk to dig a deep hole to bury her husband. Jessica Martindale hoped it was the man she was supposed to meet. She looked at her watch.

"Could I have a cup of tea, please?" Jessica attempted a smile.

"Surely. Would you care for black or green tea?" Ida Faye was the only person who drank tea within a thousand square miles. No one had asked for tea in months. She worried that the green tea had been thrown out last winter when mice chewed through the box.

"Earl Grey if you have it."

"The box says Lipton. Will that work?"

Jessica looked at Ida Faye as if she were a child. "I believe Earl Grey is a blend, not a brand, and yes, that would be fine," she said.

"Coming up." Ida Faye grinned and rushed off to the kitchen.

Joe was zipping up his fly under his apron as he stepped from the tiny unisex restroom near the far end of the counter. The men's and ladies' restrooms originally had been accessed from the outside at opposite sides of the gas station. The women's room had been lost during the remodel nearly fifty years earlier. The cracked and chipped fixtures were the originals from the late thirties. The single cold-water line served both the toilet and sink. Rusty orange stains in both fixtures were permanent.

"Christ in a nighty, Joe," Ida Faye said, putting her hands on her hips again. "You're supposed to wash your hands after putting that trouser worm away. You don't just sally out of the john flummoxing with your zipper."

"Didn't I fire you?"

"Nope, you demoted me, which begs the question of when do I get a raise?"

"When your probationary period is up, I'll consider it. Probably not." Joe winked.

"I've been here six miserable years. I'm living off of tips. And, I gotta tell you, I'm sick to death of being nice to people so as I can get a lousy dollar tip from serving up an overpriced, rancid hamburger."

"People tip the service, not the food, and by the way, don't be fighting with the customers, especially those that represent local government. They keep the lights on around here. I saw you mixing it up with the sheriff in the parking lot. If it weren't for county and state employees, we'd have to fold."

Ida Faye counted fingers on her left hand. "Let's see, we got the sheriff, one fat deputy, a snowplow jockey with B.O., and a state trooper with authority issues who whoops up on out-of-state drivers. That ought to pay the light bill."

Joe leaned forward and lowered his voice. "Between you, me, and the fence post, I hear the state has let a contract to Knife River for resurfacing the Wyoming side of the highway," he nodded toward U.S. 20 out the window, "all the way to Lusk. We'll be the only going concern for forty-one miles. This place will be a sea of orange vests and hard hats for weeks."

"God loves an optimist," Ida Faye said, shaking her head. "You know those road crews are not big tippers. I'm gonna need that raise and benefits if you expect me to scrape tar off the floor." She thought for a moment. "All the silk in China won't get me to clean that restroom after those honyaks hose the place down."

"What'd the sheriff want?" Joe asked, changing the subject.

"He was notifying next of kin, that'd be me, that my good-for-nothing husband is dead."

"I'm not sorry to hear that," Joe said matter-of-factly. "I suppose you'll be wanting time off."

Ida Faye looked at him in disbelief. "No, Joe, I'm pretty sure I can take care of things on my own time."

"Take what you need. I'll have to dock you, that is, of course, unless we can work out some kind of arrangement."

"Thanks for understanding, Joe. You know they just don't make gentlemen like you anymore. I'll be sure to tell the sheriff of your generous offer to end my connubial bliss in exchange for certain lascivious favors."

Joe smiled broadly. "God, I love it when you talk dirty."

⤛⋆⊙⋆⤜

Jessica Martindale

Looking at the Willys in the parking lot brought back fond memories. Her adopted father, the only father she had known, had one, a different color and less chrome. It looked very similar. She could still smell the distinctive odor of oil and upholstery dust with a hint of antifreeze as she bounded onto the front seat for a trip to town for parts or supplies. An ice cream cone from the Tasty Freeze was her reward for staying in the car at the John Deere dealership or the feed store. *Southeastern Iowa is the Garden of Eden compared to east-central Wyoming,* she thought as she scanned the horizon through the fly-spattered window of the cafe. She looked over the rims of her glasses at the Dr. Pepper clock above the counter. The ten, two, and four numerals were large and red compared with the smaller black numbers, the entire clock ringed in green. It was 12:10. He had said he would meet her at noon. There was no mistake. A stickler for dates and times, she remembered his telephone agreement.

Jessica pulled the heavy book from her tote and placed it on the table. A folded page corner marked what she believed was the last photograph of her parents together. Based on the copyright of the book, the photo had been taken four years before her father's disappearance in 2003. It was a fall day; the hardwoods were showing color. Her mother was wearing a light jacket, her father an open flannel shirt over a Henley. Shadows cast by the monuments of different heights with straight lines in perfect parallel indicated it was late afternoon. The cut granite stones were mostly gray. The maroon markers shone dark; the stained white ones flashed light. Her mother's family, the Peterson clan, had claimed the top of the hill. Jessica thought it strange that so many cemeteries were located on hills. She wondered if the view was for those interred or for those who came to mourn. In this case, the pastoral tree-covered shores of the Des Moines River valley meandered lazily below, providing a view for both.

It was a Catholic cemetery, lots of images of a dying Christ nailed to a cross and of the robed Madonna looking sad. She had not been raised Catholic. Her father called them guppy-guzzling, minnow-munching, mackerel snappers. He chided her mother about being a Swedish, Catholic, Iowa farm girl, especially on Fridays, when her mother insisted on serving fish as a tribute to her early indoctrination. There were great-grandparents and a grandmother she never knew buried in a neat row. Aunt Gretchen, whom she remembered, rested just a few feet away. Jessica was almost eight when Grandpa Carl died. Her memories were few, scattered snippets like pages torn from a gossip magazine that made no sense. Her mother held a bouquet of flowers at her waist. They both were looking down at the grave with somber expressions. She doubted if the photographer had asked permission to capture their image on film, let alone publish the photograph in a large-format book for the world to see.

Again, she looked at her watch. Perhaps he had stood her up, fearing legal issues. Her telephone conversation with him had been somewhat cryptic. He had been rushed. She had been impatient.

Seeing the twins was her primary reason for coming to Wyoming. They were starting their junior year at the University of Wyoming, majoring in Environment and Natural Resources with a concurrent degree in Political Science with a pre-law concentration. They would take the mock LSAT during the fall semester. Their goal was to open a legal practice that would sue the pants off corporate America for abusing the planet. It was an obvious slap in her face. Her ex, a bank president in Ames, simply shrugged. He was always more frustrated with their insistence to do everything together, the twin-thing as he called it. He referred to them as the clones. She had given up trying to treat them as individuals rather than a single living organism. Her major accomplishment had been to stop them from dressing alike when they started high school. Their rebellion ignored the enormous amounts of money she and her ex had poured into their education, all of which they considered ill-gotten.

"Here you go, hon," the waitress said as she placed a steaming coffee mug of hot water on the table in front of Jessica. "That's really hot, so be careful." She reached into the pocket of her somewhat tattered dress, the same pocket that held her cigarettes, and pulled out a Lipton tea bag. "Can I get you anything else?"

Jessica scanned the table, looking for sugar. A small plastic bowl held yellow and blue packets of sugar substitute. "Do you have any sugar?" she asked hesitantly.

"Now, down south of here in Platte and Goshen Counties, they grow some sugarbeets. They even have a sugar factory in Torrington. Up here in Niobrara County, it's mostly dryland and livestock, a bit too parched for beets."

Jessica smiled. "I wasn't asking about agricultural production. I was asking if you had some real sugar for my tea."

"Gotcha, I'll see what I can come up with," Ida Faye said as she turned toward the kitchen.

"Also," Jessica said a little too loudly, "could you bring some milk for my tea?"

"Milk? Now you've gone too far. Are you from England or what? There's coffee creamer in those little deely boppers right there." She pointed to the saucer containing the single portion tubs of liquid creamers.

Jessica looked shocked.

"I'm just funnin' ya. If you want drippin's from the underside of a cow, I'll fetch it for ya. Me, I prefer better living through chemistry." She paused and smiled. "I'll bring you some milk soon as I pick out the chunks."

Jessica attempted a smile. It came out crooked, almost a sneer as she acknowledged the strange woman's sense of humor.

⊷•≡◉✠◉≡•⊷

Sidney Dawson

"Do you think she's just kidding about her husband being killed?" Sidney asked, her eyes wide.

"What'd you have in mind?" Sam said as he shoveled a bite of coconut cream pie into his mouth.

"About what?"

"A dog. What kind of dog were you thinking about?"

Sidney gave her father a puzzled look. After a moment, her eyes narrowed, and she shook her head. "You would think I would be used to your inattentive, totally random thought processes by now." Her father could change the subject midsentence or start an entirely new conversation without divulging the topic. "I know you love bloodhounds. You've had that breed since I was a little girl. I just thought you might want to consider something less stubborn, something that didn't require a front-end loader to pick up after, something that didn't buckle your knees when it passed gas or threw slobber on the refrigerator door."

"Like what?"

"Oh, I don't know, a smaller dog perhaps."

"Did you take your meds this morning?" Sam said as he wiped the corners of his mouth with his napkin.

"Are you changing the subject again?"

"No, I'm thinking about a seeing-eye dog if you keep forgetting to take your pills," Sam said as he looked around the tiny cafe. He slid across the Naugahyde-covered booth cushion that made embarrassing sounds and revealed a patch of duct tape crossed over a tear. "Speaking of seeing-eye dogs, I need to see a man about a dog."

Sidney rolled her eyes as she watched her father make his way toward the restroom. She dug into her purse and pulled out a dark prescription drug bottle, twisted off the child-proof cap, and shook out two large white pills. Massive doses of vitamin A were the latest attempt to slow down the retinitis pigmentosa that seemed to be accelerating as part of the degenerative Usher Syndrome she had inherited. She no longer held out hope for a cure. It was not a popular disease, or was it a condition? She was unsure. Money for research was as rare as the syndrome. Gene therapy was still a possibility. For now, vitamin A was the popular approach. She had read a recent study that had reviewed almost four hundred published research papers on the use of vitamin A and fish oils to slow the degeneration of retinal photoreceptors. They found no statistically significant benefit for vitamin supplementation in stabilizing visual field and acuity loss.

She was headed for legal blindness, and she was scared. That was why she had moved back in with her father. He was all the family she had. She knew what was going to happen and was convinced there was no cure. Sam would not accept that and insisted that she continue taking the vitamins. Secretly, she knew he in some way felt partially responsible for her condition. It was much clearer on her maternal side. Her mother's lineage was easily traced back to the Ashkenazi Jews of eastern Germany. On her father's side, it was unclear to her how he had inherited the autosomal recessive. His mother, her grandmother, who she did not remember, had some linkage to a population of carriers in Birmingham, England. Sidney's best friend Annie, the love of her father's life, knew the story. She would not tell it. She said that Sam had literally buried his genetic past, and it was not her place to meddle. Annie took his secrets to the grave, as would her father.

Neither she nor her father had discussed the future. Usher Syndrome appeared not to affect longevity. She would outlive him by decades. Mostly blind and mostly deaf, she would be on her own. Being wealthy seemed more of a burden than a solution. She shuddered at the thought of being alone. Who would have her? Two love affairs, and both had tried to kill her. They, in turn, were dead. She had given up hope of finding someone to share her doomed life. Sidney took a deep breath and exhaled slowly. She thought of the student who had stood patiently in line to ask her questions about the *National Environmental Policy Act* after her guest lecture in the law school at UW. He was handsome and bright and shared her enthusiasm for the law and how NEPA was more than a burdensome government requirement that slowed capitalism. Shamefully, she used the complexity of his questions to invite him to the student center for coffee and further discussion. Fortunately, her burning ears along with her hearing aids were hidden under her hair when she discovered he was an undergraduate and probably a dozen years her junior.

She looked nervously around the cafe and sipped her coffee. A slight smile belied her concern for ethics. She had agreed to mentor him on a paper he was working on having to do with the disruption of wildlife migratory corridors from oil and gas exploration in the Pinedale Anticline, a natural gas field in northwestern Wyoming. She could tell he was attracted to her both intellectually and physically. She had caught him nervously glancing at her body. Sidney was careful to keep the relationship platonic, although she had to admit she enjoyed the somewhat flirtatious interchange that occurred during her weekly meetings with him. He, too, was distracted, frequently forgetting key points made in their earlier discussions. She told herself that if she ever dreamed of him sexually, she would end the relationship. Daydreams, however, were tolerated.

--➤━◉✦◉━➤--

Sam Dawson

The rusty throat of the ancient toilet coughed and sputtered as if it were a dying beast. It momentarily drowned out the sounds of clattering spoons against coffee mugs and the sharp ringing of the raw-boned cook's spatula as he scraped grease from his grill. Somewhere in the distance the advancing growl of a semi tractor-trailer threatened all who might be in its path. Sam exited the tiny restroom. The door screeched his presence like a curtain rising on a much-anticipated play. The cook eyed him suspiciously. The waitress made note. The lone woman at the table glanced in his direction, eyebrows raised. Sam suddenly feared he had forgotten to zip his fly. Deftly, he checked with the forefinger of his right hand as he turned toward the counter. He noted a pyramid of single-serving boxes of breakfast cereals on a shelf next to the grill. Grape Nuts, Frosted Flakes, Cheerios, Shredded Wheat, and Lucky Charms were neatly stacked next to a row of white cereal bowels, chipped, cracked, and stained, not unlike the toilet.

The woman smiled politely as he passed her table. He offered a quick smile in return and quickly averted his gaze, still self-conscious about his zipper. She was pretty, mid-forties he guessed, neatly attired in a sleeveless floral-print summer dress, a sash around her slim waist. Her ankles were crossed above sandal-like flats. She sat very straight. Her dark blonde hair was pulled back in a loose ponytail and held with a red band that matched her dress. He had not noticed the woman earlier, since his back had been toward her. Sam did the classic double-take when he saw his book on her table.

"I'll sign that if you like," he said somewhat boldly as he stopped and turned toward her.

"Excuse me?" She looked up at him over the rim of her tea mug.

Sam smiled broadly and pointed at the book. *Lost in Iowa: A Pictorial of Rural Cemeteries of the Corn State.* "The book," he said, pointing at the large-format coffee-table edition of his book. "I'd be happy to sign it for you."

Her eyes narrowed as she stared up at him. "Are you Sam Dawson?"

"In the flesh. And you must be Jessica Martindale."

"I thought you were late or that I misunderstood your directions and was waiting in the wrong cafe. You were here when I arrived. You were with someone and had your back to me." She opened the book to the back cover, exposing Sam's picture on the inside jacket. "I was looking for someone—"

"Younger." Sam interrupted with a smile. "Old book, old picture."

"No, no, I was looking for someone much older, assuming you had aged significantly since this book was published, but you, you," she stuttered and swallowed hard, "look just like the picture in the book, only bigger."

Sam shook his head. "Keep talking. I want to see how you get out of this."

"You were with a woman and I assumed—"

"Yes, my daughter is a woman, and she's tagging along for the day."

"Can we start over?" Jessica asked seriously.

"Nope, the damage is done. My feelings have been hurt. I'm afraid it's irreparable."

Jessica continued to stare at him for a long moment. Then she slid her chair back and stood with shoulders back and head up. She offered her hand and said, "Mister Dawson, it's a pleasure to meet you. You look exactly like your picture in my book. I think it uncanny that you haven't aged a bit. I would be absolutely thrilled if you would autograph the book for me, perhaps personalize it."

Sam took her hand. "Now you're talking. I'd be happy to sign it for you." He pulled out a chair for himself and motioned for her to be seated. She was even better-looking than he first thought, tall and slender with an infectious smile that dimpled at the corners of her mouth. Her lips were full beneath a perfectly proportioned nose and Nordic cheekbones.

Her radiant green eyes gave no hint of how acerbic her tongue could be when angered. Sam looked toward the booth where his daughter sat. Sidney rolled her eyes and tossed her head in disgust. He knew what she was thinking. His knack for attracting disturbed women was legend. Older and wiser now, he was committed not to making the same mistakes. He pulled a pen from one of the many pockets in his cargo pants.

Jessica, he wrote then stopped. She wanted him to personalize it. He knew nothing about her other than she was from Iowa. He was tempted to write that the photographs in the book paled in comparison to her beauty. That was much too forward for someone he had just met, although he was tempted. *Hope you enjoy the book as much as I enjoyed Iowa. Best regards, Sam Dawson.* He saw a dog-eared page near the center of the book as he passed it to her. It was like fingernails on a blackboard to him. People who folded down the corners of book pages rather than use a bookmark disrespected the book and in so doing disrespected the author. He took it personally. Sam eyed her cautiously.

CHAPTER 3
12:16 p.m.

Brad Holcomb

The hot, soapy water brought momentary relief to the swollen, arthritic thumb joints of Brad's hands. Bits of egg floated unseen beneath the foam, bumping softly on the cuts on his knuckles. The stiffness in his right hand prevented him from making a fist. He leaned precariously over the sink, his hands planted firmly on the bottom of the stainless-steel tub. He could stand that way for a long time, eyes closed, remembering all the things that were gone. Brad could become the boy on the ranch sixty-some years earlier, bucking bales to hungry cattle from the back of the horse-drawn hay sled, the mountain air slicing at his lungs. He liked becoming that boy. He wished he could stay as the boy and vanquish the later years that tortured his memory. Youth and innocence always gave way to the harsh realities of life. He took shelter in the memories of the fifties. His war, like all the generations before him, came to him as a man, a young man fighting an old man's war. Vietnam changed him forever. His youthful innocence was the last casualty of war, stolen from him as quickly as his perspective. Haunted by atrocities and threatened by those whose political ambitions trumped morality, he ran. Not before all had been taken from him.

Tormented by memories and driven by revenge, he had continued to drift from one rural crossroads to another. With each job, with each new acquaintance, he changed his name and story. From milking cows near Fairbury, Nebraska, to skinning steers on the kill floor of a beef processing plant near Ft. Morgan, Colorado, he had tried to forget his past and reinvent himself and his future. Always afraid, he moved frequently and silently, one step ahead of his pursuers. Each new relationship began with a lie and ended with the abruptness of an unexpected death. This time was different. He had not anticipated Ida Faye Mensinger.

"Are you all right, Brad?" Ida Faye said softly from behind him.

"As right as rain," he said, turning to face her. He dried his hands on his apron and smiled at her. "How about you?"

"I'm still in a state of shock. I don't know what to think. I've been hiding so long; it's like I'm afraid to come out in the open. I keep telling myself it's over, that I'm free. I can't quite believe it. I've been afraid for so long. I just don't know what to do. One minute I'm giddy, and the next I'm scared to death that this," she raised her arms as if taking in the whole of her surroundings, "is the rest of my life." She swallowed hard. "That man really got inside my head."

"Give it time. You'll figure it out," Brad said. "The important thing is that you're free. No more hiding, no more looking over your shoulder."

"Brad, I could really use a friend tonight." She placed her hand on his forearm. "Would it be all right if I stayed over tonight? I'll fix us a nice dinner. We could have a couple of beers and maybe talk about blowing this Popsicle stand and starting over someplace pretty."

He smiled tightly and looked into her pale blue eyes. They were streaked with tiny red veins, as if she had not slept. He could smell her perfume mixed with cigarette smoke. "I would like that very much." He hesitated. "But I'm not sure that's a good idea right now." Disappointment registered immediately on her face. "Hear me out," he offered quickly before her letdown turned to anger. "The sheriff wants you to ID the body and answer some questions. I think you should do that. The last thing you need is to arouse his suspicion. He's got an unsolved murder on his hands, and he'll be looking to pin it on you or someone you might be involved with. It's the classic triangle stuff. He's already seen your face, and he's wondering how you got those cuts and bruises. You said he told you that your husband was beaten to death. One look at you and he knew you weren't big enough to get that job done. He'll be looking for an accomplice."

Ida Faye's eyes darted to Brad's reddened hand.

"I'm in a bind here, Ida Faye. I can't have the law coming around here asking questions."

She nodded in acceptance. Her eyes filled with the sting of rejection. "Maybe when the dust settles," she said with a forced smile as she removed her hand from his arm.

Brad attempted to return the smile. His face seemed paralyzed. He wiped at the corners of his mouth, since he now had a tendency to drool. Sometimes he had to force himself to blink. The tremors, his balance, his memory were troubling. He could no longer dismiss them as signs of old age. He had trouble sleeping, and his depression was getting worse. It had been clear to him for some time that Ida Faye wanted a more intimate relationship. He was not sure that would be possible. That alone seemed a good reason to keep her at arm's length. He needed time to think, to sleep, to plan his next move. For so many years he had believed he would find relief with Winston Tucker's death. Not joy, just relief.

⋅→▶━◉ ⚹ ◉━◀←⋅

Ida Faye Mensinger

Ida Faye studied the Dr. Pepper clock, took a deep breath, and released it slowly. She felt like screaming, a pressure cooker about to explode. She wished these people would finish their meals and leave. Like a scene from the movie *Gone with the Wind*, Rhett Butler was putting the moves on Miss Scarlet. This was a restaurant, not a pleasure parlor. Maybe she should slap their checks down on their tables as a hint that it was time to go. The guy had written something in her book. *He's not wasting any time. Perhaps he could give a few pointers to Brad.*

She was embarrassed and could feel her ears burning. She had practically thrown herself at Brad, and he had turned her down. It was a stupid move on her part. She had been overcome with relief at the news of her husband's well-deserved death and had thrown caution to the wind. She and Brad had become close friends in the two years since he came through the door with little more than the clothes on his back. He had plucked the sign from the front window that said *Dishwasher Wanted.*

Joe immediately took advantage of him by offering room and board and no salary. He would, however, pay him ten dollars a week for doing odd jobs around the cafe like painting the entire exterior of the crumbling building, fixing the numerous plumbing leaks, and tarring the roof. The 1958 rodent-infested trailer out back was the room and the leftover swill in the kitchen was his board. Joe had told him that he could use any of the three junked vehicles scattered around the cafe if he could get one running. In the evenings, Brad had worked on an early sixties Dodge pickup. The rusted aqua and white truck rested on four cement blocks, since it had no wheels. It sputtered to life a few months after his arrival. With Joe's blessing, he had traded the other two vehicles, a wrecked Galaxy 500 and a Buick Electra the size of a destroyer, to a junk dealer from Hay Springs for wheels, tires, and a battery. Brad never complained.

He seldom talked unless asked a question, and then his responses were brief, often a single word. Yet she was drawn to him, but not like a lonely woman to a stray dog; rather, it was unbridled curiosity. He was handsome, articulate, obviously educated, and most of all, he was polite and courteous, all the things her dead husband was not. It all seemed genuine to her, although she knew there had to be a catch. It was obvious he was running to or from something or someone. He never drove the pickup on the highway, never went to town, and never came out of the kitchen if law enforcement personnel were in the cafe. She noted all these peculiarities. She never challenged him.

In the last few months, however, she had become increasingly concerned about his physical condition. Even his personality seemed to be changing. One afternoon in July, they sat together in the late afternoon shade of the cafe. Brad's left hand began to shake uncontrollably. She had seen it before and had said nothing. This time, she gently asked him if he wanted to see a doctor about the tremors. He shot back an angry "no" then offered the weak excuse of having no medical insurance. When she asked if he had signed up for Medicare when he turned sixty-five, he said "no" in a manner that indicated the conversation was over. A few minutes later, he apologetically offered that the shaking was the result of nerve damage from an AK round he took in the arm. He pulled up the sleeve of his t-shirt, exposing the nasty-looking scar tissue.

Troubled, after a long silence, she had said there was a VA hospital in Cheyenne and one in Hot Springs, South Dakota. Brad did not respond.

She looked at the clock again. With determination, she suddenly marched briskly out the back door and disappeared behind the cafe. She needed a smoke. Brad's pickup was parked next to the dilapidated 1958 Atlas Mobile Home. Forty-two feet of mouse turds; she would not spend the night there, even if he begged her. Especially not after he found a rattlesnake coiled in the dish strainer under the kitchen sink.

Ida Faye took a long drag from her cigarette then blew the smoke upward. She stared at Brad's pickup and imagined the two of them headed for Montana, their suitcases in the back, his hand on her knee. It would be a do-over of epic proportion, a fresh start with their ruined lives behind them as they drove toward the sunset. She would raise and train barrel horses and he … what would he do? She knew nothing about him. Another screwed-up veteran with no future, he would have them living under a bridge in Billings. After paying this month's rent and utilities, she would have less than six hundred dollars in her checking account.

She continued to look at his Dodge. Why was it so dirty? Brad had told her it was a '63. She remembered that because she was sixty-three. She did the math. She had been ten years old when that truck came off the assembly line. Like all children, she had her whole life in front of her. She would be the one on a sorrel mare carrying the American flag into the arena at a dead run, the crowd coming to their feet, men removing their hats. Suddenly she felt like crying.

Ida Faye turned to see Joe, who stood behind the fly-spattered screen door to the kitchen. He was watching her. He was always watching her. She expected him to call out to her, to tell her that she was fired for dereliction of duty to her customers. She was no fool. She saw the way he often looked at her. Instead, she watched him pick up the water pitcher and walk toward the cafe's dining area to fill people's glasses.

-»=● ✳ ●=«-

Jessica Martindale

"Flustered" was the word she was looking for. Agitated that he had not sought her out and introduced himself earlier and confused, since he did not resemble the mental image she had of him. With the exception of some distinguished gray hair at his temples, he really had not aged much, taller, tanned, and more robust than she had imagined. She was pleasantly surprised. Not enough, however, to allay her frustration at having to drive out of her way and meet in the epitome of a greasy spoon in the middle of this nonexistent region.

"I apologize for having you meet me here," Sam said, as if reading her mind. "I'm working under a tight deadline to get some shots near here." He smiled. "I hope it wasn't too inconvenient for you."

It was more than inconvenient, she thought. *It was downright punishing.* "Not at all," she lied. "I do have a flight to catch in Denver later this afternoon. What I wanted to talk with you about shouldn't take too long. Do you know how far it is to Denver from here?"

"Four hours," Sam said, looking at the Dr. Pepper clock above the counter. "Give or take, depending on traffic and construction south of Fort Collins. What time is your flight?"

"Five thirty," Jessica said, glancing nervously at the clock. It was just sixteen minutes past twelve.

"That'll be tight," Sam said, looking out to the parking lot at the cream-colored Toyota sedan with a red-and-white Colorado license plate that indicated it was a fleet car, most likely a rental. "Denver International Airport can be a bit a challenge. By the time you return your rental, catch a shuttle to the terminal, stand in line, check your bags, stand in line at security, catch the train for your concourse, stand in line some more … it'll be tight. You know they want you to check in two hours before your flight."

"So, what are you saying?" she said with an alarmed look.

"You can't make it."

Jessica stared at him in disbelief. "I'll call and see if I can get on a later flight."

Sam smiled tightly and pointed at the sign behind the cash register that read, *Sorry No Phone.*

She reached into her purse and pulled out her smartphone.

"I'm pretty sure you won't be able to get any cell service here," he said. He watched with a slight smile as she twisted and turned in her chair, holding the phone above her head, staring at the tiny screen.

"You've got to be kidding me," she said, sounding very agitated.

"Welcome to rural Wyoming, Ms. Martindale."

"Great! This is just great," Jessica said, shaking her head from side to side. The creases at the corners of her eyes hinted at her anger. "How am I supposed to get home in time for a very important meeting tomorrow afternoon?"

"Where's home?"

"Ames," she said as if Sam should know. "My car is in Des Moines. My flight was to Des Moines."

Sensing her agitation, Sam cautiously asked, "Can I make a suggestion?"

"Tell me this isn't the part where you tell me we're out of gas and we'll need to spend the night in the car."

"Excuse me?" Sam said, straightening in his chair.

Seeing his shock, Jessica attempted a smile. "Sorry, I don't know where that came from. What's your suggestion?"

Sam leaned forward and lowered his voice. "We're out of gas, and it looks like we'll have to spend the night in the car."

Jessica laughed. "Touché, Mister Dawson." Her eyes sparkled as she stared at him. "I'd like to hear your suggestion?"

Sam gestured with his thumb toward the window. "That's U.S. Highway 20, an east-west highway that spans the country from coast to coast. It's the longest road in the United States and stretches from Boston to someplace on the Pacific in Oregon. It's over thirty-three hundred miles long."

Jessica squinted at him. "Don't tell me, you were the last kid to sit down at the geography bee in grade school."

"Sorry, when driving that thing," he said, throwing his thumb over his shoulder toward the Willys in the parking lot, "I stay off the Interstates so as not to impede traffic. U.S. 20 is a favorite. Anyway, it will take you east across the northern tier of Nebraska, crossing the Missouri into Sioux City, Iowa and on to I-35 junction just east of Webster City. Turn south and you'll be in Ames in about ten hours. Even if you could make your flight in Denver, you're looking at about nine or ten hours before you arrive home."

"Really?"

"Really!" Sam beamed. "The added bonus is that you won't get an ulcer being treated like livestock on its way to slaughter or having to listen to the nonstop drivel of people blathering about their selfish little lives while you're wedged in between two ill-dressed, bloated walruses who can't get their tray tables down in anticipation of a tiny pack of peanuts."

Jessica's eyes were wide with astonishment. She opened her mouth as if to speak, but no words came out.

"I'm not sure you're old enough to remember when flying was fun," he continued.

"I assure you, Mister Dawson," she interrupted, "I'm old enough to remember 9/11. And yes, the consequences have been inconvenient but necessary. I'm not sure, however, I share your cynical view of the traveling public."

"Sorry," Sam said. "Perhaps we should change the subject to something we can both agree upon, like politics or religion?"

Jessica looked into his eyes for, perhaps, too long before averting her gaze. "Let's talk about this photograph," she said, opening the book to the dog-eared page.

Sam leaned over the table and turned the book toward him. "I remember this cemetery. It was in southeastern Iowa; beautiful country, very pastoral. It was above the Des Moines River, near a picturesque little community, begins with a K, I believe."

"Keotonka," Jessica said, smiling. "I grew up near there."

"That's it! I stayed at an old riverboat hotel next to the river, near a bridge."

"The Garfield." She scooted forward in her chair. "It's still there. There's a new bridge downstream. The old one here has been converted to a footbridge." She pointed to the photograph. "That's my mom and dad standing over my grandfather's grave the spring after he got cancer."

Sam studied the photograph. "I don't often take shots of people in cemeteries. I remember this couple caught my attention. They epitomized, in my mind, why we have cemeteries. They were there to respect and remember. The bouquet of daisies, the somber expressions on their faces as they stared down at the ground, were too much for me to resist. I can tell by the depth of field that I was using a short telephoto lens, probably a one thirty-five millimeter. Do you see how the light is angling through the trees? It was a late-afternoon shot, probably not much earlier than five or six." He leaned forward for a closer look. "Do your parents still live in the area?"

"Um, no," she responded after an uncomfortable pause. She felt his stare and knew that he had smelled her perfume.

"I can see a strong resemblance," Sam said.

Jessica had been told all her life that she looked like her mother. She knew her mother was beautiful and was uncomfortable with his obvious comparison. She had been thinking that if she left now, she could be home by midnight and would not have to endure any more lectures about photography or confide embarrassing family secrets in a total stranger. "I was wondering if you had other photos of them. Perhaps the ones that didn't make it through the editing phase."

Sam's eyes narrowed as he sat back in his chair and studied her face. He quickly averted his gaze when he realized she was staring back at him. He rubbed his chin before squeezing it between his thumb and forefinger.

Jessica smiled. "You're asking yourself why I would make such a request."

"On the contrary. I was thinking of the camera I used back then," he lied. "It was a thirty-five-millimeter Nikon F with a manual wind. I had a motor drive for it and seldom used it. Film was too expensive. And you're right; I usually shoot more than a single frame. And yes, I'm wondering why."

"Well, since I've missed my flight, I guess I can spare a few moments to explain myself."

⊶⊷ ✦ ⊶⊷

Sidney Dawson

Here we go again, Sidney thought as she turned away in disgust at her father's enchantment with the doe-eyed woman across the room. She slid the remains of Sam's coconut cream pie across the table toward herself. She shot a quick look at her father, who seemed totally engrossed in conversation with a perfect stranger. She took too large of a bite and covered her bulging mouth with her left hand. Maybe if he had another dog, he would stop picking up strays, she reasoned. Her father seemed to be drawn to damaged women, the ones with a sappy story, the ones on a mission of redemption. Annie was the exception, of course, and she missed her dearly. She ate the crust, scraped the plate clean, and then pushed it back to Sam's side of the table. She wondered if her mother had fit the definition of a damaged woman and quickly concluded yes. Sam Dawson was a magnet for damaged goods. She, herself, was no exception.

Her thoughts returned to the handsome undergraduate. She reasoned that if she were normal, at least physically, she would not be attracted to a man, a boy rather, who was nearly thirteen years her junior. The double standard for men like her father made her angry. Society seemed to accept older men courting, even marrying younger women. When a woman was attracted to a younger man, she was branded as some sort of sexual predator, or worse. Nothing had happened, yet she believed she had already violated the one rule she had established as a qualifier for dissolving the relationship. Last night, she had dreamed of him sexually. At least, she thought it might be sexual. In the dream, they had met at the student center, as they had in the past, to discuss his term paper on wildlife migration corridors. He had been excited by the discovery of a number of photographs that demonstrated how dependent antelope had become on oil and gas drilling sites as predator-free safety zones. When he pulled the eight-by-ten color photos from the manila envelope, she was shocked to see they were all nude photos of him in various poses, as if he were a bodybuilder in some perverse competition.

"Aren't they great?" he said with a toothy grin.

"Yes, yes they're very good," she had said, totally transfixed as she shuffled through the photographs, slowly studying each one. She had awakened with a start, fearful that someone she knew had seen her looking at the pornographic images. That fear of discovery had overshadowed any feelings of sexual arousal. Half a day later, she still felt ashamed and guilty.

"Aren't they great?" Ida Faye said slyly from beside her.

"Excuse me?" Sidney almost yelled at the realization the waitress was standing next to her.

"Mickey and Minnie," Ida Faye said as she pointed with her chin toward Sam and the blonde number. "It looks like your dad has made a new friend. Will there be anything else, perhaps another piece of pie? I've got a fresh one in the fridge."

Sidney's eyes darted toward her father and the woman, then back at the waitress. She wanted to tell this rude woman to mind her own business. She could feel the flush of anger, or was it embarrassment, turning her ears red.

"My good-for-nothing dead husband used to do that right in front of me. He never missed an opportunity to hit on some slut in heat and leave me to find my own way home."

Sidney gathered her courage. "I can assure you—"

"I'm just sayin' there's something in that Y chromosome that takes hold of 'em and makes them—"

"Yes," Sidney blurted out, "I'd like another piece of coconut cream pie for my father. Make that two pieces, and take them over to that lady's table." She looked up at the waitress with a cold stare. *I'll buy this dump, fire you, then burn it to the ground,* she thought.

"Yes, ma'am. I'll bring those pies right out."

Sidney brought her coffee cup to her lips. It was cold. She sipped it anyway as she looked over the rim at her father, who was listening intently to the attractive woman. She could not hear what they were saying. Instead, she read the woman's lips. The woman had missed her flight and seemed upset. The television above the cash register drowned them out. The media was all a-twitter with the strong possibility of the nation electing its first woman president. Sidney thought it amusing that Hillary Clinton's husband and Donald Trump had something in common regarding infidelity—a trait shared by the waitress's late husband. Sidney was starting to wonder about her father.

Sam Dawson

Sam was intrigued by the way Jessica Martindale's lips and eyes were in synchrony when she talked, perfectly choreographed in a way that held him spellbound. He discreetly surveyed her left hand. There was no wedding ring. He respected the *no tres-passing* sign of marital status, yet a slight pang of guilt whisked over him as he thought of his on-again-off-again relationship with Tommie, his rediscovered high school sweetheart. It was mostly off-again. They seemed destined to remain good friends, and Sam was comfortable with that.

Ms. Martindale seemed a little nervous as she repeatedly pulled her dress together below her neck as if to prevent him from looking at her breasts. He had not looked and was offended that she had essentially accused him. He was more interested in her eyes. They sparkled with an intensity that captivated him. He tried to look away and again found himself staring back into the hazel windows of her soul. The green was like wet emeralds, and the brown glistened sorrel as a well-groomed thoroughbred. Sam forced himself to look away. He studied the photograph again and then looked back at Jessica Martindale.

"I favor my biological father," she said. "So I'm told. I don't remember him. He was killed in Vietnam. The man in the photo is my stepfather. He was the man who raised me. My mom, a blue-eyed blonde, as Nordic as they come. I was blonde like her when I was little. My stepdad adopted me in 1978, the same year they were married. I was nine. You can do the math."

"I was forty-seven when I was your age," Sam said with a smile.

Jessica raised her eyebrows at the speed with which he had mentally calculated her age.

"That was six years ago, in case you're wondering," Sam added as if it were a footnote.

"I wasn't," she said, looking directly at him.

The waitress silently approached and placed two dessert plates of coconut cream pie in front of each of them. "Compliments of the young woman in the booth," she said, gesturing with her head toward Sidney. She pulled two clean forks from the frayed pocket of her uniform and placed them on the table. "Can I get you anything else?" Sam and Jessica leaned in opposite directions to see around the waitress toward Sidney.

"Enjoy!" Sidney called out with a smile and raised her water glass as if it were a toast.

"Here you go, big spender," Ida Faye said as she tore a check from the pad she had retrieved from the same pocket as the forks. She slapped it face-down on the table in front of Sam. "No credit cards." She winked and tossed her thumb over her shoulder toward the cash register. A hand-printed sign beneath the register read *Cash Only*. "A very large gratuity is both appropriate and expected. Enjoy your pie." Ida Faye placed a finger on her cheek. With a quizzical look, she added, "Gosh, I hope I didn't mix them up." She turned and walked away. Both Sam and Jessica looked down at their pie.

"Trade ya," Sam said. He slid his pie plate toward Jessica.

"What was all that about?" Jessica's eyes tracked the waitress, who had disappeared into the kitchen.

"I have no idea. Maybe she's from Nebraska," Sam added.

"With that accent, I'd say west Texas or the Panhandle. Regardless, that woman is strange, to say the least."

"I think she has an interesting sense of humor, that's all. Speaking of strange," he smiled, "you were about to explain your interest in this photograph." He pointed to the open book in front of her.

"Yes, I'm sorry if I didn't make myself clear. I'm looking for my father. He disappeared in 2003."

"And," Sam dragged out the word, "this has what to do with me?"

"It has nothing to do with you," she said somewhat tersely. She straightened in her chair and broke eye contact. "I soon discovered that my father was somewhat camera-shy. Actually, he was *very* camera-shy. In the almost thirty years I knew him, I can't find a decent photo of him. My folks were married for a quarter century, and there is no photographic record beyond a few shots with his back to the camera or him waving from a distance. The photo of him in your book is the best I have. I was hoping there might be others."

Sam paused before responding. She was holding back, and he wanted to know why. "As I said, I typically shoot multiple frames. I'd have to check my negative file, which is in my dark room at home. If you could give me your contact information, I'll let you know as soon as possible."

Jessica took a business card from her purse and scribbled something on the back before handing it to Sam. "Those are my home phone and my cell phone numbers. Leave a message if I don't pick up."

Sam studied the front of the card before turning it over. "Vice President for Domestic Marketing," he said, making eye contact again. "Is there a president for domestic marketing?"

Her eyes narrowed slightly, and she turned her head a couple of degrees. "No," she said as if it was indisputable.

Sam attempted a smile. It felt more like a smirk. She acted as though no one had asked that question before. Perhaps she was offended by the question, thinking that he believed there was likely a male president in her organizational hierarchy. "I assume you know that there are lots of sources to help you find a missing person: courthouses, state and federal agencies, and the like. A private investigator that specializes in locating people might be of use. There are—"

"Just the photo, Mr. Dawson; that's all I'm interested in."

There was no mistaking the clip in her voice. This was a woman used to getting her way, especially from a perceived subordinate. "Well, Madame Vice President," Sam said, looking down at the business card. "I'll see what I have and give you a call."

He scooted his chair back from the table and inwardly smiled to himself. *It will be a cold day in Hell, Lady, before I call you back.*

CHAPTER 4
12:22 p.m.

Brad Holcomb

Brad steadied himself against the back outside wall of the cafe. The smell of grease from the exhaust fan above the grill was heavy in the air. It overwhelmed the pungent aroma of sage that soothed him in the cool predawn hours when he often sat on the steps to the trailer, listening to the chorus of coyotes as they welcomed a new day. His mind raced—what to take, where to go. He would leave after he closed for the evening.

He thought it was naïve to think the feds had stopped looking for him. They never forget. They would swarm into Wyoming with renewed hope of finding him, of killing him. They knew he would be close. The last time they thought he was in Wyoming, they had called in an air strike that burned almost twenty thousand acres of the Sierra Madre Mountains in south-central Wyoming. They could care less about Winston Tucker. He was old news. They wanted the man who had stalked him for the past thirteen years. He was at the top of their list. It was a short list, a secret list. The FBI agents were the lackeys, grunts who knew nothing of the origin of the order or the rationale, only the mission. The same held true for the CIA. It was the National Security Agency under the direction of the

Department of Defense that was calling the shots. They had tried to kill him and failed. Instead, they had destroyed his life. He in turn had killed two of their own and exposed Winston Tucker's treachery to Congress and the world. Killing was easy for him. He had lots of practice.

"There you are," Ida Faye said. She let the screen door close gently. "Are you all right?"

He was not all right. He would never be all right. His world was terminally ill. "I'm fine. You?"

"It's starting to settle in. I have to pinch myself every once in a while to make sure I'm not dreaming. I'm a bit conflicted, I guess. One minute, I feel like I should be dancing in the street. The next minute, I'm in a panic about the future. Hiding in fear might have been easier than facing a new life. You know what I mean?"

Brad nodded. He knew exactly what she meant.

"I was thinking a little while ago that I had never gotten a divorce from that miserable jerk. I was too scared. So, I guess I'm still married. I mean legally. He owed money to everybody and their dog. Do you suppose I'm responsible by law to pay off his debts?"

Brad thought for a moment. "What I'm sure of is that you can find a dozen lawyers on each side of that issue." He thought it was a strange question from a woman who had changed her identity and been on the run for the past six years. Only an honest person would concern themselves with such details. He had given little thought to the operating loan he had taken out or the new tractor he had purchased before disappearing.

Therefore, he must be a dishonest person. He reasoned a fugitive has little choice: run or die.

"I guess I'll find out soon enough," Ida Faye said. "I'm a little nervous about seeing him. You know how a rattlesnake can still strike after it's dead? I keep having this vision of him reaching up and grabbing me by the throat. That's why we always separate the head from the body on a dead rattler."

He could not help looking at her throat. Her neck was long, slender, and clearly bruised on both sides. He wondered if the rest of her was as beaten as her face. He had seen the kind of man that would do that to a woman before. In this case, it would not happen again. Brad had visions of Ida Faye that he tried to suppress. He thought it strange that his mind and body were not synchronized when it came to such matters. There was something wrong with him, and he was embarrassed by it. His body betrayed his desire. Clearly, she wanted something more than comforting discussions from their relationship. She had wanted to spend the night with him, and he had turned her down. He could tell she was embarrassed by his rejection. She intrigued him. One minute she could be thoughtful and sensitive, the next minute cynical and cutting. She was an enigma. "I think the coroner will get upset if you try to cut off the deceased's head. Your ex can't hurt you anymore. Just remain calm and identify the body. Ask about getting a copy of the death certificate. You're going to need that at some point."

"I wish you would come with me," she said softly.

"We've already talked about that. It wouldn't look good. Go see the sheriff and tell him the truth. Remember, I can't be your alibi. You *do* have an alibi, don't you?"

"He was waiting for me when I got home last night after work. He'd torn the place apart. He wanted my money. That was how he controlled me, broke and barefoot, so to speak. He smacked me around pretty good, until I gave him everything I had in my rental. He didn't find my checkbook, where I'm saving up for a clean break, maybe Montana someday. Everything else is gone, and I don't care." She thought for a moment. "Say, if I'm next of kin, will they give me back the money he stole?"

"I don't think it works that way, Ida Faye. It would become part of his estate. If he had a will, it would be adjudicated through probate—"

"I'm pretty sure he didn't have a will. There was nothing legal to put in a will. He and his buddies ran a meth lab out of a junkyard in Stinnett."

Brad shifted his weight and pressed his left side against the wall of the cafe with the hope of stopping his hand from trembling. He wanted to lie down, to sleep and make everything go away. "The coroner will establish an approximate time of death. You'll need to tell the sheriff where you were when your husband was killed. Then he'll ask if anyone can corroborate your alibi."

"I never left Van Tassell. The sheriff said they found him at the Lamplighter Motel in Lusk. That's twenty miles west of Van Tassell."

Ida Faye fumbled in her pocket for the pack of cigarettes.

"You never left Van Tassell?"

"I was in no condition to go anywhere. You wanna see the rest of me?"

He did, and she knew it.

Ida Faye stretched with the confidence of a young cat. She lit her cigarette then blew the smoke upward.

"How did he find you?"

"I have no idea."

"You haven't contacted anyone in Texas?"

"Of course not."

Brad studied her. She was responding defiantly to the third-degree questioning. "Did the sheriff say how he died?"

"Somebody beat him to death." She glanced at Brad's torn, reddened hands, then took another drag from the Virginia Slim.

"Do you own a gun?"

"Yep." Her eyes narrowed, and she smiled tightly.

"Legally? Because if it's not, and the sheriff gets a search warrant—"

"Look, Brad, how on God's green earth am I going to get a gun legally? Ida Faye was my great-aunt. Mensinger was the name of my third-grade teacher. Neither you nor I even have a social security number. Joe knows it. He pays us in cash. He doesn't pay social security, unemployment, health insurance, or anything else. As far as the government is concerned, we don't exist."

"How did your husband find you?"

"You already asked me that," she said as her cigarette bobbed between her lips.

"The sheriff will ask you that. He'll want to know if you lured him to Wyoming in order to kill him."

Brad looked at her intensely. "If you own a gun, why didn't you use it?"

"Like I said, he was waiting for me when I got home. He'd found the gun in the nightstand next to my bed. He threatened to shoot me with it if I didn't give him the money. After I gave it to him, he beat the stuffing out of me, then left and took the gun with him."

Brad shook his head. "So the sheriff has the gun with your fingerprints on it."

"I guess."

"Have you ever been arrested?"

It was Ida Faye's turn to study Brad. With narrowed eyes, she glared at him for several seconds. She tossed her cigarette on the ground, turned, and slipped silently into the cafe.

--->=◆=---

Ida Faye Mensinger

Of course I've been arrested, she thought. Fingerprints, mugshot, the whole nine yards. She could change her name, color her hair, and move to Timbuktu, but those prints never change. It was Darrell they wanted, not her. She was just an accessory in the wrong place at the wrong time. The Niobrara sheriff would soon know who Tammy Jo Martin was. She hated her name. Everyone in the Panhandle knew her as T.J. Martin the barrel-racing, float-riding, hometown rodeo queen. All hat and no sense. Pug Nelson, the grossly overweight sheriff who had repeatedly asked her out in high school to no avail, subjected her to a full body search wherein they painfully probed her body cavities while he watched, panting like a boar hog. Pug, who had an IQ somewhere south of eighty, had charged her with assault and resisting arrest, since she slapped a deputy for fondling her. The judge dismissed the charges against her, since Pug had failed to get a search warrant before ripping off the door to their single-wide in his halfhearted quest to find Darrell's stash of meth. A few years later, Pug was voted out of office and indicted for his complicity in dealing Darrell's dope.

Regular beatings had turned her into a whipped dog. Submission was her only defense. Marital rape was standard. She had asked herself a thousand times why she stayed in such an unhealthy relationship. The answer was always the same: fear. The first time she found a surprise in the oven, Darrell beat her so badly that she aborted. The second time went undiscovered until she was almost five months along, when he accused her of getting fat. He threw her out of the trailer, naked, in the midst of a January snowstorm, just after breaking three of her ribs and dislocating her jaw. Pug Nelson determined that she had slipped and fallen down the three steps to the trailer. Between her parents, family services, and a benevolent obstetrician, she was kept in the hospital and a shelter for battered women until term. Reluctantly, she gave the baby, a girl, up for adoption when Darrell threatened to kill both of them if she did not agree to relinquish the child.

Over the years, she ran three times. Once to Amarillo, an easy find, then to Tulsa, Oklahoma, which took a little longer, and lastly to East Texas, where she holed up in a swamp shack at Caddo Lake for nearly three months. Darrell seemed to enjoy the hunt, almost as much as beating and raping her when found. Relief finally came when he pulled a gun on a highway patrolman. The court deemed him a habitual criminal and a threat to society and sentenced him to twenty years at

Huntsville over in East Texas. On appeal, his viperous attorney got the sentence reduced to ten years with parole eligibility in five. He had somehow managed to keep his illicit drug business functioning while in prison and regularly sent henchmen to deliver cash and threats. She used the money to start a barrel-racing clinic in Borger, where she trained kids, horses, and attempted to heal. When she initiated divorce proceedings, Darrell sent his boys and attorney to convince her otherwise. The five years passed quickly, melting into the past as if time had been reduced to a foggy memory of yesterday's dream. She bought a gun.

"Excuse me, Ida Faye," Joe said from behind her, interrupting her concentration where she saw nothing of the present. "If it wouldn't be too inconvenient, would it be possible for you to seat the two gentlemen who are standing at the door of our fine dining establishment?"

Ida Faye looked out the kitchen door at the two men dressed in black suits standing next to the cash register. She glanced to the parking lot and saw the black Suburban with no license plate parked between the vintage Jeep and the cream Toyota. They looked like the Men in Black looking for space aliens. She turned to Joe and said, "You really should bite me, Joe."

"I'd like that very much," he said, smiling, then growled like a dog.

Ida Faye snatched up two menus from the end of the lunch counter and approached the two men. "Sound it out. Take each vowel separately. Seeee..." She dragged out the long E sound as she pointed to the sign below the register that read

Seat Yourself. "Then take the next syllable Ta, Ta, short A. That's it, SeeeTa. Seat yourself gentlemen." She smiled.

The two men stared at her blankly.

"Check your weapons at the door," she said with a note of seriousness. "This is a no-kill zone."

"Is it that obvious?" the man on the left asked.

"Right out of a movie," Ida Faye said. "They should just issue you uniforms that say *FEDS* on the front and back." She placed the menus in front of two seats at the counter. "Would you like coffee? I just made a fresh pot."

⭑

Jessica Martindale

"The farm is gone now—not gone, just different owners with different ideas, different tastes." Jessica looked at Sam as if she were confiding a painful secret. Her tight smile twitched nervously. "It had been my grandfather's. He put it together after the war. Some of the best bottom land in the county, deep, dark soils that produced record yields of corn and soybeans. He added hogs sometime in the late forties or early fifties and claimed that they paid off the operating loans, bought the tractors and combines and such. Mom, an only child, grew up with those smelly things. She never liked them. But even after Grandpa passed, she kept some in his memory, cared for them as if they were some portals to the past, to happier times, her childhood, I guess." Jessica adjusted her silverware as if setting the table for an unseen guest. "It's funny how perception and reality collide with the passage of time. After Dad disappeared, my ex and I—"

She saw Sam's eyebrows jump when he discovered she was divorced. She decided not to elaborate.

"We went through all the boxes of paperwork left behind. Farmers keep everything, none of it organized, just boxes of unrelated stuff they kept for unknown reasons. Everything from birthday cards to obituaries of people we never heard of. The diplomas from Iowa State University were a shock. I never knew Grandpa went to college. Both he and Grandma were Greeks. We found the deeds and the loans from the bank, along with love letters between Grandma and Grandpa when he was stationed in France during the war. I should mention that my ex is a banker, and he quickly discovered that the farm had lost profitability over the years and was teetering on bankruptcy at the time my father disappeared."

Jessica and Sam both turned toward the door and watched silently as two men in dark suits entered the cafe. The strange waitress belittled them for not seating themselves. "She's a bit different, don't you think?" Jessica said with a smile.

Sam nodded and flashed the whites of his eyes at her as he squeezed his chin. "What happened that caused your father to leave, if you don't mind my asking?"

"It was an explosion, a freak accident. An electrical spark ignited a tank of diesel fuel that blew up the barn. I'll never forget that day. The phone rang just as I was leaving for work. It was Mary Margaret Lucritz, my mom's best friend, who lived four miles down the road from the farm. She was crying, sobbing so much that I could barely understand her. She said that my dad had called and asked her to call me. Something terrible had happened, there had been an explosion and my mother was dead, and he would contact me later to explain. He never did. More than a decade has passed, and I haven't heard a word from him." She paused and inhaled deeply, gathering her composure. "I'm boring you. I apologize."

"Not at all," Sam said somewhat weakly. He offered a hesitant smile before looking down at the table. He felt as if he were wading into murky water, unable to see the dangers below.

"You don't need to hear the sordid details of my life."

Sam smiled. "You don't know what sordid details are until you hear my life stories."

"What you need to know is that there was a special bond between my father and me. He would never abandon me. Something happened that has prevented him from contacting me. Early on when I started digging into this, I hit roadblock after roadblock. It was as though it never happened. The government was somehow involved. I was watched and followed. I think my phones were bugged. They were always one step ahead of me. When I would travel on business, they would be waiting for me at my destination. Guys in suits just like the ones at the counter." She nodded toward the two men with their backs to the tables.

"It was pretty creepy. I think I became a little paranoid. After a couple of years, it all went away." Jessica looked down and was silent for several seconds. "Enough. The bottom line is that I'm looking for my father, and I need a decent photo of him to show people, to tack on telephone poles, put on milk cartons or give to a private investigator. I'm willing to pay you for your efforts."

Sam inhaled deeply. He appeared unsure of himself and seemed to struggle as if debating what to say. He rubbed his chin. "Have you considered that he may not want to be found?"

-»=◦ ✂ ◦=«-

Sidney Dawson

She felt the same, rich, although essentially the same as she had before inheriting millions from her mother. She had tried hard not to be affected. Her attitude toward government, especially the IRS, had changed substantially. Her tax burden was so heavy that it was laughable. She hired an accountant and a tax attorney to help her save what the government had not yet taken. She was thankful that she now owned her mother's publishing company. She was able to write off its losses and amortize the equipment and facilities needed to lose money in a dying industry. She had brought Pat, her stepfather, out of retirement and placed him at the head of the small, independent publishing company. Even the big five publishing houses in New York and Germany were struggling. Sales were down month after month. Retail consolidation had crushed the book industry. Independent bookstores were headed toward extinction. The stores still in business sold more games, gifts, and coffee than books. People weren't reading. They still bought the celebrity kiss-and-tell junk but were mostly entertained by the brainless chatter on their phones and reality TV. She had to remind herself daily that her losses were a write-off. Somewhere close to the top of the list of losses were her father's books. He had no clue that his books were not selling. Even his calendars and greeting cards were gathering dust on the bottom shelves of stores. People used apps on their phone for calendars and sent cute little animations complete with music and simulated fireworks for greeting cards. The world was changing, and her publishing company was a dinosaur mired in a pit of tar. She had royalty checks sent to him every six months from an account she had created with personal funds. In her mind, she justified the deception as rent she would have paid had she not been living with her father.

Sidney squinted as she made out the hands on the gaudy Dr. Pepper clock above the counter. Her father no longer seemed concerned about losing the light that seemed so precious to him a few minutes ago. He was too busy examining the merchandise in front of him. Sam seemed to be buying whatever the pretty woman was selling. He was adding her to his collection of broken women. She, herself, was no exception.

The thought of becoming deaf and blind someday was less frightening at times. She would not have to see and hear a world unhinged that seemed bent on destroying itself. It was the waiting that depressed her. One look at the television, one look at her father, the fish about to take the bait, one look at the brash waitress clunking across the room in her ridiculous cowboy boots all told her...told her what? she asked herself. She took a deep breath and smiled at the realization that she was mildly depressed, perhaps even jealous of her father's ability to attract members of the opposite sex while ignoring the depressing news of the world. She smiled at the realization that the eve of destruction was light years away and humankind was resilient.

Her smile became broader as the solution to her depression presented itself. In lieu of a man, she would get a dog. Her father seemed indifferent to the idea. Her mind was made up, however. It would be good for him, too. Maybe he would stop looking for strays to pick up. A new dog would not replace L2. It would simply be an addition to their family. There would be no comparisons with previous dogs, no disappointments, no favorites, just untarnished memories and new ones in the making.

She looked at the clock again. *So much for the father/ daughter outing,* she thought. She was eager to get home and begin the search. She needed something to hug, something to love, and something that loved her back.

"We're getting a new dog," Sidney said, beaming with delight as she looked up at the waitress who had suddenly appeared next to her.

"Would you like mustard and relish with that?" Ida Faye asked with a straight face as she searched Sidney's eyes for context.

"I'm sorry?" Sidney said, perplexed by the waitress's sense of humor.

"Oh, some people even want ketchup on their dog; to me, that's sacrilegious, an abomination to the dog and bun. Yellow mustard is all you need in order to bring out the savory exquisiteness of the mysterious blend of animal parts in that tube of delight."

Sidney pushed up her heavy glasses on the bridge of her nose as she continued to stare at the strange person in the frayed uniform of a waitress. "Don't tell me, you were an English major in college."

"Nah, barely made it out of high school. I took a few classes at West Texas State in Canyon. I wanted to be a large animal vet specializing in equine medicine. I got knocked up instead. That didn't work out either. My formal education came from reading romance novels. You know, the ones with a muscled, half-naked guy on the cover. I'm doing postgraduate research now on the dietary preferences of truck drivers. I've discovered a positive correlation between the amount of coffee they consume and the volume of urine contained in discarded plastic bottles on American highway off-ramps. My dissertation is entitled Piss Off America."

Sidney could not contain her amusement with this peculiar woman. She smiled and leaned back in the booth. "Any suggestions as to the kind of dog I should get?"

"I like the kind that eats poop and then throws up on the carpet just outside the bedroom door. I think they call them poop-a-doodles."

Sidney laughed out loud; her depression was vanquished. She covered her mouth with her hand as she watched the waitress scuff across the floor toward the counter.

Sam Dawson

Awkward was a feeling Sam knew well. He had apparently offended the Vice President for Domestic Marketing by suggesting other means of locating missing persons. Or was it the left-handed suggestion that another person, perhaps a man, was her superior in the organizational hierarchy of Pioneer Hybrids? He had the nagging feeling that there was something, perhaps a lot of something, she was leaving out. A person of her stature would easily have determined that she could not make her flight from Denver by agreeing to meet him at this out-of-the-way cafe in the middle of far eastern Wyoming. A VP for anything domestic would know the major transportation routes across the country. Her somewhat sappy account of her childhood bond with her father seemed a bit contrived, maybe rehearsed. She could have made her request for additional photos over the phone.

Sam looked out the window as if he were taking time to determine how to end the conversation and exit gracefully. He studied her rental car in the parking lot. The side panels were covered with gravel dust. The windshield, grill, bumper, and license plate were splattered heavily with bugs. He glanced at the Willys and noted that it was relatively clean in comparison. If she had driven from Laramie at roughly the same time he had driven from Cheyenne, they would have encountered similar populations of insects in flight.

"Mr. Dawson," Jessica said, sounding like Sam's sixth grade teacher in an attempt to get his attention.

"Here," he said, raising his hand from the table.

She cocked her head slightly and looked at him curiously then quickly looked past him toward the counter. "I should be going. I have a long drive ahead of me. Is there anything else you need from me?"

Sam could not help turning around. The two men in dark suits sat patiently at the counter, their hands wrapped around their coffee mugs. He turned back to Jessica and stared directly into her eyes. "You think those guys are following you, or are you just paranoid?"

"I'm hoping it's paranoia. But you can never be too sure," she added with a slight smile.

Sam was relieved by her attempt at humor. His question was forward and could easily have incited her anger. He decided to push his luck. "You didn't say why you thought you were being followed."

"Oh, it wasn't me they were after. It was my father. I guess they thought I might lead them to him."

"And why were they after your father?" Sam said, coaxing her.

"I have no idea," she said much too quickly.

Sam smiled and looked directly into her hazel eyes. "I think you do, Ms. Martindale."

"Are you calling me a liar, Mr. Dawson?"

"No, ma'am. You're just not telling me everything. If those two," he said, tossing his head slightly over his shoulder toward the counter, "are who you think they are, they will most likely have a satellite phone in that Suburban. Even if they're not here for you, they'll run the plate on your rental as a matter of course, and presto-changeo, they'll have a new mission."

"That's very perceptive, Mr. Dawson. It sounds to me as though you've had experience in these matters."

"Let's just say I've been around the block a time or two."

"I'll bet you have. Anything else you'd like to share with me?" she said, staring back at him.

Sam leaned back in his chair. He continued to look directly at her. "Their next call will be to their home office, where they'll instruct them to contact the company that rented you that car. Most the rentals these days have GPS tracking devices installed in them. They'll be able to tell where you've been and when you've been there. And, by the looks of your car, I'd say you've been around the block a time or two as well."

She wrinkled her brow, which narrowed her eyes as she glared at him. "What are you insinuating, Mr. Dawson?"

Sam wished he had kept his mouth shut. He had pushed her too far. Her anger was obvious. "I'm not insinuating a thing, Ms. Martindale." He pushed his chair back. "I'll check my negative files when I get home this evening and leave you a message on your home phone." He picked up the two tickets the waitress had placed on the table.

"That won't be necessary, Mr. Dawson," Jessica said in response to Sam picking up the tab.

"It's the least I can do for inconveniencing you," he said. Her hauntingly beautiful eyes made it difficult for him to end the conversation and leave.

"You asked me earlier if I thought he might not want to be found. That's the question that keeps me up at night, the one that must be answered before I can move on."

Sam slid forward in his chair. He did not want to end the conversation.

CHAPTER 5

12:30 p.m.

Brad Holcomb

It was a trench cleaner, a Winchester Model 97, a pump with an exposed hammer, originally designed by John Browning as a waterfowl gun, then repurposed in World War I for trench warfare. Its short, eighteen-inch barrel, and cylinder choke could spit double ought buckshot as fast as the slide action pump could be worked while holding the trigger back. It was not his choice for a personal defense weapon. Rather, it was a cheap, no-questions-asked transaction with a truck driver in need of cash. Five in the magazine and one in the chamber would make a mess of the cafe but would buy him some time. The two at the counter would be more than dead. He would take the pickup, head southwest to Esterbrook, Forest Service roads through the Medicine Bow to Rock River, cross I-80 at Arlington, and stay in the forest until he picked up Highway 130 then all the way to Riverside and Encampment, and then Highway 70 over Battle Pass. He had the route memorized. It was all part of the plan. Ida Faye could come with him if she wanted. He owed her that much.

"Are you all right?" Ida Faye asked as she approached the large, stainless-steel sink where he stood motionless, hands deep in the soapy water. "Hello, Earth to Brad. You look like you've seen a ghost."

"The two at the counter, what do they want?" he snapped.

"I don't know. I haven't taken their order yet. They probably want burgers and fries and—"

He shot her a look that said he was serious and not to play games with him. "Who are they?" he said through clenched teeth.

"Federales of some sort. FBI, most likely. Jeez, Brad. Take it easy, would ya? All they want is lunch. If you want, I'll ask them if they're looking for you."

He ignored her. "How much money is in the register?"

"Not much, maybe eighty bucks," she said with a serious look. "Why?"

"Find out what they're doing here," Brad said with a sense of urgency.

"Um, excuse me, Ida Faye," Joe said, poking his head into the kitchen. "If it wouldn't be too much trouble, I was wondering if maybe you could take the order from the two gentlemen at the counter. They're looking as if they might leave."

"Sure thing, boss, as soon as I have a smoke and a nap."

"Thank you," Joe said, smiling as he retreated from the doorway.

Ida Faye turned back to Brad. "Can you believe the gall of that guy?"

"Find out where they're going, Ida Faye," Brad snarled. "It's important." He immediately saw the frightened look in her eyes.

Ida Faye Mensinger

"Okay, fellas, I can't wait any longer. What's it gonna be?" Ida Faye said as she poised her pencil over her order pad. They could have been brothers. Nondescript must have been a minimum requirement when applying to the Bureau, she guessed. The guy on the right looked at his watch. He was obviously irritated.

"Cheeseburger, fries, small diet cola. Can I get that to go?"

"Of course. And you, sir?" she said, turning to the guy on the left, a younger version of his partner.

"I'll have the same."

"I knew that," she said, scribbling on her pad. She tore off the page, turned, and pierced it on a hook above the grill. "To go," she said to Joe, who was already slapping burger patties on the hissing grill. She grabbed the coffee pot and returned to the look-a-likes at the counter.

Filling their coffee cups, she asked, "Where you headed?"

Neither of them responded, nor did they even look at her.

Ida Faye waited. "Don't make me ask you again. I'll spit on your burgers if you continue being rude."

The guy on the right cracked a smile and looked up at her. "What does Niobrara mean?"

"It's a Native American word, Ponca, I think, that means where you headed?"

"North," the guy on the right said, his smile a little broader.

"Montana? Me too, soon as I get the money back my dead husband stole. You best stop when you get to Plentywood, 'cause your jurisdiction ends when you cross over into Saskatchewan."

"You know where Mule Creek Junction is?" he asked, studying her.

"Yep," she answered quickly, returning his stare.

"Well?"

"Well what? Is this what they teach you at the academy? Interrogation 101?" Ida Faye put her hand on her hip. "You need to be more specific. Where you headed?"

"Mule Creek Junction."

"Well if it ain't Bud Abbott and Lou Costello playing 'Who's on First' with me."

"We're looking for the WT Ranch."

"As in Winston Tucker? We heard on the news a little while ago that somebody offed that worthless piece of human refuse. I hope you're spending my tax dollars to find the hero who finally brought some justice to the victims of his abuse. That person deserves a reward."

Both men looked at her blankly. The older guy said, "I take it you didn't like our former secretary of defense."

"Duh," she said, raising her eyebrows. She looked at the younger man. "You were just a suckling when the misdeeds of that man were finally exposed. It cost him the presidency. Thank God. I hope he rots in hell. Say," she said, smiling, "you guys are good. Look how you extracted that information from me without torture."

The older agent looked at her as if she was from outer space. He swiveled on his stool. *"Eat Here?"* he asked, gesturing over his shoulder with his thumb to the large white letters painted on the picture window. "Is that the name of this cafe?"

"Nope," Ida Faye answered with a smile, then turned and walked away.

---- ✷ ----

Jessica Martindale

"Of course, I considered that he may not want to be found," she said without looking at Sam. "Believe me, I've considered all the possibilities," she added as she made eye contact with him. "It's both funny and sad, the things you discover after a loved one is gone. He was a decorated Vietnam veteran with a whole bunch of medals still in their boxes. Two Silver Stars, a couple of Purple Hearts, and several other honors pinned upon him after battles. I had no idea he was a veteran. Mom must have known, but I didn't have a clue. He never talked about his past. I assumed he was from Wyoming or at least spent time here. Once, he took Mom and me to a cabin he had built up in the mountains, somewhere in the Medicine Bow National Forest. It was very isolated, and the setting was spectacular. I was a kid and never thought to ask him who he was.

"It wasn't until much later, when I started to notice that the fathers of childhood friends had disappeared, that I realized I knew nothing about them. The men who were perpetually driving their tractors across their fields, cussing from underneath a combine, their hands covered in grease. They were the old guys with weathered creases on their faces who would smile and wink at me at the feed store. I guess I thought they had retired and gone south or someplace where men go when they get old. Their wives were still there, some trying to hold their places together, others moving to town or moving in with their daughters and their families, never with their sons, always with their daughters. It was then that I realized how selfish and self-centered I was as a youth. I had never asked him about his past. And then one day, he just disappeared, vanished as if he had never existed. That's when things started to get very strange. The guys in suits, I called them G-men, started showing up everywhere."

"Did you ever find out who they were and why they were following you?"

"No, I assumed it had something to do with national security. Something he knew or did. Something they didn't want the public to find out. Again, it wasn't me they wanted; it was him. He must have known they would use me to find him. That's why he hasn't contacted me. I think he's trying to protect me."

Jessica paused. She sat up straight and looked directly at Sam. "None of this, of course, concerns you. I've told you way too much. I just wanted a decent photo of him, and you've been very kind to consider my request and listen to my sappy story."

Sam sat silently, staring down at the table for several seconds. Slowly, he looked up and into her hazel-green eyes. "You think he's here, don't you?"

⇥⊚⊶⊷

Sidney Dawson

Her left hearing aid squealed loudly as she attempted to adjust it behind her ear. She nervously pushed her glasses up on the bridge of her nose and looked around the cafe to see if anyone had heard the annoying high-pitched screech. They had not.

Her father was engrossed in conversation with the woman who moments earlier had been a perfect stranger. The woman appeared to be nervous. She frequently tugged at the neckline of her dress and looked down at the table as she spoke. Sidney glanced at the clock. It was half past twelve. She looked out the window and saw dark clouds building to the west. The late-afternoon showers were coming earlier than predicted. *There goes his precious light.* She was tempted to walk over to their table and not too subtly remind him of why they were there.

Sidney took a deep breath and released it slowly. Really, why *were* they there? Sure, her dad needed to satisfy the people who had funded his project. She assumed it was more than that. He wanted to publish another giant coffee table book. This one, he argued, was not a random collection of heart-rending pictures of headstones and cemeteries. Rather, it would be the definitive listing of Wyoming's burial grounds in alphabetical order by county. There would be twenty-three chapters, one for each county, each chapter, in turn, containing the alphabetical listing of cemeteries. Encyclopedic, she had complained. She wanted him to concentrate on the artistic aspects of his photography. That's what his audience wanted: stunning images of graveyards, not an inch-and-a-half-thick geographical catalog.

Pat, his publisher, had looked down at the floor and shook his head when she explained what Sam was working on. "It won't sell," he had said softly. "Bookstores won't stock a book that costs that much. Customers won't buy a book that costs that much. We can't publish a book that costs that much. We'll lose our shirts."

He was right. No matter how much lipstick you put on that pig, it was bound to lose money. They would be forced to buy back all the books that bookstores had returned because they did not sell. Her dilemma was whether to subsidize the publication of the book and fake the sales or attempt to convince her father it was an unworthy project. What Sam saw through the lens of his camera was something totally different from what consumers saw. He was delusional.

Sidney loved her father, in spite of his many flaws. She tried hard not to list them or dissect them, searching for their origin. As his daughter, it was not her responsibility to analyze or cure him. Rather, her job was to support him as he had supported her through all the trials and tribulations of attaining adulthood. She accepted him. Someday she would be orphaned. Then what? Deaf, blind, and alone were the sobering realities she faced. Her wealth was of little consequence. She looked discreetly at the woman with her father. A stepmother only complicated things. Time seemed to be running out. She was thirty-two and a half years old, with a crush on a twenty-year-old sub-adult. There were no other prospects.

"How about this one?" Ida Faye said from behind her.

"Excuse me?" Sidney jerked to attention, startled by the waitress's sudden appearance. She had not heard the woman's noisy boots clopping across the floor.

"Says here they are loyal, kind, and obedient," she said, pointing at a picture of a dog in a dog identification book that had seen better days. The *Simon and Schuster Pictorial Guide To Dog Breeds* had a broken binding, and pages were slid out here and there. "Sounds like a boy scout, huh?"

Sidney leaned forward and pushed her glasses up. "Bracco Italiano?"

"It's an Italian hound," Ida Faye said excitedly. "I just love hounds. Don't you?"

"How'd you know?"

"Just guessed. Says here it's an ancient breed that was developed back in the twelve hundreds. They're a versatile hunting dog, whatever that is, mostly used for birds. Over in Europe, they use 'em for finding truffles. So, they must have a good nose. That is unless truffles smell like Fay Ann Green did in third grade."

Sidney leaned closer to the opened book with a color picture of a dog in the classic pointing pose of a bird dog: rigid straight lines, a bobbed tail, raised foreleg, head lowered with eyes and nose pointing at something in the grass. The dog had long, drooping ears like a bloodhound and pendulous lips. It was short-haired, with blotches of rusty orange-colored fur over white, with lots of ticking. "Never heard of them," Sidney said without taking her eyes from the book.

"They're kind of rare," Ida Faye added. "They're sort of making a comeback. The breed was almost wiped out during World War II. The Italians were starving, and some folks ate 'em. Kind of makes you think twice when ordering meatballs with your spaghetti."

Sidney winced and shook her head.

"A cousin breed to the Bracco is the Spinone, not to be confused with Spumoni. You know, the ice cream," Ida Faye said, smiling. "That breed was almost wiped out, too. I guess it tasted like multiflavored gelato."

Sidney covered her mouth as she laughed out loud. "Children's books, I'm telling you. You're a natural," she said, shaking her head.

"Says here the Bracco is intelligent, docile, easy to train, affectionate with family, good with kids and other dogs. Sounds like the perfect man, doesn't it?"

Smiling broadly, Sidney studied the woman's battered face. "Yes, yes it does," she said softly.

--=◦❊◦=--

Sam Dawson

"Yes," Jessica said, slightly above a whisper. She stared at the table, avoiding eye contact with Sam. "You're very perceptive, Mr. Dawson." She looked at him briefly to see if her observation registered. Sam did not respond. "I think he's in Wyoming. I'm pretty sure he was born and raised here. He's come home."

"It's a big state," Sam said. "You could be looking for a long time."

"I keep thinking I'll see something familiar. I was just a kid when he brought my mom and me here, about the same age my boys were when he disappeared. They have very few memories of him. I guess I was hoping it would be like finding something you misplaced, car keys or earrings. If I retraced my steps... It's funny how everything in the past is reduced to snippets that seem out of context: words, expressions, laughs, sights and sounds, even smells that are remembered so vividly. The thing is they're only puzzle pieces, and you're not even sure if they're in the right box." She shook her head. "It's a bit depressing to think your entire life has been reduced to a few words or images that float past you like confetti on New Year's Eve."

Sam nodded his agreement. "I guess that's why I take photographs of cemeteries, so people won't forget. Isn't that the purpose of cemeteries?"

"I'm not sure," Jessica said. She studied Sam as if she were waiting for him to make the next move on a chessboard. "My biological father's remains were never found. His name is etched into a black granite wall in D.C. I went there once only to discover there were no memories, just a name along with fifty-nine thousand others. When Vietnam began shipping remains to the U.S. a while back, we were both terrified and hopeful. Terrified he would be among them and hopeful that he was still alive in a prison camp somewhere. What some families got were the remains of their loved ones stuffed into a plastic bag inside a cardboard box and placed in an expensive casket that they buried on some hill like that one," she said as she pointed to the photograph in Sam's book. "I don't mean to be cynical. I just think there might be better ways to remember the dead than cemeteries."

Sam leaned back in his chair and frowned. She was being cynical, and she meant it. Behind those beautiful eyes was a force to be reckoned with. "There go my book sales. I hate to admit it, but I think you are right. I can't say I haven't thought about it. What do you do with seventy million dead people every year? And that number is growing as our planet's population increases. That's a lot of biomass. That's a lot of real estate taken up by corpses. Cremation isn't the answer. Too much energy consumed and too much carbon dioxide and other pollutants released into the atmosphere. Green burials are starting to catch on. No embalming, no casket, no monuments; sort of a large-scale mulching process. You can still visit the deceased, however. In some cemeteries bodies are fitted with a GPS device. Loved ones are handed a GPS tracker when they come to visit. China is building islands or underwater reefs with dead people. You can visit your dead relatives if you know how to scuba dive. Of course, outer space holds unlimited potential. Rest assured the capitalists are working on solutions. There's money to be made from the business of dying."

"Now who's being cynical?" Jessica smiled.

"Touché."

"It appears to me that you have been successful by exploiting the dead," she said, her smile dissipating.

"That seems a little harsh. You don't think it's important to record the historically important reminders of the past, of making the past accessible to the future?"

"Okay, match point. It's my serve," she shot back. "Can you convince me that your art trumps profit?"

"I'm not sure I can convince you of anything," Sam said somewhat sternly. "I've been very fortunate. The poor, struggling artist routine is best reserved for those who refuse to compromise their often narrow view of creative ingenuity for the necessities of life. At some point you've got to put bread on the table. Call it what you want. Unlike you, Madame Vice President, I'm reluctant to say I'm a profiteer."

"Out of bounds, Mr. Dawson. Game." Jessica reached across the table and pulled Sam's plate with his untouched pie toward her. "To the victor," she said with a come-hither smile.

CHAPTER 6
12:38 p.m.

Brad Holcomb

He remembered the past. It was the present that escaped him, especially nouns. People, places, and things all familiar to him had lost their names. He was forced to describe them rather than name them. Their names would come later, often at odd moments, like a bolt of lightning from a cloudless sky. He found it difficult to converse when the words would not come. He sounded stupid. His heartbreaking conclusion was that his memories had drifted away, leaving him stranded in the present world that he found frighteningly abhorrent. Mostly, he listened. Equally disturbing was his forgetfulness of actions he had already taken. The mundane things, repetitive tasks, often disappeared moments after he had done them. He would brush his teeth and moments later have no memory of having done so. He would brush them again.

Lately, he was confusing the past with the present. He would look for an item that he had not had for years, convinced that he had simply misplaced it before coming to the realization that it no longer existed. Sometimes he would forget that he had forgotten. Time was a mystery. He had no trouble inhabiting the boy he had been more than six decades ago. The time in between had somehow magically disappeared. The details were phenomenal—sights, sounds, smells, tastes, and textures were all there. He liked boyhood better than adolescence and certainly better than adulthood. Of course there were things he wished he could forget, things he wished he had done or said. Regrets were never forgotten. Fortunately, most were pleasant memories, born of innocence and wonder. He did not know what was happening to him. It all seemed so sudden. His life seemed so compressed now that he could see the end.

"Okay," Ida Faye said confidently as she burst into the kitchen. "They're headed up to Mule Creek Junction, lookin' for the WT Ranch. I suspected as much given the news of Tucker's demise. They ain't lookin' for you. Satisfied?"

Brad looked at her blankly, as if he had forgotten the question.

"When are you going to shoot straight with me, Brad? I could run interference for you better if I knew why you were on the run."

Brad put his soiled apron back on. He winced as he tied the strings behind him; his swollen hands had lost their dexterity. Outside the kitchen he heard the alternate clank and scrape of Joe's spatula on the grill; grease popped and sputtered as he fried the burgers. Small talk drifted in, a man and a woman, their words unintelligible. A fork clattered against a plate. "Montana, huh?" Brad said with a slight grin.

"Yes," she shot back. "I know it sounds batty. I like to think of it as a fresh start, a do-over that puts the past in a drum at the bottom of the deepest lake where no one will ever find it. We could do it, Brad, just the two of us."

He looked at her sympathetically. "And we'd live off my 401K and your social security?"

"I was sort of thinking we could knock off liquor stores and banks. Heck, I don't know. Don't throw water on it. I know I'm dreaming. It's all I got, Brad. A girl has to have hope."

Brad searched her eyes. He had not had hope in nearly half a century. He knew what she meant. "I'm a septuagenarian; my only hope is to die in my sleep."

"I'm an Aquarius," she shot back. "I have enough hope for both of us."

⇥⟡⇤

Ida Faye Mensinger

"Order up," Joe yelled loud enough to be heard in South Dakota.

"Jeez Louise, Joe, you'll scare the livin' bejesus out of Snickelfritz and Bohunk here," Ida Faye said, sweeping her arm toward the counter, where the two men in casket clothes sat. Both men looked at her with expressions that said they were not amused.

"I'm sorry," Joe said, inspecting his spatula closely and pulling a hair from the crack between the blade and handle. "Sometimes the hustle and bustle of the world's busiest cafe has a tendency to drown out my proclamations."

"How long's it been since you broke even, Joe?"

Joe turned and studied her face. His eyes scanned her wounds. "A long time, and I'm here to tell you that's about to change. Between highway resurfacing and my reorganization plan, I'll be rolling in dough."

"Reorganization?" Ida Faye raised her eyebrows. "Pray tell."

"I'll be downsizing. There'll be incentives for early retirement."

"What incentives are we talkin' about, Joe?"

"Not getting fired," he said as if she should have known.

"Exactly how do you reorganize with only two employees?" Ida Faye asked, placing a hand on her hip.

"The dishwasher's job will be retrenched. The server's position, i.e. waitperson, will be retrained to do both jobs."

"So, I'll wait tables, bus, clean, put up with you, *and* do the dishes all for the same money. Is that what I'm hearing, Joe?"

"Yes. Genius, isn't it?"

"Bite me."

Joe smiled and licked his lips.

Ida Faye snatched the two paper bags and brought them to the counter. She filled two paper cups with diet cola, covered them with plastic lids, and pulled two straws from the old-fashioned straw container next to the soda fountain. "You know, folks in these parts don't cotton much to outsiders, especially from back east, comin' in and buying up family ranches that have been in the family for generations and treatin' everybody like they were stupid. If you're looking for the killer, I can assure you there will be a long list of suspects," she said, placing the bags in front of them. "That'll be two hundred and forty-six dollars plus tip," she said with a straight face.

The older man, who had not spoken, pulled a ten and two ones from his wallet and handed them to her.

"Mule Creek Junction is about fifty miles north of Lusk on Highway 85. Lusk is twenty miles that way." She motioned west with her head. "Ain't nothin' up there 'cept grass and cattle. You should have flown. I hear tell Tucker has a runway capable of landing a passenger jet."

Ida Faye watched the two men leave. From the corner of her eye, she saw the two-way door to the kitchen was slightly open. Brad also watched the two men leave. She saw him slowly release the hammer of the Winchester 97 to the half-cock position. "Take a breath, Brad," she said, pushing her way into the kitchen.

Brad Holcomb looked at her as if he had seen a ghost.

⋯►◆◄⋯

Jessica Martindale

Jessica watched the Suburban back from the parking lot and turn onto the highway. "They think he's here, too," she said, turning back to Sam.

"You think those guys were your G-men?" Sam watched the black Suburban recede down the highway to the west.

"Sure. Unfortunately, what I think and what is reality are often two very different things."

"Have you ever confronted them?"

"I used to. I was wrong most of the time. Paranoia can be very embarrassing at times. Once in Kentucky I challenged two Mormons who were on a mission. Another time, in Akron, I flipped off a couple of guys in suits in a restaurant because they kept looking at me, only to find out I had a foot and a half of toilet paper stuck on my shoe like a tail on a kite. They turned out to be Goodyear Tire executives."

"You think these guys were the real deal," Sam said, motioning to where the two men had been sitting.

"Either that or criminals. I saw the guy's shoulder holster when he reached for his wallet to pay the bill."

"So, you think he's here. They think he's here, or they think you think he's here. Hell, *I'm* starting to think he's here. What if he's not here? What I'm trying to say is what if he's, you know, no longer with us?"

"What if he's dead?" Jessica leaned back in her chair. "Sure, I've thought of that. Actually, I've thought about that a lot. Even if I knew that was the case, I think I would still keep looking for him." She looked at Sam and smiled. "I think that's what a therapist would call a need for closure. I need closure. I'm unsure of what that entails. I don't envision a group of locals standing in a semicircle singing his praises or some judicial hearing that vindicates whatever he's accused of. I wish I knew what would bring me closure. I've had a recurring dream of seeing myself trudge up that hill," she pointed again to the picture in Sam's book, "weaving between the rows of graves. I'm carrying some flowers, daises, I think, that have seen a better day. I bend over and stand them against a headstone. It's a place to visit once a year. As you say, a place to remember, a place to say thank-you."

"And if he's alive?" Sam asked soberly.

"Then I'll ask him why," she shot back immediately. "Why the cloak-and-dagger crap? What could you possibly have done or know that would cause you to abandon me? Whatever it is, it's ancient history. Let's resolve this and try to patch up all the years that we've been apart."

"You think that's possible?"

"I don't know. I'm sure it's worth trying. They say that time heals all. I'd like to think that time has healed whatever has caused him to run."

Sam straightened his fork where his pie plate used to be. She could tell something was on his mind. "You want to know if my need for closure warrants jeopardizing his safety."

"No, I want to know if you are really going to eat my pie."

Sidney Dawson

If this godforsaken place had cell service, she could use her phone to Google the Bracco Italiano breed and perhaps find a breeder that wasn't on a different continent. Sidney was interested; follow-up would have to wait until they returned to civilization. The cuteness of a new puppy was easily displaced by the realities of house soiling, destructive chewing, barking, and all the other unwanted behaviors crammed into their short lifespans. Not unlike a new boyfriend, she reasoned. She wondered if there was a more suitable name for a potential mate. The "boy" fragment of the word made her nervous. A more suitable synonym such as suitor or gentleman friend would make her feel less guilty.

Again, the disparity of cultural acceptance of men wooing younger women made her angry. She looked across the room at her father, who seemed quite comfortable making eyes at a woman who was clearly younger than him. The double standard was blatantly offensive to her. Society in general seemed to discriminate against women. It seemed that every day there were subtle hints of her inferiority. If she rebelled, she would quickly be labeled a feminist or worse. At least in this country she would not be circumcised or stoned to death for her views. So what if she had a romantic relationship with a man twelve years her junior? Would God strike her blind and deaf? Her jaw hurt from gritting her teeth.

Her mind was made up. As soon as they returned to civilization, she would let her intentions be known. At least she would accept his flirtations and reciprocate within reason. If that led to something more serious, then so be it. What could possibly go wrong? Everything, she reasoned. There would be regrets. As hard as she wished it otherwise, in spite of her sound reasoning and good intentions, there would be regrets, and there would definitely be remorse. Self-reproach had not worked in the past. She likened it to wearing those pointy-toed pumps that looked so good while they crippled her toes. She would do it again.

And what if he said no thanks? What if he said, "Are you joking me, old lady?" What if he looked at her with disdain, repugnance, tried to visualize her naked, and shivered with disgust? What if, what if, what if... *Wait, he's a man.* Well, almost a man. He would not be thinking with his brain. Men were easy to seduce. She pursed her lips and inhaled deeply through her nose. She knew it was not about seduction. She wanted something more and was unsure of what it was. Companionship, devotion, unconditional love... Sidney shook her head and smiled inwardly at the realization that what she wanted was a dog.

The waitress approached noisily, scuffing across the scarred linoleum. She grabbed Sidney's water glass and poured ice cubes and water into it from the side of her pitcher. "I had a dog, a good dog. His name was Hank. You know, after *Hank the Cowdog*."

Sidney frowned and looked at her quizzically.

"It was a series of kid's books. The author lived in the Texas Panhandle, where I'm from. Anyway, Hank was a Queensland Red Heeler, an Australian Cattle Dog. Most of 'em are blue. Mine was a Red Heeler, not really red—kind of a light brown. He was a good dog, traveled the circuit with me. You couldn't get in the pickup without him jumpin' in the back. That crazy dog would heel anything—sheep, goats, chickens, kids; if it moved, he'd heel it. I raised him from a pup, and he was pretty protective of me. He'd get between me and anybody that he thought might be threatenin' me. He was eight or nine when I got married. One day my good-for-nothin' dead husband kicked Hank so hard, it ruptured his spleen, and he died. I cried for days. That dog was my best friend. I knew then that I'd made a big mistake in marryin' that son of a sapsucker."

"That's horrible," Sidney said. "Did you call the authorities?"

Ida Faye looked at Sidney as if she were from another planet. "No, honey, I valued my spleen."

Sidney studied the woman's battered face.

"All I'm sayin' is that given a choice between a man and a dog, you might consider the one with four legs."

⊶⊷ ❈ ⊶⊷

Sam Dawson

He liked the way she ate his pie, her cheeks bulging from bites too large. Sam was tempted to reach across the table and wipe the fluffy white meringue from the corner of her mouth, a move reserved for mothers and lovers. She smiled at him unabashed then licked the corner of her mouth. He did not speak for fear of making no sense.

"You had insinuated that I'm a profiteer. I've never pretended not to be a capitalist," she said, making eye contact slowly. "Of course I'm a profiteer. That's what drives our economy. You haven't convinced me that you're not. If your profession is art, then you are either independently wealthy or a hobbyist. I'd think you'd have a hard time convincing the IRS in an audit that all the deductions you most likely claim are for the sake of art. If you're not making a profit, then it must be a hobby, and those deductions are fraudulent. We're talking major payback and fines. Maybe jail," she added with a wide grin.

Sam smiled back at her. She had a playful spirit. He wondered if she was flirting with him or was just one of those people who exhibited irrepressible joy with everyone she met. He gestured with his thumb over his shoulder toward Sidney. "They'd have to take that up with lawyer Daggett, my daughter, the she devil. She'd scratch their eyes out."

"Is that an inherited characteristic?"

"I don't know. She tends to be more verbal, while I'm a bit more physical in dealing with perceived threats."

Jessica looked at him and smiled politely.

Sam thought she was holding back. He decided not to risk misinterpreting her intentions.

"You're not one of those guys who thinks every woman he meets is flirting with him, are you?" she said, her eyes narrowed.

"I'm afraid so," Sam admitted. "My daughter tells me it's a major character flaw. I think I just like having my heart broken. I'm sort of a glutton for punishment."

"I see," she said then paused as if searching for the appropriate response.

"Once," Sam laughed, "when I was just starting out, I had this huge crush on a woman I had met at a book signing, a real looker. I was pretty full of myself, my first book and all. It was destined to become a best seller, of course. I was newly divorced and thought I had the world on a string with a rainbow over my shoulder. We dated a few times, had some laughs. I fell for her head over heels. She had a major career opportunity and moved on; took a job in Los Angeles. I thought about her for years, decades actually. You know, one of those daydreams where you ask yourself what if you'd done this or said that differently. I was pretty sure she felt the same way. Then one day I was browsing the shelves of a run-down used bookstore in Denver and spotted the familiar spine of my first book tucked away on a bottom shelf underneath a stack of old *Playboy* magazines. It had been out of print for years, with only a short run of five hundred copies. The jacket was scuffed and torn, but otherwise it was in good shape with a tight binding. I opened it up to the title page and saw the name of the woman I had dreamed of all those years."

Jessica pushed her pie plate away, the crust uneaten. "That was an interesting but totally unnecessary story, Mr. Dawson. Just to be clear, I'm not flirting with you. If this book," she said, pointing at the book on the table, "should end up in a second-hand bookstore, it will be because my heirs disposed of it. As

I've told you, it has the only photo of my father taken close to the time of his disappearance. That is my only emotional attachment to this book." She intentionally looked at her watch as if surprised to see it on her wrist. "I should get on the road. I have a very long drive ahead of me, thanks to you. Please let me know if you find any additional photos."

Sam stared at her for a long, uncomfortable moment. He now knew for sure that she was not flirting with him. Just because she was gorgeous, she assumed all men were smitten with her. He was the guy who had what she wanted, and she had wrongfully blamed him for missing her flight. The woman was schizophrenic. He would not waste his time looking for additional negatives. Her entire story was full of holes.

"Pop," Sidney said a little too loudly.

Sam turned to find his daughter standing next him.

"You better take a look outside." Sidney motioned with her hand toward the cafe window.

CHAPTER 7

12:43 p.m.

Brad Holcomb

Flashes of memory exploded unexpectedly, random and disparate from the realities of the moment. The skin on his arm below his left shoulder burned. He rubbed the raised scar tissue from a war no one had supported. It was the unseen scars that stole his sleep, the memories that he would never be rid of. Little Nail was slumped forward in his harness in the left gun bay, the barrel of his M60 pointed skyward, his jungle fatigues soaked dark red. His head bobbed with the erratic movements of the Huey as they frantically pitched away from the LZ. It was 1971 again. It was always 1971. He could smell the chopper's exhaust and the hot barrel of his M60 in the right gun bay. He could hear and feel the AK rounds as they slammed into the armored plating below his feet.

Nighttime was the worse. Forty-five years evaporated into the ethereal mist that descended upon him, vaporous whispers of the past. The dead were all around him. Rat Man, Gaseous Clay, Little Nail, and a host of others frequently flashed before him as clips in a newsreel, laughing, smoking, shouting insults in one frame, and bloody corpses in the next. He had always felt guilty that he had lived and so many others were names on a wall in Washington. Twice wounded, he had never been fortunate enough to catch the big one. "Cowboy, you lucky bastard," his best friend, Goose, had repeatedly said with a toothy grin at the end of a mission.

The past haunted him every day. Forty-five years of scattered memories of war that had changed his life. If he had been lucky, he would have died. Eternal damnation was the price he paid for living. Brad Holcomb, a.k.a. Little Nail, died in 1971. His infectious smile, his silly laugh, and gentle nature died with him. Cowboy assumed his identity in 2003.

The air in the kitchen had gone stale. Joe wiped his greasy hands on his apron as he walked to the back door. He saw the heel of the Winchester sticking out from beneath a stack of dirty dishtowels behind the sink. He had seen it before. He glanced at Brad, who leaned against the sink. Neither man spoke for a long moment.

"Do you remember when that gang of hardcore bikers on their way to Sturgis descended on us like angry wasps? They were the real deal, not those imitation wannabes that we see on their way to the rally. Remember when that fat, bearded guy with a swastika tattooed on his forehead grabbed Ida Faye around the waist and sat her in his lap, and you stepped out from the kitchen with that sawed-off shotgun leveled from your waist? The noise of the slide action being slid back, then forward, cocking the hammer and slamming a shell into the chamber of that twelve-gauge silenced everybody in the cafe. The expression on your face left no mistake that you meant business. You never said a word." Joe scratched behind his ear with his left hand. "You know, I've played that incident over and over again, and each time I regret that it wasn't me who had to defend her." Joe smiled, looked down, and shook his head.

"Seems hot in here," Joe said to no one in particular as he stepped toward the screen door, opened it, and stepped out. "There's not a breath of air stirrin' out here. That's a rare event in windy Wyoming. There's no birds flitting between the cedars or sparrows hopping around on the ground. This air is dead."

Ida Faye crossed the kitchen, thumping the side of her head with the heel of her hand. "My ears are popping like we just descended from thirty thousand feet or something." She pushed Joe aside on the small landing and looked up at the sky. "Holy cow," she said with amazement. "I haven't seen anything like this since I left the Panhandle." There was a greenish hue that had magically transformed the sky around them. The earth appeared yellow. She went down one step from the landing and turned to the west. "Guys, I think we're in for it."

Brad stood behind the screen door and eyed the approaching storm. He said nothing, as was usual when around Joe.

A black wall of storm clouds had built along the western horizon. Flashes of lightning illuminated the rolling, rain-laden clouds. The ominous sound of thunder that followed told of the intense threat to come. "I don't think this is your typical afternoon thunder boomer," Ida Faye warned. "This one smells like a tornado."

She scurried up the landing, ducked back under Joe's arm, and hurried past Brad, across the kitchen, and out into the cafe. The Scottsbluff, Nebraska weather team had interrupted their regular programming to scare the living bejesus out of their viewership with colorful radar images of a severe thunderstorm moving eastward toward Harrison and Chadron in the northern Nebraska panhandle, the two population centers just east of the cafe. There was no mention of Wyoming. The radar showed a wall of dark red surrounded by yellow and green blobs. She turned up the volume.

"Doppler radar shows strong rotations, which has prompted the National Weather Service to issue a tornado watch for the following counties..." Again, there was no mention of Wyoming. "This storm has the potential to produce heavy downpours and flash flooding, along with damaging hail." The chubby weatherman had removed his sports coat, loosened his necktie, and rolled up his sleeves to convey the seriousness of his message. "All right, all right," the excited forecaster said, holding a finger to the tiny speaker in his ear. "This just in: the National Weather Service has upgraded their tornado watch to a warning. This means that a tornado has been seen and confirmed by radar. Also, reports of baseball-sized hail and damaging winds have been received. People in the projected path of this storm are advised to seek shelter immediately. Folks, you need to go to your safe place now." He looked like he was about to hyperventilate. "Remember, if you don't have a safe place, go to an interior room away from outer walls and windows. A closet or bathroom is a good choice. Expect damage to buildings, vehicles, and livestock from the hail accompanying this storm. Stay indoors. Again, Doppler radar indicates—"

There was an eerie, stunned silence in the cafe as everyone turned to look out the window. The strange light cast no shadows. "Do you have a basement?" Sam asked as he turned toward the waitress.

"No," Ida Faye said. "There's only this cafe and that beat-up tornado magnet of a house trailer out back. Back home in Texas, you never wanted to get between a storm and a trailer court." She put her hand on her hip, her brow wrinkled. "Funny we don't have more tornadoes around here. Wyoming has more house trailers per capita than any other state."

"Where are we supposed to go?" Sidney asked, then opened her mouth wide in an attempt to relieve the pressure.

"We used to try to outrun them in our pickups," Ida Faye said. "That worked pretty well during the day. It was a bit iffy at night. In this country, there ain't enough roads to get out of the way of a storm like that. There's nothing in the vicinity going north and south; just that highway out there going east and west."

Nothing moved. Sam scanned the parking lot to see if there was anything he could park the Willys under.

"I don't see a funnel cloud," Jessica said, craning her slender neck to the west.

"Sometimes tornadoes can be more than a mile across at the bottom, even wider at the top. They just look like a bad storm until the winds hit," Ida Faye offered.

"All right," the cherubic weatherman said. "If you're just tuning in, we have a weather emergency in place. The National Weather Service has issued a tornado warning for Goshen, Platte, and Niobrara counties in east-central Wyoming and for Sioux, Dawes, Box Butte, and Sheridan counties in Nebraska. Doppler radar shows the storm moving from west to east at speeds exceeding sixty miles per hour. It seems to be following U.S. Highway 20, but most likely it is tracking the low-pressure gradient of the Niobrara River. People in the counties listed across the bottom of your screen are advised to seek shelter immediately."

The lights flickered twice then went out. The television, their only source of outside information, went dark. Joe pushed through the swinging door from the kitchen into the cafe dining area. "Okay people, listen up. The power is out, and we're on a well here. The restroom is off-limits. The kitchen is closed. I'm not about to open the freezer or refrigerator and risk losing my inventory. If you haven't paid your checks yet, you better do so now. The cafe will close in five minutes. You best be on your way."

Ida Faye thrust her hands on her hips. "That tears it, Joe, you duck butt! You can't send our customers out into a storm like this," she said, sweeping her arm toward the window.

"I'm trying to reduce my liability here, Ida Faye. I don't need somebody getting hurt and suing me."

"Suing you for what, you dumb bohunk? This whole kit and caboodle ain't worth the price of admission to an emergency room. Nothing from nothing is still nothing. That's what you've got here, Joe. They can't get blood from this turnip." She used her arm to sweep across the cafe.

Jessica, Sam, and Sidney watched this exchange as if taking in a tennis match. All eyes were now on Joe.

"You leave me no choice, Ida Faye. This type of insubordination cannot be tolerated. I'm placing you on administrative leave without pay, effective immediately. You'll need to depart the premises along with the customers."

"Not so fast, Bubba. You need to fire me without cause so I can file for unemployment."

Brad, his ear to the kitchen door, could not help smiling. Ida Faye had the uncanny ability to turn a bad situation into a comedy routine. Outside, he heard a vehicle come to a sliding halt in the gravel lot. He quickly looked at the Winchester beneath the towels behind the sink.

⇒•✳•⇐

Ida Faye Mensinger

All eyes shifted to the parking lot, where the black Suburban had slid to a stop. Totaled would have been an understatement. The windshield was pushed inward, especially on the passenger side, with large holes punched through it. The hood and roof appeared as if they had been beaten by a giant ball-peen hammer. All the windows on the passenger side were blown out. The driver jumped out and hurriedly ran around to the passenger side, his shirt wet and bloody. He was the older of the two men who had left the cafe earlier. He yanked open the passenger door and pulled his companion, who was covered in blood, from the seat. Kernels of broken safety glass fell from the younger man's suit coat and slacks. The driver slipped his head under the injured man's arm to keep him from falling.

Sam rushed from the cafe and slipped his head under the man's other arm. He saw that both men wore shoulder harnesses with handguns. Together, the two men half-carried the injured man into the cafe.

Ida Faye held the door open. "Slide him into that open booth. I'll get the first-aid kit."

Sidney pulled paper napkins from the dispenser on the table and pressed them to the large gash on the man's forehead above his right eye. Blood was still pulsing from the open wound. She pried open his eyelid. His pupil was dilated, and he seemed unable to track the movements around him. "He might have a concussion," she said to no one in particular.

"It started as rain," the uninjured man said. "It was huge drops that soon turned to marble-sized hail. Then out of nowhere these giant hailstones the size of baseballs, some the size of softballs, started pounding the car. There was no place to get out of it. I pulled over and tried to turn around. That's when the windows on the passenger side blew out. The noise was deafening."

"How far did you get?" Ida Faye asked as she slid into the booth next to the injured man. She opened the first-aid kit and was startled to find it was almost empty.

"I think we were getting pretty close to Lusk. It was hard to tell. Everything went white then suddenly black as I was turning around. I've never seen a storm like that. There was stuff, debris, flying all around us. I think there might have been a tornado or something. Hail or something came through the windshield, and Mark took a direct hit to his head."

"Try not to get blood all over my booth," Joe whined.

"Shut your trap, Joe," Ida Faye shot back. "Can't you see this man's hurt? And where in the heck are all the first-aid supplies? There's no gauze, no antiseptic, just a few lousy Band-Aids and some adhesive tape."

"What are you still doing here?" Joe said. "Didn't I put you on administrative leave?"

Ida Faye rolled her eyes.

Sidney removed the blood-soaked napkins. The wound was still pulsating blood.

"Here," Jessica said, placing her purse on the table and opening it. She pulled out a pink plastic pouch, tore it open, removed a panty liner, and handed it to Sidney. The room fell silent.

Ida Faye winked at Jessica. "Now you're just showing off. I used to need something like that. All I need now is a little estrogen or else an electric shaver."

Sidney unfolded the liner and pressed it to the man's forehead. "He needs stitches. I don't think we should use that adhesive tape. Do you have a dishtowel or something that we can tear into strips?"

Ida Faye pushed Joe out of the way and bounded off to the kitchen. Brad was nowhere to be seen. She grabbed a clean dishtowel and tore a two-inch strip from the length of the towel. She could not help but wonder why Brad was so concerned with the feds' appearance. She glanced at the pile of dirty dishcloths and noted that the shotgun she had seen earlier was gone. Returning to the booth, she wrapped the makeshift bandage around the man's head and tied it securely in the back. "Help me get his suit coat off," she said to Sidney. "We can use it as a pillow."

"Is the storm headed this way?" Sam asked the man who was unhurt.

"I don't know. It was total chaos. There was rain, hail, wind-swept dust and rocks, and a wall of black that would have engulfed us if we hadn't turned around. I've never seen anything like that in my life."

"You reckon you could remove that guy's gun?" Ida Faye interrupted. "I'm not partial to nursing an unconscious man who is armed."

The driver leaned over the booth and extracted the injured man's pistol from his shoulder holster. "Where's the nearest hospital?" he asked Ida Faye.

"Lusk has a hospital and clinic. A darn good one, I might add. I'm willing to bet they might be pretty busy if that thing," she pointed out the window with her thumb, "rolled over the town."

"What about Nebraska?"

"There's nothing in Harrison that I know of. Chadron's about seventy miles from here. They're supposedly in the path of this storm, too. Douglas is about the same distance, and that storm is between us and them. Torrington's a possibility, but I think it best you sit tight until this thing has passed."

Ida Faye surveyed the cafe. Joe was attempting to pry open the electric cash register with a butter knife. The daughter was applying pressure to the injured man's forehead. Her father was staring out the window at his vintage Jeep, and the prim woman was taking inventory of the contents of her purse. Ida Faye glanced nervously at the door to the kitchen. One agent was unconscious and the other was staring at her like a snake stares at a mouse.

"Are we all present and accounted for?" the agent asked, unsmiling.

"Yep, ain't nobody else here, just us chickens," she said, using a retort her father often used that paraphrased the old *Amos and Andy* radio comedy routine from the 1940s.

Jessica Martindale

Jessica quietly stepped out of the cafe to escape the noise and confusion. How still it had become, as if something had stolen her breath. There was no air. The highway was as flat and silent as a dead snake. It disappeared into the horizon in both directions. Her ears rang from the total absence of sound. No birdsong, no insects buzzing, not even the whisper of an afternoon breeze to stir the hair behind her ears. She gasped for a breath like a baby in the wind. She was reminded of quiet summer days on the shaded porch with her mother, the corn flagging gently behind the barn, hogs dozing in the sun, the glittering leaves of the giant cottonwoods. Those who were dead were still alive. Working, always working, never complaining. She missed them. Her mother would magically appear with a pitcher of Kool-Aid on a hot, muggy Iowa afternoon. They would talk of the future, never the past. Not that the past was bad in any way. Rather, the past belonged to each individual and was not to be tampered with. Memories were unique. They were sacred, and they took comfort there on such afternoons.

The two and a half hours between Ames and Keotonka had sufficiently separated her from her mother. One hundred sixty miles was Jessica's excuse for not visiting in the later years of her parents' lives. A demanding career, a controlling husband who viewed farmers as serfs, and twin boys, perpetually in trouble, were her excuses for not visiting the people who had raised her. She knew the real reason that now tortured her. She was unwilling to give up her life in order to be near them. The telephone was not the answer. It kept her from seeing the unpleasantness of her parents' aging. She called as often as she could, always hoping her father would answer instead of her mother. He never made her feel guilty or gave her unsolicited advice about child rearing, career advancement, or asked probing questions about her marriage. Instead, he listened, never directing the conversation.

In the earlier years, her mother's singular obsession with the government's reluctance to classify Jessica's biological father, an Air Force pilot, as MIA, KIA, BNR (Body Not Recovered), or POW always dominated the conversation. He had disappeared, presumably shot down, in 1971. Her mother blamed politics and bureaucracy. Jessica, on the other hand, sensed something else, perhaps more sinister. She had seen the extensive government cover-ups designed to protect the president who lied to the American people. She could not remember if her skepticism developed before or after her stepfather's disappearance. Jessica's friends complained about their mother's never-ending descriptions of health concerns. Her mother, however, never talked about what ailed her. She was too busy writing letters to the Department of Defense, Air Force, the State Department, the Pentagon, and the Social Security Administration. The years had softened Jessica's frustration with her mother's focus on finding the answers. Her own investigations brought feelings of regret that she had not been more sympathetic toward her mother's fixation.

The western horizon was drawing closer. Black storm clouds rolled ominously behind a curtain of white. She looked at the ruined Suburban and then the rented Toyota and wished she had purchased the additional insurance. Trying to outrun the storm was as dangerous as the idea of driving twelve hours to Ames with no sleep. She had been up all night and needed to lie down and breathe in the satisfaction of the nightmare ending.

-→=◎ ✷ ◎=←-

Sidney Dawson

Sidney unbuttoned the injured man's bloodstained collar and loosened his necktie. She studied his face. The edge of the pink panty liner poked from beneath the torn dishtowel. He was the younger of the two men, handsome and perhaps her age, she guessed. Discreetly, she lifted his left hand and placed it in his lap. There was no wedding band. She thought it strange that he would be unmarried, a man in his thirties. Three possibilities immediately came to her mind: career, divorced, gay.

His partner was in a somewhat heated conversation with the cook about a walk-in freezer, the cook arguing he would not open the door and risk losing a month's worth of hamburger patties that might stay frozen until the power was restored if the door wasn't opened.

"How about I arrest you for assaulting a federal officer and handcuff you in the back of that Suburban out there," the man said, pointing out the window toward the wrecked vehicle.

"You can try," the cook said, holding up his spatula. "I don't give a rat's rear end who you are. This is my castle, and I have a right to defend it."

"Boys," the waitress cautioned with a smile, "nobody here cares who has the larger penis. Joe, these men represent the federal government, which has all the money in the world to buy your precious hamburger patties. I suggest you do what he wants."

"I wouldn't spit on his ass if his guts were on fire. Ain't nobody gonna ride out this storm in my freezer," the cook said with finality.

"I'll buy the contents of your freezer," Sidney heard herself say. She had never before flaunted her wealth out loud. Now was no time for modesty.

"This is a cash-only establishment," the cook said with a note of acceptance.

"My daughter's good for it," her father said. He had never acknowledged her wealth to her or anyone else.

Sidney looked at him with a surprised face. Then she smiled. "You tell me the amount, and I'll write the check right now," she said, turning toward the cook again.

The cook seemed to ponder the offer in front of him. He thought it best not to question the man. "We can't get all these people in that freezer."

"We'll draw straws," the pretty woman in her summer dress said from the doorway to the cafe.

"It's my cafe. It's my freezer. I'm not drawing straws," Joe said.

Ida Faye thrust her hands to her hips. "Joe, you either play fair or I'm gonna tell these gentlemen," she pointed to the two

FBI agents, "about your totally fraudulent tax returns for the six years I've been here. I'm sure their colleagues at the IRS would be most interested."

The first drops of rain fell with exploding force. Everyone fell silent, heads cocked, looking up at the ceiling or out the window to the parking lot. Dust from the gravel lot shot upward, displaced by the velocity of heavy water slamming into the ground. Every so often a small hailstone bounced upward, first pea-sized then marble-sized, and then it quit. Sidney reached behind her ear to turn up the volume of the miniature speaker in her right ear. All was silent. It was so still outside that she could hear the breath of the man she was holding. Then a single, loud crash on the roof, as if space junk had fallen from the sky, then another and another a few seconds later. Everyone turned their attention to the parking lot. Hailstones the size of baseballs hit and bounced a foot or more into the air. The cadence quickened suddenly, going from a steady beat to a frantic drum roll. The sound was deafening, as if a thousand giants with sledgehammers were demolishing the cafe.

"Stay back from the windows," Sam yelled, barely audible above the din of jumbled noise.

Sidney pulled the injured man's head away from the table-mounted jukebox and leaned it against her chest. She felt the warmth of his breath through her blouse.

The hailstorm ended just as suddenly as it had begun. A few errant stones hit the roof or bounced off the parking lot and highway. The sun shone briefly, reflecting off the crystalline whiteness that covered the earth. The cafe was eerily silent. Darkness seemed to swallow the sun as it descended like a curtain being lowered on a stage. Sidney looked out the window at the rolling wall of destruction, nature's fury, coming down the highway from the west. It reminded her of the black-and-white photos of dust bowl storms from the dirty thirties. Flashes of lightning illuminated the black wall rolling toward the cafe. She could feel the rumbles of thunder. The cafe trembled. The floor, the walls, the ceiling shivered as if cold.

Sidney looked at the cook, who had traded the butter knife for his spatula that he now held at his side. "You better get my hamburger patties out of the freezer *now*," Sidney ordered. "Pop, help him," she said, turning toward her father. "I'm afraid we're in for it."

Sam quickly followed the cook to the kitchen as he glanced over his shoulder at Sidney. "That's my daughter," he said proudly to Joe and gestured toward Sidney with his thumb.

"Mister," Sidney called to the injured man's companion, "help me get him to the freezer."

The older man glared at her. He clearly did not like being told what to do and only reluctantly complied. They each put their heads under the injured man's arms and dragged him toward the kitchen.

Darkness at midday turned the cafe into an obstacle course as they bumped their way to the kitchen. Flashes of lightning were quickly followed by ear-splitting claps of thunder. It began to rain again. Outside, dirt, roadside litter, and tumbleweeds by the thousands rained against the picture windows of the diner. The noise behind the relentless pelting was ominous. In the distance they heard something huge coming toward them.

Sidney thought the freight train analogy that people often used to describe a tornado was accurate.

"Hurry," she yelled to her father and the cook, who were quickly pulling boxes of frozen hamburger patties from the freezer. The walk-in freezer was smaller than she had expected, consisting of a narrow walkway, maybe six feet long, between wire shelves filled with boxes and plastic tubs of frozen foods. "Pop, clear one of the lower shelves; we'll lay him on it."

Jessica and Ida Faye nervously brought up the rear of the group, all pressing toward the open door of the freezer. Ida Faye held a flashlight above her head. "Where are your straws?" Jessica yelled to Ida Faye above the roar of the storm. "We can't all fit in there."

In the kitchen, no one had disputed Sidney's command. She was in charge, a rare situation for a woman who was normally quiet and unassuming. "Listen up, people," she yelled. "We're out of time. Get in the freezer now," she barked. "Put your modesty aside and squeeze in. We can make it. Last one in, pull the door shut."

"I've got the straws," Ida Faye yelled. "I counted out seven and clipped one in half."

"There's no time," Sidney shouted. "Cram in here and bring your flashlight."

"Where's Brad?" Joe called from the back of the freezer. He had been the first person in.

"No time to worry about the dog. He'll crawl under some-thing," she said loud enough for the agent to hear.

"Push," Sidney screamed above the roar of the storm. Since she was giving the orders, she decided to be the last one in. In the dim light of the flashlight, she saw the lineup. The cook, the waitress, the agent, her father, the pretty woman were lined up single file, each facing the door as if they were in an elevator. "Suck it up, people. I'd like to join you and shut the door." She heard their feet shuffling on the floor as they crammed toward the back. She could not see the injured man on the shelf below her.

"For crying out loud, Joe," Ida Faye whined, "why'd you bring your spatula?"

"That ain't no spatula." Joe laughed.

"Come on, people. I need another six inches," Sidney shouted.

"No comment," Ida Faye said loud enough for everyone to hear.

Sidney pulled the door shut; her elbow slammed into the pretty woman's ribs. "Sorry," she said. She could feel the woman's breasts pressed against her back.

"I played women's rugby in college," the woman said. "This is nothing."

Sidney did not respond. She disagreed with the pretty woman. This was definitely something.

Sam Dawson

Ms. Martindale's buttocks were pressed against Sam's right thigh. Her head was tucked under his chin. His hands hung at his sides, appendages without purpose. He did not know what to do with them. He felt awkward to the point of embarrassment. Her hair smelled good. No, he thought, it smelled delicious, something edible. The scent of her perfume drifted upward from her slender neck, alluring and musky. He tried to concentrate on the man behind him, whose large shoes prevented Sam from moving his leg backward away from the woman's soft and fleshy posterior. Icy water dripped on his head and shoulders from somewhere above. When removing the boxes of hamburger patties, he noted the freezer had not been defrosted in years. A thick rind of crusty ice covered the ceiling, walls, and shelves. With the power off and the body heat of seven people packed inside like sardines, the ice was slowly melting. Sam immediately noticed how quiet it had become when Sidney closed the door. He no longer heard the pelting rain or the roar of the oncoming wind. No one spoke. They were listening. The tension was palpable. The total darkness hid both their fear of the storm and their uncomfortable loss of social distancing. Suddenly there was a flash of incandescent light that assaulted their eyes and transformed the mood.

"Is that better?" the waitress said. "Sorry, I forgot I had the flashlight in my hand." The light's weak beam shone at the frosty ceiling and was more than ample to illuminate the freezer and bring a measure of relief to the distressed occupants. "If it goes out, it's 'cause I've had to use it as a weapon. I'm stuck back here between randy Joe the lecher and Melvin Purvis the pervert. I'm not sure, but I may have just lost my virginity."

There was a smattering of uneasy laughter.

"You can't lose what you never had," the cook said. "What you do have is another letter for your personnel file that will document your insubordination and attempt to create a hostile work environment."

Sam could feel vibrations through the floor of the freezer as the entire cafe shook with the weight of the storm passing over it. His ears felt like he was at the bottom of the deep end of a swimming pool. He heard the sounds of pots and pans hitting the floor, of dishes breaking. He wished he were standing behind Sidney. He could wrap his arms around her and hug her to his chest as he had done so many times when she was a frightened little girl. He wondered if the woman in front of him had been consoled by the man she was attempting to find. He hoped so. That was the duty of a father.

The shaking stopped as suddenly as it had begun. There was total silence. Jessica, obviously uncomfortable, tried to twist away from Sam's leg. She only succeeded in pressing her hip into his groin. Sam groaned and involuntarily jerked backward, setting off a chain reaction of movement through the bodies pressed impolitely together.

"Sorry," Jessica offered weakly.

"Easy does it, J. Edgar," the waitress warned the agent in front of her.

"How will we know when it's safe to come out?" Jessica whispered to Sidney.

"I have no idea; probably when it's safer out there than it is in here."

"Let's have a look, Sid," Sam said. "I think it passed over us."

"Yeah, Sid, let's have a look," the waitress mimicked. "Go to the light."

Sam could hear Sidney rattling the push bolt he had noticed when entering the freezer. A long bolt with a round, three-inch diameter plate welded at its end was designed to be pushed. The other end of the bolt was attached to the freezer door handle on the outside. "What's wrong?"

"I don't know," Sidney said. "It won't open."

"Push, don't pull," Sam ordered.

"I am. It's not working."

"Push harder."

"It won't budge. Maybe something fell and is wedged against the door handle."

"Oh yeah," the cook said from the back of the freezer. "That darn thing would rattle every time the compressor came on. It drove me crazy, so I disconnected it."

"You did what?" the waitress yelled. "And didn't tell anybody?"

"It's my freezer. I don't have to tell anybody."

"Ever hear of OSHA, you fool? You're supposed to provide a safe and healthy workplace. What if the power comes on? We'll freeze to death."

"Oh, we'll run out of oxygen long before that," the cook said matter-of-factly.

Stunned silence swept over the group.

"That shouldn't take too long," the cook added calmly. "With seven of us gulping for air it won't take any time at all. Whose dumb ass idea was this, anyway?"

"It was mine," the agent behind Sam said.

"Somehow I knew the government was involved," the waitress said.

Sam had brushed against the hard grip of the man's gun that he carried under his left arm. "What's in your shoulder holster?" he said, turning his head to the side.

"Glock Nineteen, Generation Five, nine-millimeter," he said immediately.

"How many rounds?"

"Fifteen in the mag, one in the tube."

"Will it shoot through that door?"

The man was silent for several seconds. "Depends on what it's made of and how thick it is."

"Looked to me like aluminum. Probably over Styrofoam maybe three inches thick. What do you think?"

"Piece of cake," the man said without hesitation.

There was silence in the freezer as everyone listened intently.

"Well, there you go, folks," Sam said cheerfully. "Sixteen holes in the door ought to give us enough air to breathe."

"Fifteen," the man behind him corrected. "I'm saving one for the woman behind me."

"Very funny, mister G-Man," the waitress said.

"You want to pass your gun up front? My daughter knows how to shoot," Sam lied.

"Not on your life," the agent shot back without explanation. "I'll need to work my way up front."

"That's not going to happen on our first date." Jessica laughed. "I expect dinner and a movie before I let you take those kinds of liberties."

Sam could not help smiling. The woman had a sense of humor after all. He was beginning to like her.

"Honeybunch, you're not thinking of cheating on me with miss hot to trot up there, are you?" the waitress said with a flinching grin.

"Make that fourteen rounds," the agent said.

A metallic click was heard from outside the freezer, followed by the release of the door seal, a sound like tape being pulled from something smooth. Startled, Sidney gently pushed the door open. No one was there. They silently strode out single file, each glad it was over and feeling a little ridiculous.

CHAPTER 8

1:05 p.m.

Brad Holcomb

Memories were all he had. He blocked the bad ones during the day. At night they slithered under the door like a poisonous snake, found him sleeping, and crawled into his subconscious. He would experience them in living color, their elliptical eyes black and unblinking as they waited for their opportunity to strike with paralyzing venom. Brad watched for them during the day, always careful where he stepped. They were mostly nocturnal. Daytime memories were pleasant for the most part. Lately, however, they often left him with feelings of regret, unfulfilled experiences from a previous life that made him sad. He worried that he was becoming depressed.

It was his short-term memory that was most alarming. Every day, repetitive functions seemed to disappear without a trace. At first, he thought it was simply age-related forget-fulness. He would retrace his activities to find what he had misplaced or forgotten. That process no longer worked. It frightened him that there was no memory at all of having accomplished a common task. He would do it again. More recently, he found evidence of half-done daily duties, things he had walked away from, easily distracted by something equally unimportant. He tried writing checklists on a small notepad he carried in his pocket, then quickly forgot that he had it. The distant past was still intact, sometimes with frustratingly minute details. He could remember the names of first-grade classmates, what they wore, how they smelled. He could see the oil level in the breather of his dad's '49 Chevy truck, the amber color, oily smell, and insects floating in the sticky liquid. He heard the rapid clicking of a sticky valve from more than a half century ago. Yet he had no idea if he had brushed his teeth after breakfast. He knew all the words to the songs of the sixties and most of the fifties, yet could not remember the names of people he had just met. When pressured to provide the name of a person, place, or thing, he would resort to describing it rather than naming it. He was quick to anger when he could not think of the words.

Dementia scared him more than the physical changes that were slowly limiting his ability to function. There were, however, names he could never forget, names that were inextricably intertwined with the events of his life. Names that had been the driving force behind his quest for the past half century. Now they were all dead. Soon he would join them and there would be peace, not justice, just peace. His name added to those who would soon be forgotten.

He had ridden out the storm in the well house, a cement-block structure the size of a small privy that sat between the cafe and his trailer. Perpetually dank, it was a favorite place for snakes during the heat of summer. In the winter, a space heater kept the pipes from freezing while attracting rodents and an occasional stray cat through the partially opened doorway. Brad watched the storm pass to the north, black and threatening. The hail pummeled his house trailer, huge stones bouncing on and between the tires that had been laid on the roof to keep the Wyoming wind from tearing it off. There would be leaks.

The temperature had dropped at least ten degrees as he picked his way through the huge hailstones between the well house and the back door of the cafe. Quiet had settled over the landscape like the prelude to an opening scene of a play. He stopped in the kitchen to listen. Muffled voices from inside the freezer and the rattling of the door handle gave away their hiding place. He thought briefly of retrieving the shotgun, although he knew there was no need. If the feds wanted him, they could have him. He was tired of running. Winston Tucker was dead and could join Nixon in Hell, if there was such a place. He would see them there.

Ida Faye Mensinger

Ida Faye knew who had opened the freezer, yet she said nothing. She hoped Joe would dummy up as well. They shuffled out, taking baby steps. She was surprised to see little damage. A few of the hanging pots and pans had fallen from their hooks on the wall. "Good work," she said loudly to the young woman with thick glasses. "You must have jiggled it just right." She glanced around the kitchen to make sure Brad was no longer there. Everyone squinted as if blinded by a photographer's flash, their eyes adjusting to the subdued light filtering in from the back door that hung open.

The young woman hurried back into the freezer to attend to the agent on the shelf. "He's awake," she said to the older agent who had entered behind her.

"I think I'm going to be sick," the younger man said as he struggled to sit up. "Where am I?"

Ida Faye laughed from the doorway. "You're nowhere, my friend. This is Wyoming."

"We're in the cafe's freezer," Sidney said. "There was a bad storm, and we took refuge in here."

The man squinted, barely opening his eyes as he tried to see who was talking to him. "Who are you?"

"My name is Sidney Dawson," she barely got out before the older agent pushed her aside.

"Mark, let's go. Can you walk?" the older man asked brusquely.

The younger man looked at him as if he were a stranger with bad news. "I think I'm going to barf," he whined.

Sidney turned to the older man. "He's sick to his stomach, confused, groggy, and sensitive to the light. I'm pretty sure he has a concussion."

"I concur," Ida Faye said from over their shoulders. "I've had a few of those in my day. He's probably got a monster headache too."

"Come on, Mark," the older man said. "I'm taking you to the nearest hospital. Ladies, can you help me get him up and out to the car?"

"Clear a path," Ida Faye ordered as the older agent and the young woman assisted the wounded man from the kitchen.

"Does anybody have an Aspirin? My head is about to explode," the injured agent begged.

"No," Ida Faye said, looking at the older man rather than the younger agent. "I don't think that would be a good idea. He's possibly had a traumatic brain injury. We don't know the extent of it. Aspirin could cause bleeding, which ain't good, not to mention upsetting his stomach even more."

"Good points," the older agent said. "We'll let a doctor decide what to do. Is there another hospital?"

"Go a couple of miles west and take 159 straight south to Torrington. They've got a community hospital and an emergency clinic. I've a feeling Lusk will have their hands full, even if you could get through."

The group fell silent when they entered the cafe from the kitchen. In the subdued light they saw the windows and door were buried in tumbleweeds. Otherwise intact, with the exception of the pyramid of single-serving cereal boxes, the cafe appeared completely encased by wet and broken tumbleweeds that had blown under the flat, overhanging roof. Light filtered through the tangled mass of tan weeds with a kaleidoscopic effect that created a spidery web of shadows on every surface of the cafe.

Ida Faye, her mouth open, was strangely speechless.

"Mister," Joe said to the girl's father, "come with me out back and we'll see if we can clear a path to their car."

"I'm glad those things are wet," Ida Faye called after them. "Talk about tinder, this place would turn into a giant sparkler. Here," she said to the older agent and young woman, "put him in this booth." She pointed to the center booth next to the window.

Minutes later, she heard the scraping of a shovel against the concrete approach to the cafe door. Soon she saw movement as Joe and the girl's father clawed at the tangled wall of hail-smashed tumbleweeds, pulling them back from the door along with hailstones the size of fruit.

"Okay," Joe called as he pushed open the door, "bring him out. The parking lot is clear. The weeds are all piled up against the west side of the building."

The group watched as the injured man was laid on the back seat of the Suburban. The injured agent and the young woman talked briefly, and the agent handed her a business card.

"Two miles that way," Ida Faye called to the driver and pointed west, "then 159 south." The agent nodded his acknowledgment. No one spoke as they watched the black vehicle disappear down the highway to the west. Joe and the girl's father pulled some of the battered tumbleweeds from the windows of the cafe before replacing the cartons of hamburger patties into the freezer. Joe complained that he had put off buying a generator until times were flusher and now regretted his decision.

Silently, everyone peered out the windows at their damaged vehicles.

"I should have bought the insurance," the pretty woman said. Spider webs of cracked glass covered both the front and rear windows. Large dents appeared like lunar craters on the hood, roof, and trunk.

The young woman's father stared at his vintage Jeep. There was surprisingly little damage. The straight up-and-down windows were unbroken. The roof and hood had some dents, although nothing like the pretty woman's Toyota or the dirty Ford Fiesta and late-model pickup parked in front of the cafe.

"We'd had a better chance," Ida Faye said, "if we had parked round back on the leeward side instead of out front so as to look like the place had customers."

Joe paid no attention to her. He was busy twisting a small transistor radio in the air in an attempt to get some news of the storm.

"Who wants ice cream?" Ida Faye called out. "It's gonna melt if we don't eat it."

No one responded.

-→=◎ ✦ ◎=←-

Jessica Martindale

Sam was solid and textured, like a man. He smelled like one, too. The awkwardly close confinement in the freezer had resulted in a connection to a man she barely knew. She could not describe the attraction that seemed to grip her by the shoulders and fog the frontal lobe of her brain. It was a long time since she had experienced that type of fascination with someone. She liked the feeling.

"You okay?" Sam asked, suddenly appearing in front of her.

"I'm fine, thank you," she said somewhat curtly. She could not make eye contact with him. She felt as if he had seen her naked, and she was now embarrassed. She turned away from him.

The cook's transistor radio blurted unintelligible fragments of speech and music as he twisted and turned while attempting to tune in to a station with news of the storm. She was reminded of her grandfather's huge 1939 Zenith console radio that her parents called the green-eyed monster due to the magic green tuning eye centered within the large dial. Her father would gently adjust the tuning knob until the shutter-like eye would glow bright green as he tuned in WLS in Chicago or KOMA in Oklahoma City.

They would dance and twirl around the living room. It was one of the few times she heard him laugh. He had taught her how to do the two-step to his favorite oldies, the slow love ballads of the late fifties and early sixties. Her mother would sometimes cut in, and she watched as the two of them nestled close, floating around the room. Those were the ideal times, the best of times etched into her memory that replayed over and over again, always the same. Her parents' relationship was the gold standard she could never achieve.

Individually, her parents' lives were troubled. As a little girl, she was frightened by her father's frequent bad dreams. He would awake screaming, shaking, and sweating with a terrified look on his face. Her mother would sometimes alternate between sobbing and frustrated anger when opening the mail or slamming down the telephone receiver. They seldom showed such ill-tempered emotions toward one another. They loved each other, a tender happiness Jessica was never able to find in her marriage. Some outsiders had speculated foul play since her father disappeared. The chief of the volunteer fire department was positive he had seen her father headed west on the highway as the fire truck was heading east toward their burning barn. Locals knew the special bond between her mother and father and never considered pointing an accusatory finger toward the only father she had known.

When her grief turned to anger, Jessica took up her mother's mission of discovery. She believed there was a connection between her mother's relentless probing of government ineptness and cover-up of her biological father's status and her stepfather's disappearance. On a sunny fall day, when the leaves had turned gold and yellow in Ames and the ISU Cardinals were on the field for homecoming, her life was changed irrevocably. After years of slammed doors and dead ends, she received a surprise visit from an older, silver-haired woman named Shelly Robinson, who represented the president of the United States.

⊷═◈═⊷

Sidney Dawson

His name was Mark Johnson. Sidney glanced at the official-looking business card. The Department of Justice was written across the top edge. The printed words did not register. A gold badge with the eagle holding an olive branch and arrows in its talons above a large U.S. made it intimidating. He was a special agent. The card meant nothing, a blur of words and symbols. It was the memory of his face, his eyes that mattered. The way he held his mouth rendered her speechless. She stared out the window and followed the highway to the west until it disappeared on the horizon. Maybe there was a bridge that had washed out or storm debris that blocked the road, and they would have to turn back. She could give him her name and number hastily scribbled on a napkin. She did not have a business card. There was no need. Thick glasses and hearing aids were her calling card.

"You think it's too soon to give him a call?" the waitress said from behind her, a large, round container of ice cream tucked under her arm.

Sidney tucked the card into her jeans front pocket as she turned around. She smiled.

"I have to admit he was a looker, all right," the waitress said. "If I were thirty years younger, I'd fight you for him."

"If I were thirty years younger, I'd be two and wouldn't care. You could have him."

The waitress smiled. "I'd be thirty-two and in my prime and married to a S.O.B. meaner than a snake who would have gunned me down."

"In that case, I would have asked him to wait for me," Sidney said, turning back to look out the window, the tortured tumbleweeds still piled against most of the glass.

Her newfound wealth could not buy her what she wanted most. There had been few men in her life, only two that she had taken seriously, and both had betrayed her and worse. They had paid the ultimate price for their deception, and deservedly so, while she had been left with nothing except a broken heart. She was thirty-two, handicapped, and lived with her father who still treated her like a teenager. Someday he would die, and then what? It was hard to hope for love when it never came. She looked out the tall windows again. The sky had turned radiantly blue, and the sun shone between the tangles of weeds on the window, raindrops turned into prisms.

"You want some ice cream, hon? It'll take the heat of defeat right out of ya. It's cherry vanilla, the only thing in this room with a cherry." The waitress giggled.

Sidney shook her head and smiled at the irreverent waitress. "I'm Sidney, by the way. And yes, I'd love some ice cream."

"Ida Faye." The waitress beamed. "I'm pleased to make your acquaintance, Sidney." She placed a cereal bowl on the table and scooped the already soft ice cream into it. "I hope the co-op over in Lusk can get the power back on soon. Otherwise, we're gonna have to eat everything in the cooler, that you own, by the way," she added.

"Keeline and Manville got clobbered," the cook called out, the portable radio on his shoulder. "They're saying it was most likely an F3 or F4, unheard of in this country. It swung north and just clipped the edge of Lusk. The Wyoming Women's Center and the Lusk Cemetery took direct hits. It sounds like the town was pretty much spared. It headed off toward Chadron then ran out of steam. The northern panhandle is just getting rain and light hail."

Sidney surveyed the room. No one spoke. There seemed to be a collective sigh of relief by all except Ida Faye.

Sam Dawson

Jessica made him nervous. They both avoided eye contact. Sam repeatedly rubbed his chin whiskers as if he were checking the need to shave. He cleared his throat in preparation to speak. He said nothing. What was it with Iowa women that turned him into a speechless, slobbering idiot? Annie had been from Iowa.

He had never loved anyone like he did her and never expected to again. This woman was not Annie. He needed to repeat that to himself over and over until his attraction or infatuation or whatever it was subsided. He should go back to his daughter, who was eating ice cream and eyeing him suspiciously from across the dining room. That was easier said than done, especially since his feet seemed stuck to the floor.

"I should get on the road," Jessica said half-halfheartedly, almost in a whisper.

"Your windshield is shattered. Every cop between here and Des Moines will pull you over," Sam said with authority.

Jessica's eyes narrowed, and she studied his face. "Tell me this isn't that same routine you tried earlier about running out of gas, and we'll need to spend the night in the car."

"Tempting, but no." Sam smiled. "I'm thinking you might want to forget your meeting for tomorrow. You're most likely not going to make it. We'll give you a ride back to Laramie, and you can make other arrangements. That is, of course, if you don't mind a quick trip to a cemetery to take a few photos, assuming it's still there. It's just down the road a few miles."

"What about my rental?"

"When we can find cell service, you can call them to come pick it up. There's a shuttle from Laramie to DIA, or if you don't mind puddle-jumpers, you can fly to Denver from Laramie. You can catch the next flight home."

"You sure it wouldn't be an imposition?" she demurred.

"Not at all. We live midway between Cheyenne and Laramie. Heck, you can camp out at our place, make your reservations, and we'll run you to the shuttle or airport in either Cheyenne or Laramie the next day. I'll be able to check my negative files and print you whatever I find."

"Do you have cell service?" she asked skeptically.

"Sometimes if you stand on the front deck, turn around three times, click your heels, and hold your mouth just right. Better yet, we have a land line."

Jessica looked down, her bottom lip gripped between her teeth. "My boys' apartment looks like a science experiment gone bad. I could get a room in either Cheyenne or Laramie," she said, thinking out loud.

"No need," Sam said. "My daughter and I would be happy to have you."

"You could be an ax murderer or something."

"Not anymore. I see a therapist for that."

"What about her?" Jessica said, nodding toward Sidney.

"She's paid her debt to society and no longer poses a threat." Sam motioned for Sidney to join them.

"All right, belly-up to the table," the waitress said as she approached with the container of ice cream still tucked under her arm. "Cherry vanilla on the house." She placed two bowls on the table and proceeded to scoop the soft ice cream into them. "Nothing takes the taste of humiliation out of your mouth better than cherry vanilla ice cream," she said with a wink toward Sam.

"Make mine a double," he said.

CHAPTER 9
1:13 p.m.

Brad Holcomb

The midday heat had been washed away. Huge hailstones littered the drought-brown landscape. Birds had begun to chatter and flit from the scrubby cedar trees between the cafe and trailer. Soon, the prairie grasses would turn green, if only for a few days before resuming their relentless struggle to survive. The sun pierced the gray clouds with beams of light as if shot from a celestial ray gun. A scruffy cat, a yellow tabby with a bent tail that lived under his trailer, scurried by, its tail straight up with the end at an acute right angle. He thought of days of achingly hard summer work when he was young that were suddenly transformed by a cool mountain rain and his only thoughts were finishing one task in order to start another. The earth was vivid, and he knew he was dying.

He had been dying since the day he was born. Vietnam had robbed him of the fear of death, along with compassion for those who did fear it. He had come within minutes of relieving himself of life's agony when absolution was finally granted, not by any representative of a god, but rather by the woman he loved. It was as if his wife had traded her life for his—killed in his stead by an unmerciful government that traded life for political gain. It was nothing new. Killing for power had been going on since his ancestors clambered out of the primordial ooze. Killing for revenge followed. Guilt had to wait for religion to be invented.

"They're gone, Brad," Ida Faye said as she stepped from the back door of the cafe. She shook a cigarette from the pack in her uniform pocket and fumbled for her lighter.

"I saw them leave. There will be others."

"Maybe it's time to move on. For both of us," she quickly added.

He noticed her hands shaking as she lit her cigarette. "Are you all right?"

"Too early to tell." She blew smoke upward by funneling her lower lip outward. "I don't think my cracker box in Van Tassell got sucked up to Oz. I bet this hail did a number on it, though. Sure as heck, I'll bet my rent goes up." She flicked her ashes off to the side. "Thanks for opening that freezer door, by the way. Can you believe we got seven people in there?" She took another drag on her cigarette. "I kind of made up my mind while I was jammed in there waiting to die that if I made it out alive, I would start over—a new beginning. Head out for greener pastures. Keep driving north until I run out of gas. That fat slug of a sheriff will be so busy cleaning up after this storm that he won't miss me until I'm long gone."

Brad watched her closely. She was a handsome woman who, at one time, had been beautiful. She was trim and well proportioned, with a face that captured his attention. She had transparent blue eyes, a pert nose, high cheekbones, and lips that demanded to be kissed. "Why are you here, Ida Faye?"

She cocked her head slightly and looked at him with narrowed eyes. "I needed a smoke," she said skeptically.

"You know what I mean. Why are you here?" he said with the emphasis on the word *here*. "Of all the places you could have chosen to escape a bad marriage, why this godforsaken place?"

"Same reason you're here, Brad. You think I don't know you're looking for somebody? I don't know who, and I don't know why. What I do know is you can't get on with the rest of your life until you find them. I ain't stupid. I suspect it has something to do with the law. I'd be willing to bet this person either owes you something like money, or maybe it's just simply revenge or vindication or forgiveness. All I know is that your past, whatever it is, has prevented you from seeing the future. There's gonna come a time when you have to choose between whatever justices you're seeking from the past and a future that lets you take some comfort in your life."

Brad stared at her for a long moment before speaking. "You've obviously thought about this, and I suspect that while it might be applicable to me, it also fits your situation. You haven't answered my question."

Ida Faye tossed her cigarette and ground it out with her foot. "I guess what you're saying is—you'll show me yours if I show you mine."

⊷➤❈❖⊷

Ida Faye Mensinger

She could not remember how old she was when she first heard those words; maybe five or six. The Tobias brothers were several years older and eagerly convinced her to pull down her shorts and panties with the promise they would do the same. They sweetened the deal with a Milky Way candy bar. They stared in stunned silence and then ran from the barn laughing without holding up their end of the bargain. She would never go first again.

"Okay, Brad, let's see what you got," Ida Faye said and placed her hands on her hips. "You be honest with me, no bovine feces. You tell me why you're here, who you're runnin' from or runnin' to, and I'll come straight with you. I won't judge. I won't say a word. When you're done, I'll tell you why I'm here. I'll tell it to you bare naked if you want."

They both turned their heads toward the kitchen's screen door at the unmistakable sound of a vehicle sliding to a stop in the gravel lot at the front of the cafe. "Somebody's in a big hurry…" Ida Faye started to say, turning back toward Brad, only to find he was no longer there. She twisted around, scanning the cluttered area between the cafe and trailer. "Where does that man go?" she mumbled to herself as she entered the kitchen. She heard a woman call out from the dining room.

Two women in blaze orange pants and matching short-sleeve blouses stood just inside the door near the cash register. The acronym *WDOC* was printed in bold black letters across their backs. The same acronym was displayed on the door of the pickup truck in the parking lot.

"Jeanie?" Ida Faye said softly, her eyes wide with surprise as she stared at her middle-aged daughter. "What are you doing here? How did you—"

"A bad storm hit the Women's Center. I think it was a freaking tornado." She pushed back her short, dark blonde hair

from her angular, hard-looking face with piercing eyes. "It tore
the place all to hell. Me and Luisa were in the Aquaculture
Building when the alarms went off. It ripped the roof right off.
Tilapia and catfish were everywhere, a real mess." She looked to
the other woman for support.

"*Si*," the short, dark Hispanic woman said. "The fish were
wiggling all over the floor," she said with a strong Mexican accent.

"Why are you here?" Ida Faye repeated, still shocked by
Jeanie's presence. "Please tell me you didn't escape."

"Why am I here?" the woman said, shaking her head slowly.
"That question makes me want to scream at the top of my
lungs. I've asked it every day of my life." She looked at Ida Faye,
squinting. "You tell *me* why I'm here. I want to hear it. Oh, by
the way, I'm fine," she said, her words dripping with sarcasm.
"Thanks for your concern." She brushed back the crooked
bangs of her dishwater-blonde hair with dark roots from her
eyes, the homemade tattoo of a star between her thumb and
forefinger clearly visible.

"I can see that," Ida Faye conceded. She shook her head
and frowned. "But why are you here?"

"Since you obviously don't have a clue, I'll tell you why,"
she said as if everyone in the cafe, who stood watching in
stunned silence, should know. "I've had lots of time to discover
the answer. I'm forty years old, and I've spent most of my life
in one form of a prison or another. Foster homes, shelters,
juvenile detention, county jails, detox units—you name it, I've
been there. A bag of weed, a stolen car, breaking and entering,
assault, you name it; it's all there on a rap sheet that looks like
a diploma from Hell. Believe me, I've asked that question a

thousand times. I'm here, *Mom*," she spat the word like venom from a viper, "because you gave up on me when I was born. Why am I here? I'm here because you screwed the first guy who put his tongue in your mouth and wouldn't accept the responsibility of being a mother. I'm here because you failed me as a parent. I'm here because you chose yourself and not me. That's the answer to your question, *Mom*." She again splashed the word as if it was distasteful. "It ain't random. The probability was high that I'd turn out like I did. And, by the looks of you, I'd say this apple didn't fall far from the tree."

She smirked and nodded slightly. "Then you come waltzing into Lusk six years ago, as if I had been a lost dog in an animal shelter, and I'm supposed to wag my tail and lick your face. A little late, don't you think, *Mom*? Why am I here? I'm here because I need money and a car that doesn't say Department of Corrections on the doors. You think that's asking too much? Do you think that would be an imposition?"

"Jeanie, don't—" Ida Faye pleaded.

"And some clothes," Luisa added eagerly.

Jeanie looked around the cafe. "I believe these state-issues are a little conspicuous." She sized up Jessica and smiled. "I'll take that dress, lady."

"No, you won't," Sam said, his voice confident and stern. He stepped in front of Jessica. His jaw muscles rippled as he clenched his teeth, and his body seemed to swell with a foul, rustic temper.

Jeanie laughed. "What is it with guys? Do you train for this, or does it just come naturally?"

"Oh, it comes natural, part cultural, mostly probably hormonal, I'd bet," Joe said, reaching under the counter and pulling out a shortened baseball bat.

"No, don't, Joe," Ida Faye ordered.

Jeanie pointed a finger at Joe. "I don't want any trouble, old man." She reached behind her and pulled a pistol from her waistband. She pulled the hammer back on the snub-nosed .38 Smith and Wesson and pointed it at the cook's greasy apron. "Drop the bat and hand over the cash, you old fool."

"Better do as she says, Joe," Ida Faye cautioned. "She's got her daddy's mean streak. Wait a second. How'd you get a gun?"

"Shut the hell up, Mom. I want your car keys. Give 'em to me, now," she yelled.

"I can't get the cash register open without electricity," Joe said.

"My old Fiesta is running with the spare doughnut on the right rear. It shakes terrible at anything over forty. You won't get very far with it," Ida Faye said.

Jeanie glanced between the sagebrush piled against the windows. "Whose Toyota with the smashed windshield?"

"Mine," Jessica said with weak resignation. "Take it."

"And give me that dress. I won't ask you again."

"I want your clothes, too," Luisa said, pointing at Sidney.

Jessica picked up her purse from the table.

Jeanie swung the gun from Joe to Jessica. "Don't try anything funny, lady."

"Car keys," Jessica said, pulling them out and holding them up for everyone to see. "There's a suitcase in the back with enough clothes for both of you."

"I want everyone's cash," Jeanie demanded and snatched the keys from Jessica.

"Don't do this, Jeanie," Ida Faye pleaded.

"Yours, too," Jeanie said to her mother. "Don't you think it's the least you can do?"

The loud, metallic cocking of the Winchester pump caused everyone to turn toward the kitchen door. The twelve-gauge's barrel poked from the partially opened door and pointed directly at Jeanie.

"Brad, no," Ida Faye screamed and burst into tears. "She's my daughter. She's my daughter."

Brad did not respond. The ominous black tube with its bead sight on the end did not move.

Jeanie and Luisa backed slowly to the door. "I ain't your daughter, you stupid bitch," Jeanie snarled. "You lost your right to call me that a long time ago. I hope you rot in Hell for what you did to me."

Ida Faye looked as if she had just seen a dog run over by a truck, unable to move, unable to speak, wanting to turn away, still hoping for a miracle.

No one spoke as the group watched the two women back from the cafe and scurry to the smashed Toyota. The sedan slid sideways, gravel flew as they spun from the parking lot, and the tires squealed as they hit the highway, headed east. Everyone except Ida Faye turned toward the kitchen door. The gun was gone. Ida Faye plopped into a booth and sobbed quietly. She pulled napkins from the dispenser and blew her nose. "She's my daughter," she said weakly. She took a deep breath that shuddered in her chest, then she shook her head slowly. "I didn't even get the chance to tell her that her good-for-nothing father was dead."

⤞⬥⬥⬥⤝

Jessica Martindale

"I suppose Hertz is going to have trouble finding their car," Jessica said, still looking out the window, not speaking to anyone in particular. Her dyed, dark-blonde hair appeared lighter in the natural light, gray roots at her temples.

"I'm sure their GPS tracker will tell them where to find it. The authorities will hone in on it like a chicken on a June bug," Sam said with a forced smile.

"I guess I'll take you up on your offer of a ride, if it still stands," she said, turning to look up at him, her green eyes misted as she held back tears. The lump in her throat was visible as she attempted to swallow it.

"It does," Sam said. "We'll need to contact the sheriff when we can get cell service. They'll want all the particulars on your rental."

"The paperwork is in my briefcase in the back seat," her voice trailed off, "along with my clothes, underwear, and makeup." She thought of her meds, the statin for her high cholesterol, the Femhert for the low estrogen associated with menopause, her various night creams that kept her face from looking her age, her toothbrush, and floss. She swallowed the lump with obvious difficulty. "It was a Toyota, sort of cream-colored, and I think this year's model. It had less than twenty thousand miles on it. That's about all I know."

"Not to worry, Hertz will have all the necessary information. At least you still have your dress."

She could tell he was trying to sound upbeat, even though he knew she was stressed.

"Tell you what," he said, still trying to minimize her tension, "we'll stop by the mall in Cheyenne. Dillards will have everything you need to get you home. We'll even throw in a toothbrush."

His words seemed hollow to her. She felt faint as the realization of discovery threatened to engulf her, settling over her shoulders like a heavy wet blanket. "Do you think that car really had a GPS tracker in it?" she asked, looking out the window again.

"I do," Sam said. His enthusiasm seemed forced. "They'll get their car back, or whatever is left of it. The law doesn't take kindly to escaped cons, especially when they're armed. There could be a Bonnie and Clyde ending for those two."

She wanted to place her hand over his mouth as soon as his words came out. The waitress stood behind him, tears spilling down her cheeks.

-⊷≡◉✕◉≡⊶-
Sidney Dawson

"You did what?" she said, her brow creasing as if trying to understand.

"Look," her father said, "they stole her car and all her stuff. We'll give her a ride back to our place, and she can catch a flight in the morning."

"Here we go again," Sidney said, keeping her voice down. "Sam Dawson's Rescue Mission for Disturbed Women."

"That's not true," Sam objected with a wounded look.

"You know, Pop, you have this propensity for taking in lost and abandoned waifs that only bring trouble."

"Don't you think you're exaggerating?"

"Let's see, there was Blair, then there was Aimee, followed by Glenna, a.k.a. Cricket, then Tommie, and let's not forget Valentina. Even Annie had her problems."

"Now you've gone too far," Sam said with a note of seriousness.

"Are you forgetting Horse Creek Creepy and the paranormal visions she had?"

"She had a brain tumor," he shot back. "And she saved your life, for crying out loud."

Sidney could tell by the set of his jaw that she had stepped over the line. "Granted, take Annie off the list," she conceded. "But do you see the trend? You can't deny your history, Pop. You're a magnet for disturbed women."

Her father stared at her as he squeezed his chin between his thumb and forefinger. She had lived with him long enough that she knew when he was holding back. He was undoubtedly considering his next move. Would he bring up the totally disturbed men in her life or simply add her name to the list she had just laid before him? After all, she was the maiden daughter, a barren doe who still lived with her father.

He took a deep breath and exhaled slowly. "Point taken," he said almost cheerfully. "However, the offer has been made and can't be retracted."

There was an uncomfortable silence as she pushed her glasses up her nose. She knew his mind was made up, and there would be no changing it. He did not need her to remind him of all his mistakes. Although that had always been her job. She was the keeper of the past, always there to remind him of how similar the dangers of the past were to whatever trouble he was likely to encounter on his present misguided course of action. He was an optimist, and she had assumed the role of a pessimist out of necessity.

She could see him plain as day, standing on the back deck, staring off to the valley below, a slight smile on his lips as he considered all the wonderful possibilities of some hare-brained decision he had just made. He did not need her to remind him of the past. Her father saw only the good of the future. "All right, then," she said with a smile and then looked at her watch. She would change the subject. "Pop, am I the only one here concerned about that shotgun that was poked out from the kitchen? There's someone else in this cafe that we haven't seen. Brad, the waitress called him. I think it's the same person who opened the freezer door."

"A Good Samaritan, indeed," Sam said, still smiling. "And I share your concern. I think it would behoove us to vacate the premises as soon as possible. In other words, let's git while the gittin's good. First, let me introduce you to Jessica Martindale," he said, gesturing with his head toward the pretty woman at the other end of the cafe.

"Martindale," she asked, tapping the hearing aid behind her right ear. "Did you say Martindale?"

Sam Dawson

He did not need his daughter to remind him of where he had been. He knew. There was always something familiar about wading back into a relationship with a woman. He had fished that stream before. The slippery rocks, the push of current, the snags that threatened to deter him were challenges that only added to the anticipation of the catch. The catch of a lifetime always waited in the swirling calm of a deep hole on the downstream side of a boulder. He thought of it as gambling with a fly rod. It was an addiction. Perhaps Sidney was right about him being some sort of a magnet. He liked his fishing metaphor better. He could justify his addiction with the notion that you can't catch a fish unless you have your hook in the water.

Naming the women involved in his love life surprised him. The realization that his daughter, of all people, had accurately kept tabs on his romantic escapades was troubling. A father should not be embarrassed by his daughter's assessment of his failed relationships. He could easily justify how he was taken in. He knew it all boiled down to sexual attraction. A wink and a nod were his undoing. He could blame pheromones, the chemical attractant that influenced his bad decisions, even though he was a complex, intelligent organism that could override those primal urges. Easier said than done, he believed.

Blair Tennyson, the stunningly beautiful geneticist, had seduced him in an attempt to divert him from discovering America's dark history of genetic manipulation and the mass murders of young women. When he closed his eyes, he could still smell her scent and hear her voice coaxing him toward her lethal embrace.

Aimee Pond was not who she pretended to be. Older and more calculating than the other women in Sam's life, she had hidden her sins of the past while posing as a benevolent caregiver. Sam was haunted by the memories of her and the discoveries of her dark and brutal history. He tried not to think about her.

Annie George was and remained the love of Sam's life. He still regretted the time lost to exploring the boundaries of his complex relationship with Annie rather than openly telling her how much he loved her. She helped him navigate the treacherous waters surrounding the uncompromising complexity of relationships. She could not have seen the deception and consequences that traded her life for Sidney's. He lay awake at night thinking of the things he wished he had said to her and the things he wished he had not said. She had died in his arms before he could tell her the truth. The regrets were an open wound, a pain that frequented him every hour of every day. A pain as if stabbed in the heart without the complications of dying. Sometimes when half asleep he thought he heard the floor creak or a door quietly close as he sensed her movement in the darkened room. He still dreamed of her.

Cricket, Gleana McMurdy, the effervescent attorney and Annie lookalike, had beguiled him with her allure and stories of her family's past. She had easily enlisted him in her odyssey to correct history. Nothing was as it seemed as the two of them delved deeper into the underworld of politics and confusing legal entanglements that had hidden the truth for generations.

He still blushed with excitement when remembering the complexity of their relationship.

Tommie Tucker was Sam's first love, the first girl he had kissed romantically. She had stolen his heart in his junior year of high school. They had fumbled their way through a teenage love affair that he was convinced would last a lifetime. When immature people deal with mature concepts, when biology and reason collide head-on, Sam realized that being forced into adulthood with all its responsibilities meant abandoning his dreams. He had selfishly walked away without explanation. It had taken him thirty-two years to muster the courage to face her and tell her why. He believed Sidney had unfairly categorized Tommie as disturbed. Her only crime was she had once loved him.

On the other hand, Valentina Thompson, the seductively alluring dark-haired beauty who had relentlessly stalked him, was a professional temptress who deserved the "disturbed" label. He could see her in her evening attire, the knobs from her girdle that held her stockings up clearly visible beneath her skin-tight dress. His youthful indiscretions had led both he and Sidney to being victimized by a dangerously unpredictable psychopath who had changed their lives forever. It was as though he had signed a pact with the Devil and now must live with the consequences of his mistakes.

Sidney had conveniently not mentioned her mother when listing his failed relationships. Marcie had grown up privileged and deserved the title of Jewish American Princess. He, a gentile, could not provide her with the lifestyle she refused to abandon in favor of a marriage with him, a perpetual underachiever.

She had dedicated her life to transforming him into someone her parents would forgive for marrying their daughter. Her persistent attempts to shape him into something he was not ended in failure. Just like the marriage.

Like the lyrics from the Eagles song, he thought. He had seven women on his mind, some of whom wanted to own him, a couple of others who wanted to stone him, and only one who said she was a friend of his. Maybe Sidney was on to something. There seemed to be justification for her to believe he possessed some irresistible attraction to troubled women. Sam rubbed his chin. He would proceed with caution.

"Jessica Martindale, this is my daughter, Sidney."

An awkward moment passed before Jessica offered her hand.

"I'm pleased to meet you, Sidney," she said with what appeared to be a forced smile.

CHAPTER 10
1:28 p.m.

Brad Holcomb

There was too much noise and too much confusion. His world had tilted on its axis. He wanted to rest, to hear the wind as it rippled the roof of the trailer, the branches of the cedars gently scraping the sides. He wanted to see the gentle kiss of the sun's touch as it rose on the eastern horizon, the pink frosting smoothed over the coarse Nebraska panhandle, the smell of silver sage, wet with morning dew, clinging to his nostrils. His previous life was out of the question. He would settle for yesterday, unperturbed by the World Wide Web, the constant chatter of those pretending to report the news, and the constant fear of being discovered. It was time to leave, to crawl off into a burrow and die peacefully, unlike those he had killed, some so close he had seen the terror in their eyes. He could not kill enough.

So many years, so much time, yet the ghosts of the past still haunted him. Most of those who knew what he had done were gone. Now Tucker was dead. Soon, there would be no one to tell of the politically motivated murders he had committed. History would be pasteurized, shaped, and molded into something the public could accept, something that supported their feel-good beliefs about the present. But he would know. He would always know. Only death would wipe the slate of memory clean.

First, however, he needed to surface long enough to tell his daughter why her mother had died and who had killed her. There was no need to incriminate specific individuals. They were dead. His mission had come to an end. He would assign the blame to something amorphous like the government and a long-dead president who had resigned in disgrace. Maybe she would understand.

Brad stood in the center of the musty living room, surveying the sum of his existence. He held his few personal belongings in his arms. Old, thin, and forgetful, he had nothing to show for his life. A few pairs of underwear no longer white, t-shirts stained and frayed around the neck, tube socks that had given up their elastic, and a pair of faded jeans with frayed cuffs. He held his few toiletries in a plastic Walmart bag. He wore the scuffed wingtips from the Goodwill store in Scottsbluff, and his stained barn coat hung by the door. The roll of dollar bills, almost two hundred of them, held together with a rubber band, was the total of his earnings for two years of scrubbing grease from dishes and mopping floors. The bulge it created in his pocket was uncomfortable. He hoped it would buy enough gas to get across Nebraska.

"Just like that, you're gonna leave," Ida Faye said from the other side of the screen door.

"It's time," he said, turning to face her. The screen softened her features, even though he could see she had been crying.

"I have a daughter too," he said weakly, his voice cracking. "It's been thirteen years." He paused and swallowed hard. "It's time," he said again. He wanted to say there was nothing to hold him any longer. He wanted to tell her that his quest had been about absolution and vindication. He knew that would be a lie. It was revenge and reconciliation that he had sought. Now there was no need. It was time to reunite and tell his daughter why. But Ida Faye had her own problems without solutions. She did not need to hear his.

Ida Faye opened the screen door and stepped inside. She straightened her uniform where it had ridden up on her hips. Her eyes were glassy with tears. "You heard all that in there?" she asked with a slight jerk of her head toward the cafe.

Brad rubbed his chin with his shoulder; the clothes in his arms occupied his hands. The scraping of his beard stubble indicated he had forgotten to shave that morning. "Don't worry about it. I'll forget about it in a little while. I'm pretty confused lately. I think lots of people are confused. Some mornings I can't remember where I am or how I got here. I figure it's nature's way of cleansing itself, of getting rid of all the stuff that doesn't matter anymore. I'll wake up in the middle of the night and remember the phone number of my apartment when I was in grad school. Did you know I have a master's degree? And then it's gone. Bits of trivia that for some reason rise to the surface when you least expect it. Things are jumbled, all clogged up. The dead from the past who rise up and point bony fingers at me, they keep me from the future. Believe me, that's not a metaphor."

Ida Faye cleared her throat. "I'm not a girl anymore, Brad. Seems like I've been waiting all my life for my future to begin," she said, looking up at him. She huffed. "Did you know I was a lady in waiting for a whole year once before I became Boomtown Queen? That was before I was Miss Panhandle. Then the logjam happened. I made mistakes, some really stupid ones. I thought Darrell was the biggest one of all. Later, I realized it was me. I let that rotten piece of human trash talk me into giving up my baby, and you saw how that turned out."

Tears streamed down her cheeks. She took a deep breath. "It's easy to look back on innocence from a distance. I think the future is now, Brad. I've been waiting my whole life for it. Let's not go it alone. Let's do it together. You and me, a big do-over. We can take care of each other. We can find our souls together." Her lips quivered. "We can find our quieter place in the world."

His left hand began to shake as he stared at her. He had sought solace from her. He knew the comfort in shared sorrow was temporary. She had touched his heart. Not in the same way it had been touched by his wife a lifetime ago. Rather, in a way that allowed him to see what he had become and to realize that he must bury the past in order to gain passage to the future. "I'm not sure I have a soul to be found," he said, shaking his head slowly. "You deserve more, Ida Faye, so much more than I can give you." He saw her close her eyes. Her head descended to her chest as she sensed his rejection; her dreams were shattered for a second time in a matter of minutes.

"My name's not Ida Faye," she said softly, her voice catching as she fought back sobs. "It's Tammy, Tammy Jo Martin.

Everybody called me T.J." She wiped her nose with the back of her hand.

Brad smiled. He believed her revelation paled in comparison to his secrets. He was not yet willing to give his up as a show of mutual confidence. He had used many names over the years; each was the name of a fallen comrade from a previous life that he could not forget. Brad Holcomb had died forty-five years ago. His nickname had been Little Nail. "I had a nickname," he offered softly as a token gesture. "Everybody called me Cowboy."

⇢⊷◈⊷⇠

Ida Faye Mensinger

"Cowboy," she said as if discovering the name of something new. She wanted to ask him how he had been given that moniker but was hesitant to ask. Brad had offered it as a gesture in response to her divulging her nickname. She had confided in him. "Look, Brad, this ain't no poker game where I up the ante, you see my bet, and call me. My cards are on the table. I'm all in. You better show me what you're holdin'." She wiped a tear from her cheek. "Or else," she threatened, placing her hands on her hips. She had been turned down again and did not know how to exit the embarrassing situation. The pain of suddenly realizing she had lost again by going first swept over her. She had showed him hers, and he had not reciprocated. The memory of the Tobias brothers laughing as they left the barn sent a shiver down her spine.

"I'm from Wyoming, grew up here, I went to school here. It's the Equality State. Most people know it as the Cowboy

State because of the bucking bronco on its license plate. I was eight thousand miles from home, and nobody knew anybody from Wyoming. They had seen the license plate. So, they started calling me Cowboy, and it stuck."

"All right then," Ida Faye gushed. "Now we're getting somewhere." She wanted to press him for more but hesitated for fear of being greedy. "Here's what we got so far: your nickname was Cowboy." She paused. "I'm gonna need some time to digest all this information," she said sarcastically. She suspected, given his age and the scar on his arm that he had admitted was a bullet wound from an AK, and that he had been eight thousand miles from home, he was most likely a Vietnam veteran. "Wait, you have a daughter and a master's degree and could use some new socks. Anything else you'd like to share with our viewing audience?" She paused again as she studied his face. "Are we all in and all done? Going once."

"Sorry," Brad said, looking at her sheepishly. "My silence is what has kept me alive all these years. The less you know about me, the safer we'll both be. I know that sounds paranoid. Let's just leave it at that."

"Going twice," she said, looking directly into his eyes, then paused. "No sale," she declared softly and shook her head. "This was a no-reserve auction, Brad, and your goods didn't sell." Her chest convulsed as she fought back her tears of grief. "You're my friend," she sobbed. "We're growing old, dying a little every day. We'll never be young again," she said, her eyes glassy with tears. She knew it was her last chance for a new beginning. "I wish you all the luck in the world, Brad. Send me a postcard when you get to wherever it is you're going." She turned and scuffed noisily out the trailer.

Outside, she inhaled deeply as she walked toward the cafe. She brushed the tears from her cheeks with her fingers and fumbled in her dress pocket for her cigarettes. She thought about going around front and getting in her car and driving away, far away, maybe Montana. A trucker from Plentywood had told her a good-looking woman like her could find a job there, and it was only fifteen miles from Canada, where the fishing was great and the people friendly. Pulling out her cigarettes, she dug deeper and retrieved the only cash she had left, six dollars and change. Looking up, she saw Joe watching her from the back door of the cafe. He said nothing before turning and disappearing inside.

⊸⟡⊷

Jessica Martindale

Sam's daughter was a woman, early thirties, with beautiful skin and a trim body. Not what she expected. Her long, dark hair glistened with the radiance of a Clairol model. Her features were perfect, thrown off only by the thick glasses she wore, her eyes appearing unnaturally large, child-like. Jessica searched Sidney's face, looking for some trace of Sam Dawson. She did not find it and quickly assumed the woman favored her mother. She was tall and angular, like her father, and shared his somewhat intimidating presence, although she did not resemble him. Her smile was forced when Sam introduced her.

Jessica offered her hand awkwardly late. "I'm pleased to meet you, Sidney." The young woman's stare unnerved her as she took her hand. An uncomfortable silence followed. "Thanks for the pie," she offered to break the tension. Still nothing as the younger woman studied her. "Your father told me you're a lawyer." There was no response other than the start of a tight-lipped smile. She wondered if the woman was shy or just being rude. "Where did you go to school?"

"University of Wyoming," Sidney said matter-of-factly. "Forgive me for staring, but you have an amazing resemblance to a young man I've met at the university who shares your name, Martindale, Jeffrey Martindale."

Jessica smiled broadly. "Well, he should look a little like me. He shares fifty percent of my genotype. He's my son. That one's a rascal. How do you know him?"

"I'm sometimes a guest lecturer in the law school. He sought my advice on a paper he is writing about the disruption of wildlife corridors in the Pinedale Anticline." Sidney stopped short of telling her that she had met with him several times, that she was infatuated with him, that she daydreamed about him constantly, and that she had made up her mind to take their relationship to the next level.

"I swear those boys chose their major in Environment and Natural Resources as a slap in my face for working with Pioneer Hybrids. They believe agriculture is poisoning the earth." She shook her head while holding her smile.

Sidney's eyes narrowed, and she tilted her head as if she did not understand. "Boys?"

"You've not met David, Jeffrey's brother?"

"No," Sidney said, her brow slightly wrinkled.

"I'll bet you have and didn't know it. It's a little joke they've been playing ever since they started school. If you think Jeffrey looks like me with fifty percent of my genetic contribution, you should see the two of them together. They share one hundred percent with each other. They're identical twins, and even I sometimes struggle to tell them apart. Their father never could. They're two peas in a pod. You would think Pioneer engineered them."

"I haven't met David," Sidney said weakly, her voice cracking.

"Sure you have." Jessica beamed. "They delight in switching identities. If one of them doesn't feel like attending class, the other will substitute and no one's the wiser. In high school, David took Jeffery's date to the senior prom and vice versa. When I found out, I threatened to tattoo their names on their foreheads. Those boys are rascals just like farmyard dogs, to be sure."

Both Sam Dawson and his daughter stood silently, seemingly stunned by her revelation.

Jessica looked at each of them and back again. She saw the terror in their eyes at her disclosure. She looked at Sam. "You've met them," she said softly.

"No," Sam said quickly as he tried to recover. "It's just that … you know how some people are afraid of clowns or snakes— not that your boys are either—it's just that I'm sort of afraid of twins." He looked sheepishly down at the floor. "Actually, I'm afraid of triplets, quadruplets, quintuplets, sextuplets, all multiple fetuses. I get goosebumps just talking about it."

Jessica stared at him with disbelieving eyes. "Have you thought about getting professional help for that?" The moment she spoke, she wished she could take it back. By the look on his face, she knew it was true. He was a stranger, and she had suggested he seek mental health assistance, which to most people is a deeply personal decision. Yet his fear seemed so irrational, especially since she was the mother of twins. "I know what you mean." She laughed. "I break out in a cold sweat at the thought of a den of snakes or an alley of clowns. Multiples of things that all look alike can be a little scary."

She turned toward Sidney. "I'm used to my boys' pranks. Looking back, those antics seem humorous and benign. Hopefully, they've outgrown those juvenile behaviors." She paused as she searched Sidney's face for a hint of understanding. She saw alarm and disbelief. "I'll make sure Jeffrey introduces David to you properly," she said softly, realizing it was too late to soften the blow she had delivered.

"That won't be necessary," Sidney said as she turned and walked away.

⊷═❋═⊶

Sidney Dawson

Sidney, quiet as a nun, had taken the woman's hand and stared into her green eyes, the same green eyes as Jeffrey Martindale. *I am not who you think I am,* she thought. *I am much more than his daughter. Neither of you will ever know who I truly am. Words of introduction are superficial. I am the woman who has been stalking your son, the woman who has betrayed both of you. I'm the woman who has taken Jeffrey Martindale into her arms and secretly seduced him, if only in my imagination. I have stared into his eyes, your eyes, Jessica Martindale, and whispered all the unsaid words between two lovers. Please tell me this is not happening.* She had rudely walked away without explanation. She had to.

Sidney stopped at her booth and stared out the window. She surveyed the storm's damage. Broken windshields, dented hoods and roofs were the reminders of the storm's ferocity. Hailstones, pearly projectiles, nature's weapons, lay melting, scattered across the landscape like her dreams. Her chest convulsed with emotion as she breathed. She replayed her meetings with Jeffrey and how he seemed to forget important details from previous discussions. She had been scammed, treated like a fool by the man—boy, rather—she had secretly fallen in love with. She felt suddenly ill, as if she had been gut-punched. She wanted to leave, find a hole and crawl into it, to laugh and cry at the same time. She had been the butt of jokes all her life. This one was particularly hurtful. How they must have laughed at her as they planned their next assault on the four-eyed beast with hearing aids. Her mind raced. *Why me?* She began to shake as she thumbed through the memories of the men she had fallen for. Her eyes burned, and she knew she was about to cry.

Dr. Tom Stevens had successfully wooed her by convincing her that he was the mild-mannered animal behaviorist who saw past her physical shortcomings and loved her true self. She had believed him. She had trusted him. He was smart and hand-some. When she closed her eyes, she could smell his aftershave and feel his beard stubble against her cheek, the warmth of his breath on her ear, and then the shiver of fear when she realized the truth. It was Sam, her father, whom he wanted to hurt. She was the pawn sacrificed in his deadly game of retribution. Annie

George, her father's true love and Sidney's best friend, had tried to save her and died for her efforts. Sidney felt strangely responsible for Annie's death and her father's inability to move on. Sometimes, she wished it had been her instead of Annie.

Deputy Nick Alexander had convinced her not once, but twice that he was in love with her. That did not stop him from betraying her. She had fallen hard for the handsome young man. It was a bitter pill to swallow when she finally learned his true motivation. She had unwittingly been trapped in his family's tangled web of deception. Again, she was collateral damage for the intended target, her father. She still could not determine if her tears had been for herself, her father, or for Nick, who had been used as much as she had. She had truly loved him.

Really, she wanted to shout out loud. *How stupid could I be?* She had been used and abused by men she had trusted, men who, she believed, had loved her. In desperation, she had fallen for a boy, obviously not yet a man, who had played sophomoric tricks on her. *Really,* she thought again as she slowly shook her head. She felt her heartache turning to anger. Being mad at herself solved nothing. Thoughts of revenge, on the other hand, gave her momentary relief. She would get even. Tit for tat seemed appropriate. Various scenarios surfaced, partially thought-out and rejected. Too elaborate; too time-consuming; too mild or too harsh. She could use their mother to her advantage, since she seemed immune to their shenanigans. The three of them, mother and sons, would laugh off such an attempt. Then, as if struck by lightning, she knew what she would do.

Sam Dawson

The sun streaked through the kaleidoscope of smashed tumble-weeds piled against the cafe windows, slanted rays that illuminated the scuffed checkerboard of tiles on the floor. Sam stared at the floor as he recalled the terror of discovering identical twins from the twisted eugenics experiments in Colorado and how he and his daughter had been victimized by the clandestine society of twin descendants.

Remembering the discovery of more than a hundred unmarked graves in an asylum cemetery, the broodstock of forced embryo donors, a mass murder that no one cared about still kept him up at night. He had buried the records of lineage, more than a hundred sets of octuplets spread across eight states. His mother had been one of them. He was a descendant, an unknowing member with a racist pedigree. They had killed his sister, culled because of a genetically transmitted hearing defect. They had tried to kill both him and Sidney and anyone else who threatened to expose their warped efforts to improve the human race by controlled selective breeding. People who looked alike made him nervous.

"Was it something I said?" Jessica asked. She looked past Sam toward Sidney, who stood looking out the window at the other end of the cafe, the shafts of sunlight stabbing at everything around her.

"Oh, no, I'm sure it was nothing you said. It was something she heard," Sam said. He turned and looked at his daughter. "She doesn't hear very well and probably thought the conversation was over. She has a condition," he believed "condition" sounded better than disease or syndrome, "that is slowly destroying both her hearing and vision. She misinterprets things all the time," he lied. He knew his daughter was the most perceptive person he had ever known. Despite her sensory impairments, she saw and heard things that most people missed. He was sure something Jessica had said sparked Sidney's sudden exit. He had no idea what it was. Sam nervously glanced over his shoulder at his daughter, who had her back to them. He knew he was digging a hole, and he needed to change the subject.

"All right, people," Joe half-yelled in order to get everyone's attention, "pay your bills, cash only. The cafe closes in five minutes. You'll need exact amounts, since the cash register is locked." He wiped his spatula on his apron as if it were the gavel falling in an auction or a court proceeding.

"Jeez Louise," Ida Faye whined, her hands placed squarely on her hips. "You ain't some high–and–mighty muckety-muck who can just sally out here and bark orders at people."

"I'm the king of this castle, and my order stands. You have four and a half minutes, people." He pointed his spatula at Ida Faye. "Your insubordination will not be tolerated. If you persist, your employment will be terminated, and I'll have security escort you to the door."

"You heard the man," Ida Faye said, turning toward the pretty lady and the father. "Pay those bills kersplickety-splick. This going concern closes in four minutes. And don't forget the gratuity," she added as an afterthought, with an exaggerated wink.

Sam used the opportunity to climb out of the hole he was digging. He stood, picked up both checks from the table, and reached for his wallet.

"You don't need to do that," Jessica said. "I still have my purse. My car, my clothes, and all my other stuff are gone; everything except my purse."

"It's the least I can do for the inconvenience of having you meet me here. I hope you understand that my attempt to have a father-daughter day took precedence. I was only trying to accommodate your request to meet with my scheduled day with Sidney."

Jessica studied Sam's face for a long moment before standing. "I'll let you buy my lunch, Sam," she said, "if you promise not to feel guilty for this unfortunate series of events."

"Deal." He smiled. "I don't believe meeting you was an unfortunate event." Sam immediately wished he had not said that. It was much too forward of him. However, it was done, and there was no taking it back. He stood there awkwardly, waiting for her response. He squeezed his chin and looked down, embarrassed by her silence.

"I agree," she demurred and also looked down shyly. "But," she said a little too loudly as she looked up, then lowered her voice, "let's see how the rest of the day goes before we come to that conclusion." Her smile was warm and inviting as she held eye contact with him until he looked away.

He surveyed the scattered remains of pie crust that littered the table. The waitress and fry cook bantered sarcastically in the background. Their language was foreign. The odor of grease hung heavy in the air that had suddenly gone stale. He made a conscious decision to breathe as he fought the panic that settled over him heavy as night air on a moonless night, his desire resurrected as if he were sixteen again. He had thought it impossible that someone could captivate him the way Annie had. "Is it hot in here?" he heard himself say, a voice distant and unlike his.

Jessica studied him, surveyed his face with her head tilted sideways, and her eyes narrowed. "Stuffy, perhaps," she managed.

He could taste her words on his tongue, a mixture of sugary sweet and something tangy that were as addictive as buttery popcorn during a suspenseful movie. He wanted more. He wanted to touch her and was unsure why. Her green eyes softened, and dimples appeared at the corners of her mouth. She was smiling at him with radiance as bright as midday sun, an expectant energy that said, *It's okay, and you can touch me.* Sam reached out for her.

CHAPTER 11
1:32 p.m.

Brad Holcomb

B rad had watched Ida Faye as she slowly walked back to the cafe, her head bowed. Disappointment had been with her most of her life. He wanted to call out to her, to tell her he was sorry, that she was his inspiration for moving on, for embracing the future and letting go of the past. He wanted to wrap his arms around her, hold her to his chest, and confide his secrets trustingly, like a child admitting guilt. He would ask her not to be afraid and that he was done killing people. He wanted to tell her to pack a bag and meet him out front, their future was waiting and their past would soon be forgotten. The words did not come. He stood there helplessly, ashamed that he had hurt her.

Brad looked around him at the stark interior of the trailer. There was nothing else. He picked up the Walmart bag and grabbed the Winchester. The shotgun was heavy in his hand. He debated whether to take it. Anger replaced his shame. Perhaps he was not done killing after all. Would they still come for him? There was no need to protect Tucker. He knew they would never forget the two he had killed for their botched attempt to silence him permanently. He decided to take the gun.

His pickup was parked in front of the cafe. Joe insisted that everyone park in front to give the illusion that the cafe was busy. The plates and registration on his truck were out of date by years. He had no driver's license or any other form of personal identification. He had no plan if he were ever pulled over. It was too risky. Even more dangerous was being finger-printed to determine his identity. The nonexistent Special Forces group, SOG, had required his prints in order that he have the clearances necessary for his covert operations while in Vietnam. TS, SI, SOG (Top Secret, Special Intelligence, and Special Operations Group) were the highest security clearance granted. The Army, Department of Defense, and National Security Administration knew more about him than he did. The CIA and FBI were the footmen that mindlessly carried out the international and domestic investigations. His fingerprints would cause the FBI to swoop in and snatch him up like an eagle catching a fish. There would be no trace. He would never make it back to D.C.

Brad looked beyond the cafe at U.S. 20 that stretched to each horizon, east and west. There was no traffic. The storm had stalled any plans he had of hitchhiking. The realization that he needed Ida Faye was not a new revelation. He had repeatedly dismissed the idea, fearing for her safety. The thought of using her because she had a car and driver's license was reprehensible. She deserved much more than that. Brad realized he needed her. Not just for transportation. There was something else. He was unsure of what it was. It was more than emotional support, which he had not needed since losing his wife. He would have never guessed that a man his age could be sexually attracted to a woman, especially one as mouthy and irreverent as Ida Faye. He certainly had not ruled it out. Doubts about his inability to consummate such a relationship should not stop him from pursuing a physical connection which, he believed, was secondary to the emotional bond necessary for two people to love each other. Time was running out. He had borrowed more than his share of time. What was he waiting for? He could find comfort with her, even though she was like a nervous hummingbird with too much energy, always moving, never still. She would speed from one flower to another with a cigarette protruding from the side of her beak. Her idle chatter was like the hum of the tiny bird's wings.

Something was wrong with him. He was unsure what it was, but he suspected it was neural. Muscle control was becoming an issue. Resting tremors, especially when falling asleep, caused his entire world to shake. He shuffled his feet when walking and found it difficult to straighten up, unconsciously leaning forward. His greatest fear was dementia. He was not convinced his forgetfulness was simply age-related. Brad believed it was possibly symptomatic of something more progressive. His sleep patterns since Nam had been strange. Now they were disturbing—awake at night and totally exhausted during the day. He frequently fell asleep while standing over the sink, his hands submerged in soapy water. The hallucinations he experienced after Vietnam were like daydreams compared with the realistic illusions he saw now. He feared his time was running out. He had considered a detailed, explanatory letter to his daughter that he would give to a trucker to mail from some distant state. Between the tremors and the strange cramped writing that often disappeared by the end of a sentence, he had given up on a letter. Whatever was wrong with him was reason enough to protect Ida Faye from becoming his caregiver. The problem was he was in love with her.

-•══ ❋ ══•-

Ida Faye Mensinger

"I don't have the exact change," the young woman's father was saying to Joe as Ida Faye entered the dining area from the kitchen. He looked flushed, his ears a hot pink, and a rosy glow extended down his neck. He nervously glanced over his shoulder at the pretty woman with whom he had been talking. He cleared his throat as he looked into his wallet. "I have two bills each with President Grant's picture on them, and I'm not about to give you a fifty for—" Sam spread out the three tickets on the counter and roughly added them up. "I don't have the exact total. It looks to be less than thirty bucks."

"Don't forget the twenty-dollar gratuity," Ida Faye said as she passed by and winked at Sam, her eyes puffy and red.

"Pop, I have my checkbook," the young woman said, sliding from the booth. "I'll add it to the check I'm writing for the frozen hamburger we pulled out of the freezer."

"No checks, no credit cards," Joe loudly proclaimed and pointed his spatula at the sign below the defunct cash register.

The pretty lady slid her chair under the table noisily. She smoothed the front of her dress. Everyone turned to look at her as if expecting a solution to the bill-paying dilemma. "What?" she said with a startled look on her face. Ida Faye noticed the same rosiness in the woman's cheeks as the young woman's father at the counter. "I'm just going to the restroom."

"The restroom is closed," Joe said with authority. "We're on a well here. Without electricity there's no water. We've got one flush, and I'm saving it for an emergency. Harrison, Nebraska is that way," he said, pointing his spatula east. "Lusk, Wyoming is that way." He swung the spatula to the west.

"Now that tears it, Joe," Ida Faye said, thrusting her hands to her hips and stepping in front of him. "I'm about to take that spatula and put it where the sun don't shine if you don't start treating people better."

"You're fired."

"Thank goodness. Now, I can file for unemployment. Oh, wait! You've never paid unemployment insurance."

"I don't have to. You're a private contractor. You should have been paying your own unemployment insurance," Joe said with a smug smile.

"I really need to use the restroom," the pretty lady said. She bit her lower lip for emphasis.

"You go right ahead, honey," Ida Faye said with a smile. "I'll handle this lummox." She turned back to Joe with a look that said, *Try me.*

Joe recognized the look and knew it was futile to argue with her. "You're not really fired," he said softly.

"Yes, I am. You can't take it back this time, Joe. I'm out of here." Her eyes became glassy with tears again. "I can't take anymore." She took a deep breath, shook her head slowly, then looked up into Joe's eyes. "You know, the day started out pretty good with news of Darrell getting himself killed. It was my big chance to get myself free; a new life. I was fixin' to go to Montana and start over. He took all my money. Then my daughter shows up and takes the very reason I was here in the first place." She took a deep breath that was jagged with emotion. "Brad's leavin', too. Not with me, however." She swallowed the lump in her throat. "I can't take any more rejection, least of all from you, Joe. You've been good to me all these years. You're an odd duck, a bit of a weirdo, but I've stuck with you 'cause in your own way you've been kind to me, and I appreciate it."

"I'll go with you," Joe said.

A reflective glint from sunlight on chrome flashed against the darkened wall above the cold grill. Gravel popped from beneath the tires of the Suburban as it rushed to a stop in front of the cafe.

"Well, look who's back, Mutt and Jeff. Now there's a mismatched pair to draw to," Ida Faye said, purposefully ignoring Joe as she looked out the front window through the tangle of tumbleweeds at the battered Suburban. "Like a bad penny, they just keep showing up."

The young woman with thick glasses, Sidney, stood up and rushed to the door and held it open as the older agent assisted the handsome younger man to the door.

"Easy, Sidney," Ida Faye cautioned. "Remember, they're armed."

The two shuffled through the door. Their blood-spattered white shirts appeared polka-dotted from a distance. The younger man still had the makeshift bandage wrapped around his head.

"If it ain't Bud and Lou back for more rural hijinks," Ida Faye said her hands still on her hips.

"We're closed," Joe ordered. "Unless either of you have change for a fifty," he added politely.

"Flash flooding west of here took out the road," the older agent said. "There was no way around it. Mark is feeling much better and suggested we come back here until things open up."

Mark glanced at Sidney.

She absently tucked loose hair behind her right ear, which caused her hearing aid to squeal shrilly. She pushed up her glasses on the bridge of her nose, stepped forward sure of herself, and took the younger agent by the arm. "Agent," she said, nodding slightly to the older man. "Mark, why don't you have a seat over here." She gestured toward her booth.

"Excuse me," the bandaged agent said, looking at her queerly. "Do I know you?"

"Nice try, buster." Ida Faye laughed. "I suppose you forgot proposing marriage to her too. And by the way, your wife called and said don't forget to bring milk home for the kids."

The agent grinned broadly. "It was worth a shot. I just wanted to see the expression on her face."

Sidney's dumfounded expression quickly surrendered to one of mild amusement. "You have a sense of humor, Special Agent Johnson. That's a significant improvement from earlier today, when you asked me for my phone number."

"Now why would I ask you for your phone number, Sidney Dawson, Esquire, of 1199 Highway 210, Cheyenne, Wyoming?"

Sidney raised her eyebrows. "So, you've been checking on me."

"How 'bout my phone number, young man?" Ida Faye asked. "If you substitute experience for age, I'm your gal."

"You can be my lady in waiting, first on the list." Mark smiled.

"Story of my life," Ida Faye said. "Story of my life," she repeated softly as she scuffed dejectedly toward the kitchen.

-⊷═�֎═⊶-

Jessica Martindale

If the cafe felt stuffy, the tiny restroom was downright hot. She stared at her reflection in the cracked mirror. Her nose was shiny and her face reddened. She took a deep breath and exhaled it slowly. It was not hot; she was flushed, blushing with embarrassment. Sam Dawson, a perfect stranger, had reached out and taken her arm in his hand as if he were assisting her as she arose naked from her bath. Normally, she would have jerked her arm away from such an uninvited gesture. Jessica had steadied herself by grabbing the table's edge before sitting back down. It was as though an electric current had passed through her body and found ground deep within her loins. She had not felt anything like that since her first kiss when she was fifteen. *This can't be happening*, she thought. *Not now.* She tried to convince herself that it was exhaustion. It had been a long night without sleep. Absently, she twisted the faucet handle on the sink. She wanted to splash cold water on her face and wake from the unsettling dream that had overpowered her rational thinking. Nothing happened. There was no water. She looked at the clear water in the stained toilet bowl. She had lied about needing to use the restroom. Privacy was what she had needed;

time to collect herself, to justify her actions, and to focus on the future, both immediate and long-range. She flushed the unused toilet.

Muffled conversations from the cafe exploded suddenly when she opened the door.

"Jessica Martindale," the older man in black almost yelled as she stepped from the restroom.

From the look on his face, he was as surprised to see her as she was him. "Yes," she said slowly.

He reached inside his coat, produced a gleaming gold badge, and flashed it at her too quickly for her to read his name. He glanced out the window toward the parking lot and then back to her. He seemed confused. She quickly surmised that he believed she had driven away in his absence, since her car was no longer there.

"I have some questions I need to ask you," he said in an official voice.

Jessica noted that he did not say he would like to ask her questions or inquire if she had the time or would she mind if he asked her questions. He forcefully said he needed to ask her questions. "Okay," she said hesitantly.

Stunned silence hung over the cafe's dining area. Five people looked as if they had just witnessed a murder. Finally, Sam took a step forward toward the agent. "What's this about?"

"Stand down, Dawson," the agent commanded. "This is not your concern."

"The fact you know my name is a concern," Sam said. He stiffened, which made him appear even taller.

"We've got quite a file on you, Dawson. The words 'approach with caution' stand out. Assaulting federal officers should have put you away three years ago. If you try any of that crap with us, I'll put you down." The agent's cold stare and set jaw told Sam that he meant business.

"Pop," Sidney called to her father. "Don't interfere. He can nail you with obstruction."

"Yeah, Pop," the waitress chorused. "I ain't cleanin' up after you two. Near as I can tell, you don't have a dog in this fight. Come on back here and have a seat. I'll scrape up another piece of pie for ya."

"Dawson," the agent lowered his voice and looked at Sam from under a lowered brow, "listen to your daughter. She knows the law. You don't need a fine or jail time for interfering with a government proceeding."

Jessica smiled at Sam and nodded. Again, he had tried to protect her.

"Where's your car?" the agent asked, his voice official and his eyes focused on hers.

"It was stolen a little while ago by two escaped convicts."

"Borrowed might be a more accurate description," Ida Faye added quickly.

"At gunpoint? Really?" Jessica shot the waitress a wide-eyed look.

"Where were you last night?" the agent said, ignoring the stolen car issue.

Jessica stared at the agent. She thought about lying but then realized it was futile. She had not taken the time to fabricate an alibi since finding out the car had a GPS locator. "You know where I was."

"I need to hear it from you."

"I was north of here, sitting on a knoll overlooking the WT Ranch."

"Why were you there?"

"You know why I was there. Why the interrogation?"

"I need to hear it from you." The agent used the same measured voice.

"I was hoping to find my father."

"Why would your father be there?"

"Because today is the anniversary of when your kind ruined his life."

-·-➣◉✶ ◉═◄·-

Sidney Dawson

Sidney watched the agent's face. He seemed unfazed by Jessica's accusation and never averted his eyes from hers. "What time did you arrive at the WT Ranch?" he asked.

Jessica took a deep breath. "Look, you've obviously charted my locations and times from the GPS tracking device in my car. Since you haven't read me my rights, I assume I'm not under arrest. I don't mean to be rude, but I must insist on having legal representation before I answer any further questions."

"Are you armed?" He looked her up and down and then glanced at her purse on the table.

"That's enough," Sidney called out from across the room and slid from the booth, leaving the younger agent, who was still smiling, by himself. She confidently approached Jessica and the older agent. "As her legal counsel, I'm advising her not to answer any more questions until I've had an opportunity to confer with my client." Sidney smiled reassuringly at Jessica then turned toward the older agent. "You know as well as I do that reasonable suspicion does not allow for arrest or even the issue of a search warrant. I'm citing Terry versus Ohio, 1968."

"Is she your attorney?" the agent asked Jessica.

Surprised, Jessica stared at Sidney, her eyes wide, brows raised. She then looked to Sam, who nodded once. "Yes," she said softly.

Sidney positioned herself next to Jessica and faced the agent. "Don't confuse probable cause and reasonable suspicion as far as the rights of my client are concerned. Without a search or an arrest warrant, you better be darn sure that the circumstances reasonably show that my client is guilty of some breach of the law. I suspect you don't need to be reminded of Goldberg versus Texas, 2002."

"You go, girl." The waitress held her fist in the air.

"I can have that warrant flown in here by chopper in a couple of hours," the agent said, holding his ground.

Sidney looked at the dead Dr. Pepper clock above the grill. It was still dead. "No, you can't," she said, turning and looking without blinking at the agent. "Probable cause is all about probabilities. You're going to need a lot more than just suspicion to convince a judge." She smiled at the agent and then leaned toward him as if to confide a secret. "Since you're a federal agent, I assume you're an attorney and that you understand, I'm trying to protect more than just my client here. You know I'm trying to protect both you and the law. All I want is to verify the correctness of the process."

"You're in way over your head, girlie. You're a tree hugger specializing in environmental policy. Our attorneys will eat you alive. You better stick to whales, ferrets, and endangered toads."

"Despite your disparaging remarks about my age, gender, and occupation, I will welcome the opportunity to debate the law with you and your agency's attorneys. Now, if you'll excuse me, I wish to consult with my client in private."

Sam stepped forward again, his hands clutched into fists, his nostrils flared. He looked straight into the agent's eyes and through clenched teeth said, "If you disrespect my daughter like that again, I'll throw you through that window." He nodded sideways toward the cafe's large-plate glass window.

Jessica's arm shook in Sidney's grasp as she led the frightened woman back to her table. The woman's mouth was partially open, as if she was trying to find the words to speak. Sidney looked over her shoulder and saw her father hovering over the older agent in a threatening posture. "Pop," she said loudly. "Could you come here please?" Her request was not presented as a question. It clearly came out as a directive.

Sam dutifully obeyed, leaving the older agent looking somewhat stunned as he scratched behind his ear.

"Pop, don't make a bad situation worse. If you threaten a federal officer, either verbally or physically, they'll restrain you and haul your sorry butt off to jail. How many times do I have to tell you not to hit the good guys? Now, go over there and talk to the younger agent. His name is Mark. See if you can find out what's going on."

"Can't I stay here? I'll just listen."

"No. Ms. Martindale's conversation with me is protected by attorney-client privilege. Anything you hear is not protected, and you could be forced to divulge incriminating information. So, cool your jets and try to be nice to people."

"He's been nice to me," Jessica said softly, her eyes fixed on Sam.

Sidney looked at her father. He had the same puppy-dog expression on his face that Jessica did. She was reminded of the dog characters in Disney's *Lady and the Tramp* from the 1950s, dogs that were opposites yet attracted to each other. "Great," she said with a disgusted expression. *Here we go again,* she thought.

⋅→═◉ ✳ ◉═←⋅

Sam Dawson

The younger agent, Mark, looked as dazed as Sam felt when Sam slid into the booth next to him. The older agent gave them both a threatening look as he stormed out of the cafe and disappeared behind the smashed and darkened glass of the Suburban's windshield. "You've got a satellite phone in there, don't you?" Sam said.

"Yep," Mark said without looking at Sam. His gaze was fixed on Sidney across the room.

Sam waited for the bloodied agent to say something. Instead, he continued to stare at Sidney. "So, what are your intentions, young man?" he asked. It was the standard question he always asked of men interested in his daughter.

The agent finally acknowledged Sam's presence by looking at him. He smiled broadly. "First, let me remind you that I am armed," he said without averting his gaze. "Second, I've been advised to approach you with caution. And third, throwing caution to the wind, I'd like to ask for your daughter's hand in marriage."

Sam grinned and chuckled while shaking his head. "Your sense of humor will serve you well when dealing with Sidney. She can be a handful. Don't you think you're being a little premature in your approach?"

"How long have you known Jessica Martindale?" he said, still grinning.

"A little more than an hour." Sam's eyes narrowed.

"Might I ask you what your intentions are?" the young man said somewhat brashly, still staring intently at Sam.

"Touché, Mark." Sam leaned back against the Naugahyde, which squealed like a wounded rodent. "You know, the approach-with-caution advisory is somewhat unjustified. If you knew the circumstances, I think you would agree with me."

"I don't need to know the circumstances, Mr. Dawson. You assaulted agents three years ago. If you assault my partner, he will subdue you. If you assault me, I'll shoot you." Mark's face lost the amusing smile, and his stare was threatening. "Are we clear on that?"

"Crystal-clear," Sam said. "You should know, however, that my daughter had been kidnapped not once but twice by a deranged psychopath who was being protected by feds like you. Just know that I will do what it takes to safeguard my daughter."

"Fair enough; spoken like a good father. Now, tell me about Ms. Martindale's car. Which direction did the suspects go when they left here?"

"East; does your head hurt?" Sam saw the pained expression in the agent's eyes.

"Only when I'm awake." He attempted a crooked smile.

Sam reached across the table and grabbed Sidney's purse. "My daughter gets headaches sometimes," he said as he rummaged through the miscellaneous debris that most women kept in their purses. "Here we go." He held up two small bottles. "This one's got ibuprofen, which will take care of your menstrual cramps," he said, shaking the bottle, the pills clacking noisily. "And this one's got naproxen for longer-lasting relief from brain injuries." He shook that bottle too. "I suggest ibuprofen followed by naproxen in a few hours. If she had some acetaminophen in here," he shook the contents of her purse and looked inside again, "you could mix it with the ibuprofen sooner than you could combine it with naproxen. Or is it the other way around?" Sam cocked his head sideways and pursed his lips. "Most likely, none of them will cause your head to explode. Maybe just a little brain bleeding and some paralysis. If you're worried about it, you could just man up and quit whining."

The agent pushed the bottles and Sam's arm aside. He gulped water from Sidney's glass and wiped his mouth with the back of his hand. "I should arrest you for practicing medicine without a license."

"You'd arrest your future father-in-law?"

"Yep."

"Pop," Sidney called from across the cafe. "Don't be giving him anything."

"Like drugs?" Sam called back.

"Nothing."

"How about information?"

"Nothing," she repeated strongly.

"I can't undo what's already been done."

"What did you give him?" Sidney demanded.

Sam grinned at his daughter and waved his hand in the air. "Your hand in marriage," he answered.

CHAPTER 12
1:41 p.m.

Brad Holcomb

New beginnings drifted over the land that ponderous glaciers had smoothed flat, leaving the high plains unremarkable. Hail, cold and round, was piled where wind and gravity had sent it. The earth was as cold as the hand of a forgotten lover whose familiar scent peeled away the years of longing. Birds seemed to have forgotten nature's cruelty. They sang as if happy as they flitted between the haggard cedars whose limbs were as unruly as morning hair. Tiny white butterflies, oblivious to danger, floated on unseen currents. Brad slipped along the side wall of the cafe, listening, seeing. The conversations from within were muffled. Ida Faye and Joe argued, as usual. Men's and women's voices rose and fell, the tone serious. The feds had returned and suspended his plan of taking Ida Faye by the hand and leading her into an uncertain future. His romantic scheme was as lifeless as a wet towel thrown in the corner of an abandoned locker room.

The dented Suburban with the smashed windshield was parked in front of the cafe. One of the two men was sitting behind the wheel, talking to his rearview mirror. Brad's thumb unconsciously found the hammer of the Winchester. He looked down the row of dented vehicles parked unevenly in the puddled lot. Ida Faye's Ford with the skinny doughnut tire on the rear was faded and tired-looking. Joe's burgundy Silverado had taken a beating. The windshield and a side window were blown out. A tan, late-model pickup with state plates and *WDOC* painted on the sides was parked near the cafe's door. The Willys wagon appeared unscathed, unmoved by the whole affair, sixty years of foul weather behind it, but it would not win a race. His pickup, unlicensed and weathered with fenders of different colors, looked no different than it had before the storm. It was mechanically sound and had fifty years under its Dodge hood. He would steal the Suburban.

Brad slowly backed away from the cafe and returned to the trailer. He quickly closed all the windows and doors and then scurried out the back door and opened the water heater compartment. Using his Leatherman, he undid the compression fitting that held the quarter-inch copper gas line to the control valve and pulled the gas line free. The sulfur-scented propane filled the compartment immediately. He gently closed the door. Returning to the kitchen, Brad dug through the junk drawer and produced a large candle. He lit it, picked up the Walmart bag, the sum of his existence, and quietly exited the trailer.

Ida Faye Mensinger

"To hell in a handbasket, I tell ya," Joe said to Ida Faye. "This country is well on its way to Third World designation. From manufacturing to service, you'd think we were in some godforsaken 'developing' country. China is eating our lunch. They own this country. They hold our debt. A debt we can't pay back short of war with those commies."

Ida Faye stared past him. She had tuned him out as soon as he began his rant. He would sum it up with his sheep theory, shake his head, and walk away in disgust. She had heard it all before. Doomsday, Armageddon, the end-is-near speech; she did not care. She would be the last to die in some isolated valley in Montana—alone.

"Have you seen the next generation?" Joe's voice was louder. "They dress like homeless vagrants. If it weren't for T-shirts and jeans, they wouldn't have anything to wear. They don't own a necktie or a dress. Their bodies are covered in tattoo graffiti that makes them look like they're wearing the funnies from the Sunday paper. They have rings in their noses and lips, giant plugs in their ear lobes, and purple hair. They live at home because they don't work. Their parents give them a smartphone as if it were a pacifier for overgrown babies. Sheep, I tell ya. They spend all day baaing and bleating to each other over their phones. If one goes one way, they all go that way. Their parents are no better. They spend their entire life following instead of leading. They all drive the same color car, the men don't shave, the women wear yoga pants, they watch the same mindless reality shows on TV, and believe everything the media and politicians tell them. They're fat little sheep following each other and their phones all the way to the slaughterhouse. Sheep, I tell ya."

Ida Faye thrust her hands onto her hips. "And if I were a ewe, Joe, you'd be my ram? Is that what you're trying to tell me?

Or are you just another dried-up old man spouting off like you have all the answers?"

Joe's eyes darted back and forth as if he was unsure of himself or had lost his place in delivering his manifesto. "If I were your ram, I'd never hurt you," he said softly. "But I'm not a sheep. I have a brain, a brain not clouded by drugs. The drug pushers in this country need to be exterminated," he offered as if an afterthought. "I'm not stupid, like most of the people in this country who just follow and can't think for themselves." His voice reached a higher pitch. "Mindless little drones that mimic what they see or what they're told. They'll follow anybody who tells them what they want to hear. Think of the greatest orators of the last century and their messages of hope and rectification."

"Rectifiwhat? Now there's a big word, Joe. Sounds like something you put Preparation H on."

Joe ignored her and continued his rant, invoking the names of FDR, MLK, Marx and Engels, and TV evangelists. Again, he proclaimed that everyone but him was sheep.

"Uh-huh," Ida Faye said, rolling her eyes and turning away.

"Don't you see it?" Joe said emphatically. The wattles between his chin and neck quivered. "Our society is ripe for leadership. We're in a downward spiral, economically, politically, socially. It's the Roman Empire all over again. Where's the progress, where's the innovations, where's the work ethic? People don't want to work; they just want to be entertained. If some do-gooder says drink the Kool-Aid, most of America will do it. We're sheep, Ida Faye."

"Baaa," Ida Faye bleated. She was in no mood to be lectured to, especially by a guy wearing a greasy apron and holding a spatula as if it were a scepter. *Crazy old coot*, she thought. She turned around to see Sidney's father and the younger agent staring at her and Joe as if entranced by the soiled fry cook's summary of world events. "Don't pay any attention to him." She motioned with her chin toward Joe. "The cord was wrapped around his neck when he was born, and he was oxygen-deprived. I've had goldfish smarter than him. Can I get you anything before it spoils or melts?"

She placed her hands on her hips again and studied both men, Sam and Mark. "You know, we do wedding receptions here. We can accommodate up to fourteen people here in the banquet hall. Musical entertainment is provided by Seeburg and the Wall-O-Matics, two plays for a quarter. The dance floor is over there." She motioned toward the table where Sidney and the pretty woman were sitting. "Unless, of course, you're Southern Baptist and view pre- and post-nuptial courtship behavior, a.k.a. dancing, as upright fornication. Food, service, and decorations are all provided for a tidy sum. Turkey legs and funnel cakes are always a hit. Gratuities, while not required, are strongly recommended. I can MC the event for an additional fee. Think on it, but not for too long. Our calendar is filling fast." She looked at Sam. "We can do a double wedding at a discounted rate. We'll have to limit the guest list a little."

"And who would officiate?" Sam dared to ask.

"Mother Teresa there," Ida Faye tossed her thumb toward Joe, "does the Catholics. He cooks up a mean plate of fish sticks and provides an open bar of Old Milwaukee and Schlitz.

I do the Protestants and bake a humble pie served with a large scoop of guilt."

"What about Hebrew?"

"Not a problem. I know a guy who works on the kill floor of a small slaughterhouse in Wheatland. He's Jewish and does all the kosher stuff. We'll order some Mogen David wine—it comes in a box now—and Abraham there," she again gestured toward Joe, "will cook up pork tenderloin sandwiches made with turkey burger."

Both men nodded. Mark raised his eyebrows and said, "Sounds good. Sign us up."

"I'll need a deposit," Ida Faye said seriously.

"Mark," the older agent barked as he entered the cafe. "They've enhanced the satellite images, and we've got a positive ID on the vehicle."

⊷═◉ ⚹ ◉═⊶

Jessica Martindale

"I've told some of this to your father," Jessica said between rapid and somewhat ragged breaths. Nervousness had given way to fear; her eyes darted from side to side.

"Better tell me," Sidney said softly with a comforting smile of reassurance. "That older agent seems set on arresting you. And you should know I'm not a criminal attorney. I know the basics and, perhaps, can keep you from incriminating yourself." Sidney pushed her glasses up on the bridge of her nose and looked into Jessica's eyes. The resemblance to her son or sons was distracting.

"I don't know where to begin."

"Just like they say in the movies, start at the beginning," Sidney said. "I'm not here to judge. I'm here to defend. Since you accepted me as your legal counsel, anything you tell me is privileged."

Jessica swallowed hard and folded her hands as if she were about to pray. "My father disappeared in 2003, thirteen years ago today. There was a fiery explosion at our farm in Iowa."

"Do you suspect—"

"No, of course not. My dad loved our farm, and he loved my mother. I've never known anyone so much in love as my parents. They were inseparable, joined at the hip." She stared intently into Sidney's eyes. "He would never have blown up our barn, especially with my mother in it." She leaned back in her chair and took a deep breath. "I should mention that my dad was my stepdad who adopted me when I was nine. My biological father was an Air Force pilot who was shot down in Vietnam and classified as MIA. My adopted dad was my best friend. He helped me through those difficult years of adolescence. I could tell him anything, and he kept my secrets. He listened and never preached or condemned. Although I didn't realize it at the time, he was an extremely private person. It wasn't until after his disappearance that I started to piece together some of his past. I say some of his past because I kept running into brick walls. It was as though his past had been erased. He was a highly decorated Army veteran, and he was from Wyoming. While I didn't understand it at the time, he suffered from post-traumatic stress disorder. He had unspeakable nightmares and hallucinations. He never talked about it, and my mother and I never asked him to explain. Instead, my mother spent years trying to get closure on my biological father's death. The official term was KIA/BNR: Killed in Action, Body Not Recovered. None of it offered closure to my mother, who had run into so many roadblocks that she sensed some sort of government cover-up. The Department of Defense, the Air Force, the State Department, the Pentagon, the Social Security Administration, right up to the president all had different stories, and they all had the same ending.

"Imagine my frustration having both my dads disappear without a trace. The one thing I know for sure, though, is that my adopted dad was trying to protect me by not contacting me. My mom's best friend, who farmed down the road from us, called me on the day of the explosion and tearfully told me that my dad had asked her to call me and that he would contact me to explain what had happened and that he loved me. Later on, I found a Senate Select Committee on Intelligence subpoena in their living room. It summoned my dad to Washington. I had no idea what for. I waited for years for him to call or write or to somehow magically appear on my doorstep and make sense of it all for me."

Across the room, the waitress made a sound like a sheep. Sidney and Jessica turned to look at the strange woman, who was in some animated argument with the cook. Sidney turned back, pushed up her glasses, and said, "Then what?"

Jessica leaned forward as if divulging a secret. "One day, an older woman by the name of Shelly Robinson showed up at my door. She was some sort of special assistant to the president of the United States, John Roberts. She had known my adopted dad when she was a Red Cross volunteer in Vietnam.

She told me that dad was the bravest man she had ever known and that the president owed his office to him. You can imagine my surprise. I thought my dad was a corn and soybean farmer from Iowa, and this woman was telling me the leader of the free world was indebted to him." She shook her head. "I was stunned. The man who used to help me carve jack-o-lanterns and bought me ice cream cones at the Tasty Freeze in lost in the woods Keotonka, Iowa, was in some way the benefactor of the president of the United States. She spent an entire afternoon with me and told me things that changed my perception of this country and soured me on politics for the rest of my life.

"The common denominator for years of deception and lies to the American public was Winston Tucker. When he headed the National Security Administration, he had falsified the location of loss data for American casualties in Cambodia and Laos. When he was secretary of defense, he interfered with and undermined the legal process for settling status determinations of POWs and MIAs by declaring them Killed in Action, Bodies Not Recovered. The Senate Select Committee that had subpoenaed my adopted dad adjourned without a single indictment after two months of investigating Senator Tucker's involvement in the alleged assassinations of American servicemen during the Vietnam War, supposedly ordered by former President Nixon. I learned that my adopted dad was the unidentified, protected witness whose testimony destroyed the political future of Winston Tucker that resulted in John Roberts becoming president. Do you remember any of this?" she suddenly asked, her brow wrinkled and eyes squinted.

"I do," Sidney said, nodding. "It was the start of my junior year in college, and I wrote a paper about it for a political science course I was taking. I remember using it as an example of George Hegel, the German philosopher's, concept of dialectic, the idea that all human progress is driven by the conflict between opposites. He believed that every political movement was imperfect and eventually gave way to a counter movement that takes control, which itself is imperfect, and succumbs to yet another opposing movement, and so on and so on."

"Uh-huh," Jessica said with an edge of skepticism. "In all cases, the roads led to Tucker as the evildoer who was responsible for the death of my biological father and the destruction of my family. Tucker was after my adopted dad to keep him from testifying in the Senate Select Committee on Intelligence." She paused and took a deep breath. "No indictments were handed down as the politicians maneuvered to protect themselves and the process. They couldn't take back my dad's testimony, and the damage was done. Washington distanced itself from Tucker and let the media feed on his carcass in front of an apathetic public. The rest, as they say, is history. Tucker was just another tainted politician who was quickly forgotten." There was a sharp edge to Jessica's voice and a piercing look in her eyes. "I'll never forget the lack of justice that allowed that man to go free," she said through tight lips.

Jessica looked away and took a deep breath. "Apparently, my dad mistrusted the witness protection program that had been offered to him, and he simply disappeared." Her eyes had glassed over when she turned back to Sidney. She looked as if she were about to cry. "I'll never forgive myself for not trying harder to find him. It was a difficult time in my life. The boys were seven or eight and more than a handful. I was in a demanding job and attempting to build my career, all while stuck in a bad marriage that was spiraling downward toward divorce. There were simply not enough hours in a day to take on what seemed like a lost cause. When the boys went off to college, I was finally able to catch my breath and think about how to find my dad."

"Why Wyoming? Why here?" Sidney interrupted.

"My dad grew up here. He went to school here. Wyoming is home to him. The only vacation we ever took when I was growing up was to Wyoming. I did some poking around and discovered that he had both undergraduate and graduate degrees from the University of Wyoming, an education I never knew about. My boys had grown up hearing me talk about that one vacation and how beautiful the mountains were and the cabin my dad had built in the forest. I think that was one of the reasons they chose to come to UW."

"Is the cabin still there?" Sidney asked.

"No, it was lost to a suspicious forest fire shortly after my dad disappeared." Jessica stared out the window, transported in time to a favorite place. "Then," she said suddenly, turning toward Sidney, "I discovered that Winston Tucker was here in Wyoming. I suspected that I might find my dad here too."

-→⊨⊙✳⊙⊨←-

Sidney Dawson

Sidney was silent for several seconds. She kept her poker face and did not avert her gaze into Jessica's eyes. It was time for the tough questions.

"Who are you trying to find, your dad or Winston Tucker?" Sidney asked, her voice serious and her expression expectant. She knew the answer, and her next two questions would follow in rapid succession.

"My father, of course," Jessica said, her brow wrinkled with annoyance at the absurdity of the question.

"Why were you at Tucker's ranch last night?"

Jessica leaned forward, her eyes fixed on Sidney. "I told you. I was looking for my father. And I'm not sure I like your tone." She had lost the doe-eyed, love-struck look she had displayed for Sidney's dad.

"Did you kill Winston Tucker?" Sidney paused for a second then added, "Don't answer that. As your attorney, it makes little difference to me. I'll still defend you until you can replace me with a criminal attorney of your choosing. The point I'm trying to make is if they can place you at the scene of the murder, you'll be asked that question repeatedly in one form or another. You just admitted that you were at the victim's ranch. GPS tracking only indicates your rental car was at the scene. They didn't know who was driving it until you admitted you were there looking for your father. My advice to you is not to answer any questions without your attorney present. Some questions, like 'Have you stopped beating your wife?' are designed to incriminate you. It's best to not say anything and ask for your attorney. So, based on what you've told me so far, you had both motive and opportunity. From their point of view, you're definitely a person of interest. It wouldn't take much more for a judge to issue a warrant for your arrest."

"You need to understand that I had no intention of coming to this godforsaken place until your dad asked me to meet him here." Jessica leaned over the table slightly and kept her eyes focused on Sidney's. "It was fortuitous, that's all. I thought since I was here, I might as well take a look around."

"You told the agent it was the anniversary of your father's disappearance. You told me that you believe Tucker ordered the attempt on your father's life. Further, you inferred that your father might use this date as justification for seeking revenge. I have to tell you that a fortuitous look around sounds pretty weak." Sidney leaned toward Jessica and raised her eyebrows. "Do you see where this is going? Stop talking! Anything you say can and will be held against you in a court of law. That's Miranda 101."

"And I have a right to an attorney," Jessica said as if she were annoyed at being told what to do or was challenging Sidney's ability. "And yes, I can afford one," she added with a tight-lipped stare, addressing the last of the Miranda rights.

"You can't afford me, lady. I guarantee it." Sidney leaned back and started to push her chair back from the table. "I'm not for sale."

"Wait," Jessica implored, her attitude shifting suddenly. "I didn't mean to offend you. It's just that I don't like being lectured to. I've been told I have some authority issues." She attempted a smile and looked down at the table. "I'm vice president for domestic marketing at Pioneer Hi-Bred International, and we get sued regularly. I have two full-time attorneys assigned to me, and I keep them pretty busy with both internal and external legal issues. This isn't my first rodeo."

"Then you understand the difference between civil and criminal litigation," Sidney shot back immediately. "We're not talking about disputes between people or organizations. We're talking about a criminal case that's considered harmful to society as a whole. Killing somebody is a crime against the state."

"Is it still a crime if the victim deserves it?" Jessica asked with a note of seriousness.

"The short answer is yes. It can get complicated when considering such things as self-defense or protecting someone who is in imminent danger." Sidney paused. She bit her lower lip. "Look, I've told you I'm not a criminal attorney. I'm only trying to protect your rights under the law here. Again, my advice to you is to be cordial and cooperative within bounds. If you ask an officer of the law if it's okay to kill someone who deserves it, that question will come back to haunt you. Less talking, more listening is the rule. Look for those incriminating questions."

"You mean questions like, 'Are you still having sex with my son?'"

⊸⊶◉⊱✶⊰◉⊷⊸

Sam Dawson

The explosion seemed to suck the air momentarily from the room before the entire cafe shook with a thunderous roar. All eyes had been turned toward the cafe doorway as the older agent hurried in and announced that enhanced satellite surveillance had yielded positive vehicle identification. The blast knocked him to the floor, pushed by the plate glass door he had been holding. The picture window bowed inward then rebounded with a shudder. The noise was deafening. Sam's eardrums felt as if he were at the bottom of a deep swimming pool, the pressure almost painful. The few items that remained on shelves behind the counter fell to the floor. The noise of pots and pans bouncing off the kitchen floor sounded as if a Spanish mission had been bombed, the bells ringing uproariously. Outside, planetary debris rained downward on the cafe roof and parking lot as though it was raining dirt and gravel. A large piece of aluminum siding crashed to the ground, narrowly missing Sam's already bruised Willys. Yellow tufts of insulation floated downward like a snow globe that had been turned upside down and shaken. The silence afterward was eerie. Dust particles filled the rays of sunshine that filtered through the smoke in sharp downward angles in the cafe's interior, distorting the images of people who stood silently, mouths open, dumfounded by the surprise of the unknown. Then, as if someone had rung the recess bell, everyone silently rushed toward the door and filed outdoors. They scurried around the side of the cafe to the back.

Seven people lined up shoulder to shoulder behind the cafe, surveying the smoldering remains of a trailer house. A chaotic debris field fumed in and among the cedars and around the area between the cafe and the trailer's undercarriage.

The waitress was the first to step forward, a fearful look on her face. She screamed, "Brad," then, "Oh my God, Brad," she repeated as the tears rolled down her cheeks.

Sam held Sidney's hand tightly at the realization that someone may have been inside the twisted and charred wreckage. "This just keeps getting better by the minute," he whispered in Sidney's ear. "This place is turning into a real freak show. Let's go before the authorities arrive and hold everybody for questioning."

The distinctive sound of a vehicle starting caused everyone to orient toward the cafe. They moved quickly around the side of the building, stepping over smoldering rubble as the Suburban backed away from them.

"Hey," the older agent yelled as he fumbled for the weapon he carried under his left arm.

"Brad," the waitress shouted again.

The man behind the wheel stared at them through the unbroken half of the windshield. He seemed to hesitate as he shifted from reverse to drive. He sat motionless for a moment, staring at the line of people who looked back at him with anticipation. He looked away and then spun the steering wheel as he floored the accelerator. The vehicle fishtailed sideways then straightened with the squeal of tires as it hit the highway and sped eastward, almost drowning out Jessica's bone-chilling scream. The word "Dad" hung in the air, plaintive and revealing.

CHAPTER 13

1:47 p.m.

Brad Holcomb

It could have been a hundred years, and he would still have recognized his daughter. The tears came slowly. His chest heaved as he clutched the steering wheel, his knuckles white. Their eyes had fixed on each other. All else was irrelevant. He saw only her. Thirteen years disappeared in an instant. She appeared as the same little girl who had watched him leave so many times before. A trip to town for combine parts or hog vaccines or to pay an overdue bill, she always magically appeared in the driveway with that same look on her face. A look that said *take me with you, I'll be good, please let me ride along.* It was the same little girl face on the woman standing in front of the lonely cafe. A father will always recognize his daughter. The years cannot deny him that.

The four men and three women had stood helplessly in the parking lot of the cafe as he sped away, dust engulfing them. Looking in the rearview mirror, Brad watched the cafe disappear on the western horizon as he drove eastward into Nebraska. The wind roared through the windshield on the passenger side. The feds had undoubtedly scrambled to find a vehicle to pursue him. He glanced at the ice pick on the front seat that he had used to puncture two of the four tires on every vehicle in the parking lot except the Willys. It could not catch him. The stock of the Winchester bounced above the seat, its barrel toward the floor. It gave him reassurance.

Just before Harrison, he pulled over. The Nebraska Panhandle was as stark as the moon. There was no place to hide while he considered his options. Jessica's presence had more than changed his plans; it cleaned the slate. His breath came in ragged surges. His ears rang. He looked behind him, he looked ahead. He could go no farther. His time was running out. The sun had jostled the black and blue storm to the north and broken its will. A line of birds flirted with the taller grasses of the borrow ditch filled with storm water and hail. Barbed wire strung tightly between wooden posts paralleled the highway; their straight lines converged in the distance without destiny. Life went on, renewed by the Earth's rotation and the warmth from above. His time had run out. He could see the future. He knew how this would end. He would not be young again. His life was behind him. Memories were all that he had, and they would not sustain him.

He turned the car around.

⇥═◉ ⚹ ◉═⇤

Ida Faye Mensinger

The pretty woman stood in the parking lot, staring at the desolate highway, her clenched fists at her side. All except she and Ida Faye had filed back into the cafe. The two women, each aware of the other, did not speak. Both women brushed tears from their eyes. Ida Faye swallowed hard and seemed about to say something. Instead, she remained silent. *Brad has a daughter too,* she thought.

"Funny what you remember about a person, especially a parent," Jessica said without looking at Ida Faye. "Even funnier is what you remember about yourself. It seems all my memories involve me as a dumb kid." She shook her head slowly. "I was invincible and hopelessly concerned with myself and the totally unimportant things that kids believe will affect their lives. I never asked him who he was. I never thought that he might have a past or a future, for that matter. He was just there to provide for me, nothing else. I've often wondered if all kids were like that."

"I think we're still like that," Ida Faye said as she turned and studied the younger woman. "I've known your dad for a couple of years and never thought to ask if he had children. 'Course, I never told him about mine, either." She paused. "As far as knowing our parents, remember, we were just kids back then. We sort of took each day as it came without much thought of how it got there. We were young. We didn't have a clue about the future and couldn't have cared less about the past. Sure, we thought about ourselves and not much else. There's no sense in kicking our rumps about it now. Nothing good will come of it. We were just girls—girls with secrets that we never shared, just like our parents."

Jessica looked at the waitress for a long moment and then smiled briefly. "I can't help thinking that there's something broken inside, something that's never healed, that somehow I've betrayed my dad by not knowing more about him. It's a feeling that will haunt me even more than all the other mistakes I've made in my life."

Ida Faye laughed. "Honey, you don't know what mistakes are. I wrote the book on it. I used to think they were all somebody else's fault and I was just a victim. It took me years to understand that it was me. I made bad choices in my life. Simple as that! I'm still making them. They should give an annual award for stupidity. I'd have a whole room full of trophies. My point is that you can't go on beating yourself up for things you did as a kid. The past is over and done with. You can't change it. As bad as it might have been, without it there wouldn't be a present. We are who we are. Accept it and move on. It's the future that counts."

"I wish it were that easy," Jessica said with a tight smile. "I'd like to think that if I had it to do all over again, I would get it right." She shook her head. "I'm not so sure. Just because I'm older and tamer doesn't mean I'm any smarter."

"I guess that's true," Ida Faye said, squinting. "Why else would you be standing here talking to a beaten-up old waitress in a dirty uniform?"

"Because we have a lot in common," Jessica said warmly. "We both love the man who left us."

⋯⊷⊷ ✵ ⊶⊶⋯

Jessica Martindale

Philosophical discussions with a waitress in a tattered uniform seemed, on the one hand, a waste of time. On the other hand, her somewhat crude observations on life in general were accurate, although somewhat melancholy. Jessica could not help feeling sorry for the woman who shared with her love for her father. She was curious as to the seriousness of this entanglement.

A scrap of paper floated to the ground. The smell of burned propane and dust descended over the cafe. Jessica picked a tuft of insulation from the waitress's hair and dropped it to the ground. "Did you ever have one of those dreams where you could fly?" she asked without warning.

Ida Faye nodded ever so slightly. "I tried my hand at trick riding when I was still in my teens. I had this recurring dream of standing in the saddle at full gallop as I entered a packed arena, my arms outstretched like wings, the leather fringe on the sleeves of my jacket trailing like feathers, my long hair flowing behind me. Slowly, the sound of the crowd and the announcer faded away. It was just me and the horse, then total silence as I gently lifted off the saddle and flew above the arena, circling above the stands, the spectators standing quietly, awestruck. I swooped back down and landed in the saddle, the horse slid to a stop facing the crowd, and with my arms still outstretched, we took a bow. The stands erupted in thunderous applause." She smiled. "I was always happy when I woke up."

Jessica smiled, too. "That's a beautiful dream. I'd bet a psychoanalyst could write a book about that one. Mine were never that pleasant. They always started out with splendor and amazement with the discovery of my newfound talent. My flying was more like weightlessness where I could bounce higher and higher. They often began as I was starting down the stairs in the farmhouse where I grew up. One bounce in the middle of the stairway, and I would be at the bottom. Then I was out the front door, where I would bounce over trees and buildings. I was always looking for someone or something. The cornfield between the farmstead and the river was dark and mysterious. I would catch glimpses of someone running down a corn row. I could never determine who it was. I liked to believe it was my dad. I saw a therapist after he disappeared, and she thought the same thing. She would poke and prod and lift up every rock in search of daddy issues. She never found any. She concluded that the dream was a repressed desire to find out who he really was, facilitated by the fact that I never knew my biological father and that he, too, had disappeared without a trace. All this, of course, was complicated by my husband who had abandoned me in favor of a nubile young bank teller in a tight dress who thought withdrawal was a form of birth control. My therapist convinced me I was an orphan, a waif in search of someone to claim me. She suggested I find my adopted dad and ask him who he was. That cost me a little over three grand and a loss of self-respect for not figuring out for myself what the real issue was."

"Did you figure it out?" Ida Faye asked as she turned to look at Jessica, her brow knitted. "'Cause if you did, I'd really like to know. The man is a total mystery."

"No." She shook her head. "Just bits and pieces, all of it second-hand. It was like finding a jigsaw puzzle without the box and many of the pieces missing. I had no idea who or what the picture was on the lid."

Ida Faye waited. She stared at the pretty woman, her eyes searching the woman's face with anticipation. "That's it?" she said, jerking her chin back. "That's all you got?"

"Sorry, but my attorney has advised me not to talk with anyone without her being present." She turned and saw Sidney watching her through the cafe's picture window. At the door, the older agent watched her even more intently.

"She any good?" Ida Faye asked with a nod toward the cafe window. "I have a feeling I'm going to need one before this day is over."

"She seems knowledgeable."

"Watch this." The waitress smiled, leaned around the pretty woman, and faced the window of the cafe. "Bracco Italiano," she whispered.

Jessica scrunched her eyebrows together, narrowed her eyes, and tilted her head downward. She watched as Sidney smiled and nodded while giving the thumbs-up.

"She reads lips," the waitress said, covering her mouth with her hand. "Be careful what you say."

⊷━◉�֍◉━⊶

Sidney Dawson

"I assume you know something about genetics, since you work for a giant plant breeder," Sidney said without warning. Jessica Martindale had just returned indoors. She and the waitress had lingered in the parking lot after the man they had identified as both Brad and Dad sped away in the stolen Suburban.

"Just what I pick up in my briefing papers and the break room," Jessica said, somewhat defensively. "I don't see what that has to do—"

"Let's just say hypothetically that a woman becomes pregnant and is unsure of who the father is when she learns that she has been sleeping, unbeknownst to her, with identical twins who have duped her into a sexual relationship—"

"Are you—" Jessica blurted.

"Let me finish," Sidney interrupted. "The woman had been deceived into thinking she had a monogamous relationship with a man, only to find out that she unwittingly had engaged in sexual intercourse with two men, each an identical twin of the other. Is there—"

Jessica opened her mouth; her eyebrows were raised, and the whites of her eyes revealed tiny red vessels that appeared about to burst.

Sidney raised her index finger on her right hand. "My question to you is, is there a genetic test to determine paternity between identical twins?"

"I–I don't know for sure," Jessica stammered. "There's something called a DNA fingerprint that has to do with the sequence of base pairs called the Variable Number Tandem Repeats. Theoretically, there are probably some minute differences in those VNTRs. But—"

"Well, for the moment, let's leave that to the eggheads." Sidney smiled. "What I really want to know is which twin should be sued civilly for paternity and which twin is criminally liable for rape?"

"Rape," Jessica said much too loudly. The muted conversations across the cafe stopped suddenly, and all eyes turned toward the two women at the far end of the diner.

"Isn't it interesting how some words when spoken with the right inflection evoke an immediate response by people?" Sidney smiled without taking her eyes from Jessica. "Fire, help,

stop, snake, ouch, and look, to name just a few. Rape gener-
ally refers to unlawful or forced sexual intercourse. I believe
that a case can be made that would include sexual intercourse
resulting from misrepresentation. The victim of such deception
surely has some legal recourse. The ruling, if it hasn't already
occurred, would be precedent-setting, don't you think?"

"I don't know what to think," Jessica said with a stunned
look. "I had no idea you and my…"

Sidney stared at Jessica without blinking. The scarlet streaks
that ran up each side of the woman's neck and the flushed look
on her face told Sidney that she had succeeded in getting her
attention and partially exacting her revenge for being the butt
of her sons' cruel joke. "I barely know your son or sons. My
relationship with him or them has been purely professional. The
point I'm trying to make, Ms. Martindale, is that their harmless
little pranks could have serious consequences. My hypothetical
question was just that, as, I assume was yours, when you asked
if I had stopped having sex with your son. Additionally, I
wanted you to see how a small amount of personal information
can be used to intimidate you. Those two guys over there,"
she said, pointing with her head, "are trained in interrogation
techniques. Stop answering their questions. Got it?"

"Got it," she said with an edge to her voice. "But I don't
appreciate being made a fool."

Sidney leaned forward toward Jessica. "Neither do I," she
said with an emphatic look. "I hope you convey that message
to your sons."

"Understood," Jessica said without averting her gaze.

"Now," Sidney said with a smile. She scooted her chair closer to the table and rested her head on the heel of her hand. "Let's get down to business. Tell me, what exactly are your intentions with my father?"

Jessica stifled a laugh and grinned broadly. "I imagine they're the same intentions you have for the young agent over there." She pointed with her nose toward the booth.

⊷⊸⧓⊷⊸

Sam Dawson

Sam surveyed the cafe. With the exception of Sidney and Jessica, who talked in muffled tones at the other end of the dining area, there seemed to be stunned silence between the other people. The cook, his spatula still in hand, stood staring blankly at his grill. The waitress, quiet for a change, looked out the door toward the littered parking lot and abandoned highway. The older agent had a vengeful scowl on his face as he appraised the crippled vehicles, their mass listing toward punctured tires. He scrutinized the Willys then approached Sam.

"Don't even think about it," Sam said from the booth as he looked up at the agent. "Better yet, don't even think about thinking about taking my ride."

"Legally I can," the agent shot back.

"It's temperamental. You wouldn't get out of the parking lot."

"I've been told to approach you with extreme caution, Dawson. Basically, that means I could shoot you a couple of times in order to persuade you to cooperate," the older agent said with a menacing stare.

"My cooperation doesn't have anything to do with her cooperation," Sam said, gesturing over his shoulder toward the Willys with his thumb. "That dog only hunts for me."

"You can drive."

"It's not what I'd call a pursuit vehicle."

"I'm not pursuing. I just need to get to a landline or someplace with cell service. We'll let local law enforcement pick him up. He can't outrun a police radio."

"What about my daughter?" Sam said.

"Mark here will keep an eye on her."

Sam looked suspiciously at the younger agent.

"Don't worry, Mr. Dawson," Mark said. "If she tries anything funny, I'll subdue her and take her into custody."

"You can try," Sam said with a smile. "She's kind of wiry."

"Let's go, Dawson," the older agent commanded.

Outside, Sam immediately noticed both hood latches on the Willys were undone. "That's not good," he said out loud. He lifted the hood and slid the brace forward while he inspected the engine. The distributor, tucked up against the firewall and below the oversized chrome air breather, caused him to do the classic double-take. The distributor's cap lay askance; the spark plug wires held it roughly in place. He lifted the cap and peered inside the distributor. "We're not going anywhere," he said disgustedly. "He took the rotor."

"Do you have a spare?" the agent asked.

"You're not a mechanic, are you?" Sam said cynically.

"I'm a lawyer. Can you borrow one from one of these other vehicles?" the agent said with a sweep of his hand across the parking lot.

"That's an insightful question, counselor. The short answer is maybe. If there was another Chevy HO Deluxe 350 with a HEI distributor, it would be a simple matter of borrowing the rotor. Unfortunately," Sam said, looking around the lot, "that's not the case."

"Can we exchange wheels; take the good tires and—"

"No," Sam said. "The lug pattern, the wheel size, and the hub bore diameter are all different between each of these vehicles."

The agent looked at Sam menacingly, his eyes narrowed. "Are you joking with me? You think I'm stupid, Dawson?

Sam smiled and shook his head. "No and yes."

"You think I'm stupid because I don't understand all your mechanical mumbo-jumbo?"

"No," Sam said with an icy stare. "Because you didn't approach me with extreme caution."

CHAPTER 14

2:07 p.m.

Brad Holcomb

B rad took a ragged breath as he clutched the steering wheel of the Suburban and turned off the ignition. The curtain was coming down, the drama over. It was time to exit the stage. There would be no final bow, no applause for this tragedy, just stunned silence. The sky had cleared, and the sun shone again as if nothing had happened. Thirteen years disappeared like the pages of his poorly written script that now fluttered in his wake. His purpose had evaporated. He had made a career of killing time, and it was now time to retire. *Ain't no use in lookin' back, Jody's got your Cadillac. Ain't no use in feeling blue, Jody's got your girlfriend, too.* He remembered the cadence drill from boot camp and thought it appropriate to his present circumstance. His time was all in the past, and there was no changing it. He needed to accept it and move on.

The wind slipped through the cedars without noise; their scent lingered deep within his memory as fresh and clean as Elizabeth's skin the first time he held her in his arms. All these years later, his senses had not forgotten. It was as if she were still there. He heard her voice telling him to take a breath; he felt her warmth and the tickle of her hair on his cheek. When he closed his eyes, he could feel the beat of her heart against his chest, a heart that had been stilled instead of his. He swallowed his pain.

Brad had nestled the Suburban behind the few cedar trees that had surrounded the now destroyed trailer and sneaked to a vantage point where he could view the back door of the cafe. The trees around him appeared festive, decorated with tufts of insulation and strips of aluminum. The highway in front of the cafe was eerily quiet, abandoned like his future. There was no turning back, no going forward. He would wait.

Ida Faye appeared, as he knew she would. The spring of the back door of the cafe cried out before the door slammed behind her. She lit her cigarette, released a plume of smoke, then surveyed the damage. Her left arm was folded across her midriff, the hand tucked under the elbow of her right arm. She worked the cigarette with her right hand as she scanned the line of cedars behind the burned-out hulk of the trailer's frame. Brad stood staring at her. When she saw him, it appeared as if she thought it an apparition. He brought his forefinger to his lips then motioned for her to come to him before he slipped behind the trees.

Ida Faye hurried in jerky movements across the debris field, stepping over and around the fragments of the trailer. An arm suddenly reached out from behind a cedar and pulled her behind it. Brad engulfed her, his arms wrapped around her slender body that had been pulled tightly against his. His lips found hers, and he kissed her deeply, then he pulled away and looked into her eyes. She was speechless.

"Whew," was all she could muster.

"We're going to Montana," he said.

"When?"

"Right now, but first I need you to do something for me. My daughter is in there, and I have to talk with her before we can go." His voice quivered and his hands shook.

"There's a whole bunch of people in there that want to talk with you before we go," Ida Faye said. "Those feds know who your daughter is, and I suspect they know you're close by. The young woman in there is an attorney, and she's protectin' your daughter. They think she might have had somethin' to do with Winston Tucker's murder. That's the way I understood it. Cripes, Brad, are you going to tell me what the heck is going on?"

"Later, I promise. Right now I need to talk with Jessica. Think of something, some reason to send her out here by herself. I've got thirteen years of explaining, make that about half a century of explaining to do, and only a few minutes to do it in. When she comes back in, you come back out and we'll be on our way to a new life in Montana. I promise," he added again.

Brad could see that she was skeptical and that she viewed his promises in the same way he viewed the sales pitch of a used car salesman. Her eyes continued to search his. She wanted the truth. She *deserved* the truth. "I promise," he repeated.

-→=•)✳(•=←-

Ida Faye Mensinger

His kiss was tender. It lingered sweet and tangy as she gently licked her lips. Ida Faye looked back over her shoulder as she reached for the screen door to the kitchen. He was gone. She was sixteen again, with the promise of a future not darkened by the present. The lingering odor of grease and French fries drifted outward, mixing with the after-storm perfume of sage and cedar. She was starting over and was excited, even grateful. She could feel the warmth of his body pressed to hers, her lips brushing against his ear as she convinced him they had made the right decision. In a thousand years there would be no trace of them, not even a memory. Today was the only day that mattered, and there was possibility. They both knew they were no longer young. Their healthy years were behind them. She wanted to believe that somehow their love and a new beginning in Montana would make them invincible and the messiness of life inconsequential.

Voices rose and fell from the dining room. Her kiss-endorsed superiority made her feel sorry for all those people who had not found hope. They seemed mired in the present, more concerned with what she now believed was trivia. She, on the other hand, had an agenda. No more past. She would not let Darrell's rotting corpse or Jeanie's hate stand in her way. She was on a mission.

Joe was still trying to pry open the cash register with a butter knife. The two agents in their black suits had their heads together, talking in muffled tones. The young woman and her father were in a more animated conversation at the other end of the dining room, something to do with the Jeep that the father repeatedly gestured toward. The pretty woman was by herself, sitting at her table, staring out the window. A band of unfiltered sunlight shone through the cafe window, a spotlight

that illuminated her like an Italian fresco painted on the wall
of a church. She looked older. Ida Faye walked confidently to
the woman's table and positioned herself with her back to the
others. "Listen to me very carefully," she said quietly as she
pulled her order pad and pen from her pocket.

Jessica looked up, startled by the waitress's sudden
appearance.

"Your dad is out back and wants to talk to you."

Jessica's eyes opened wide, and she started to speak.

"Don't say a word," Ida Faye cautioned. "Just sit there and
listen carefully. I'm going to create a diversion at the other end
of the dining room. When everyone's attention is on me, get
up quietly and go through the kitchen and out the back door.
He'll be waiting for you in that grove of cedars behind where
the house trailer used to be. Got it?"

Jessica nodded almost imperceptibly.

"When you come back in, tell them that nature called." Ida
Faye placed her pad and pen back in her pocket, turned, and
walked toward the cash register. As she passed the agents' table,
she stopped, staggered, and then fell to the floor.

The first thing she heard was the butter knife clanging as
it fell from Joe's hand to the floor. There was a confusion of
scuffing and shoveling feet, squealing Naugahyde, and chairs
being pushed back. Joe was the first to reach her. He smelled of
grease and sweat, the rendered fat from squashed hamburgers
and the spices of a man excreted through his pores. She was
reminded of the Borger Burger Basket on a Panhandle hot
Saturday night, carhops in white shorts on roller skates, onion
rings falling from their trays as they raced to hook them on the

windows of the pickups lined up like cattle at a feed trough. No place else was open at midnight. Cigarette smoke curled upward from their cabs, and tiny scarlet dots glowed from their Marlboros beneath straw Resistols that bobbed to the music as Tommy James and the Shondells sang "Crimson and Clover" from the bug-spattered speakers that seemed to amplify their longings; the desires of teenagers on nights they thought would last forever. Nights that ended too soon.

Someone poked a finger under her jaw at the side of her neck. "She's got a strong pulse." She recognized the older agent's voice. Someone patted her cheeks. "Ida Faye, Ida Faye, wake up. Please..." It was Joe. She could hear the concern in his panicked voice.

"Is she on any medications?" It was the young woman's father.

"No, not that I know of," Joe answered.

A large hand covered her forehead. "This woman's burning up." It was the voice of the older agent again. "Let's get these clothes off her. We need to get her temperature down."

Ida Faye opened her eyes.

"I thought that might bring you around," the agent said with a broad grin.

⊷⊷◉✴◉⊶⊶

Jessica Martindale

She had not gone to either of her class reunions, one at ten, the other at twenty. She remembered the past. Things seemed simpler then. She saw her friends and classmates as they were nearly thirty years ago. They were still slender, without combovers, divorces, or fabrications of success. They still moved awkwardly across the gym floor, their prom dresses shimmering in the subdued light of her memory. Her excuses were weak. Small-town gossip, speculation that had quickly become reality, had her father as the mad bomber. She was forever linked to the stain on Keotonka's otherwise unblemished history. Jessica had gone out of her way to avoid the past. Now, she was about to confront it. Thirteen years was a long time to be without a father.

She stepped around a flattened water heater and the jumbled remains of an interior wall. Long staples projected outward like the quills of a frightened porcupine. No nails, no screws, just staples. Shards of glass, insulation, chunks of wallboard, broken dishes, bits of carpet, and a dish towel all randomly deposited in a landfill-like scene from an apocalyptic movie lay out before her. Her heart beat wildly, thumping a muffled bass in her ears, the pressure alarming. She could smell the acrid odor of propane.

"Jessica," he said softly as he stepped from behind a cedar.

Without hesitation, she rushed to him. "Dad," she exhaled, and the tears started immediately. They embraced tightly as though wringing out the years that had separated them.

"We only have a minute or two," he said, pushing her back and looking into her eyes as she blinked through her tears to see him. "There is so much I need to tell you."

"You don't need to tell me anything, Dad. Shelly Robinson visited me years ago and told me everything."

"Not everything." He clutched her upper arms firmly as he held her away from him. "She didn't know everything."

"It doesn't matter anymore. The bad guys are all dead now. Everything is history. It's over, Dad. You can come home now."

He smiled tightly. "I've wished for that every day of my life for years, to see you again, to tell you what happened and why. I've dreamed about it every night." He paused and looked deeply into her eyes. "There is no home. It's a dream, a dream within a dream. Home doesn't exist anymore. It's an illusion as temporary as the future. The only thing that's real is the present. It's the only thing that matters."

"I agree that we can't change the past, Dad. I believe the present only exists for the future. That's what counts. Let's figure out a way to put the past behind us and start living for tomorrow."

"I wish I could, sweetie. I've been trying for forty-six years to forge—"

"It's over now. Tucker is dead. There's no one else to account for what happened."

He studied her face. He longed for the monotony of teaching her to read, the repetitive reciting of multiplication tables, the frustration of teaching her to drive. Now, she was the teacher attempting to shift the burden of blame to the dead. "There's one more," he said. "One more to be held accountable."

Jessica's brow wrinkled. She turned her head slightly, her eyes narrowed. "Who?"

"It's me, sweetie. It's always been me," he said sorrowfully.

⊷⊶⊙✿⊙⊷⊶

Sidney Dawson

Sidney wondered if there could be any more drama left in the cluster of strange people in the tiny cafe in the middle of nowhere. Everyone was gathered around the waitress, who was struggling to sit up and looking disoriented.

"You look like the kind of guy who'd take advantage of a passed-out woman," the waitress said to the older agent, her eyes attempting to focus.

"Lady, you're not my type," the agent grumbled.

"Oh, and what's your type, J. Edgar?" Ida Faye snarled. "I'm bettin' it's cheap hookers. Does your wife know?"

"Take it easy now, Ida Faye," Joe cautioned with a sense of urgency. "Stand back, folks, give the woman some room. Can you get yourself up?"

"Yeah, I can, but I have my doubts about Mister Hoover over there," she said, gesturing toward the older agent.

Sidney watched the younger agent, Mark, who seemed genuinely concerned about the waitress. He stepped forward and offered her his hand. The cook brushed Mark's hand away then grabbed both of Ida Faye's hands and pulled her to her feet. The waitress smoothed her dress and quickly looked around the cafe before thanking the cook and continuing her caustic banter directed toward the older agent. It was then that Sidney realized Jessica was gone.

"Are you sure you're all right?" the cook asked the waitress. "You know this wasn't workplace-related. I'll need you to sign a statement to that effect."

The waitress looked at Sidney.

Sidney smiled, shook her head, and silently mouthed, "No."

"If you need some time off," the cook continued, "I'll have to dock you since you are out of both sick leave and personal days."

"Thanks for your concern, Joe," the waitress said, smiling. "That won't be necessary. I'm submitting my resignation, effective immediately."

"Your contract calls for at least two weeks' notice and the signing of a nondisclosure agreement."

Again, the waitress looked to Sidney.

Sidney rolled her eyes and shook her head. She noticed that Mark was smiling broadly at her. She smiled back at him. She saw her father eyeing both of them suspiciously. The Martindale twins seemed a distant memory, no longer important. She knew it was for the better. The future of a relationship with a man, a boy, rather, thirteen years her junior was destined to failure. Someday the twins would outgrow their childish pranks and realize the hurt they had caused others. She absently pushed a wisp of hair behind her ear as she diverted her eyes shyly downward. Her hearing aid screeched loudly.

"Where's Martindale?" the older agent shouted in a voice that could crack concrete. He looked at Sidney accusingly.

"Did you get your warrant?" Sidney asked as she fixed her eyes on the older agent. She did not like the man and could not help challenging his authority.

"Martindale," he called out again as he turned away from Sidney.

"What?" Jessica said with annoyance as she stepped from the kitchen. It was obvious she had been crying. Her eyes were reddened and her makeup smeared. "Can't a woman get some privacy around here?"

"Where were you?" the older agent snarled.

"Nature called, so I stepped out back. Are you going to arrest me for peeing in public?"

"She's not admitting to urinating in public," Sidney quickly said as she walked toward Jessica. "She's merely asking your intentions." She held a finger up in front of Jessica to silence her. Sidney knew that public indecency was a misdemeanor that was punishable by imprisonment for up to six months and fines up to seven hundred and fifty dollars. She wasn't sure about public urination that differed from state to state and by local ordinances. What she did know was the agent was looking for any excuse to detain Jessica while he put together his case for murder. "Allow me to advise you," she said, turning to the older agent. "If you pursue this, I'll force you to bring similar charges against every person in this room should they relieve themselves outdoors while we wait for electrical power to be restored to the well."

"Don't be ridiculous," the agent said with a sneer. "You're the only one I'll arrest." He paused for a moment. "I'll be waiting and watching," he added with a lecherous grin.

-»▬◉▬✠▬◉▬«-

Sam Dawson

"Pop," Sidney called out as Sam loomed over the older agent in a threatening posture.

"That's twice you've disrespected my daughter," Sam said, glaring at the agent. "If it happens again, approaching me with extreme caution will not save you. Are we clear on that?"

"You know, Dawson, if I was to take your threat seriously, I could arrest you right now for threatening a federal agent. It's a felony."

"That's right, Pop," Sidney said as she stepped between the two menacing men. "I'm sure the agent meant no disrespect toward me." She smiled. "Just because he taunts me like an adolescent schoolboy doesn't mean you can threaten him." The agent shot her an angry look. She slipped her arm under her father's and guided him toward Jessica's table at the other end of the cafe. "You can say disparaging things about him, just don't threaten him," she said under her breath. She glanced upward toward his face. He was smiling, his eyes shining with the radiance of new love. Sidney looked at Jessica. She had the same expression, a Cocker Spaniel look. It was Lady and the Tramp reunited. Sidney exhaled loudly.

"I'd like to take you up on your offer of a ride back to Cheyenne or Laramie or to any place that's civilized," Jessica said, her glassy eyes about to spill over with the history of her personal torment, the chapters of her life about to flutter forth like the pages of a book caught in the wind.

"I would love to take you anywhere," Sam heard himself say before he could stop the words. His eyes searched her face for forgiveness. "I mean, yes, I'd like to leave here, too," he said in an attempt to recover some form of dignity. "But—"

Jessica offered a smile that twitched at the corners of her mouth. "Have you ever read Willa Cather?"

"*My Antonia* and *O Pioneers*," Sam blurted as if it were a game show question.

With narrowed eyes, she studied his face, surprised by his response. "She once wrote that she thought it strange there were only two or three human stories, and they go on repeating themselves as fiercely as if they had never happened before. She likened it to meadowlarks that go on singing the same five notes over and over again as they have for thousands of years." Jessica paused. She did not take her eyes from his. "Do you think this is just one of those stories?"

Sam was unsure what she was asking. He wanted to believe it was about them, him and her, the story that has kept the species surviving for millennia: love and war with all the subplots thrown in for flavor. He wanted to list all the possibilities then announce the answer confidently. All that left his lips, however, was a simple "yep" that caught on his Adam's apple and caused him to swallow embarrassingly.

"Oh, how I wish that wasn't the case," Jessica said, the tears finally spilling over. She sat down and stared up at Sam. "I don't think I can take any more surprises."

"Lady, you don't know what surprises are," Sidney said seriously. "You hang around Don Quixote here," she said, gesturing toward her father, "who believes chivalry isn't dead and who aspires to be a hero, trust me, you'll be in for some huge surprises."

Sam looked at his daughter. "I don't think that's a fair characterization. I was only trying to—"

"Yes, it is," Sidney interrupted. "You can't help yourself. You're a hopeless romantic who—"

"Stop," Jessica said forcefully, looking up at both Sam and Sidney. "This isn't about either of you. It's about me." She looked out the window then turned back to them. "I thought I understood it for what it was. It wasn't simple. It was complex. It took me years to figure it out. And I did it. At least I thought I had. I saw the puzzle with all of its pieces and parts as one thing, a combined image of the whole. I was sure the worst was over. Little did I know," she said with a frightened look on her face, "that I would have to reconsider everything, that I would have to question my love for the man who raised me, my faith in humankind, my faith in God, what little was left." She shook her head. "We really are a hopeless lot, you know. We do the damnedest things to each other. We truly are our own worst enemy." Jessica wiped the tears from her cheeks with each hand. She stared at them as if pleading for their understanding. "His name was Cain, you know, and he was forever condemned to be a fugitive."

Sam attempted a tight smile. He inhaled deeply through his nose. He was tempted to say that questioning her relationship with her father was just one of the few notes sung by the meadowlark, a repetition of a common human story. Instead he exhaled slowly and said, "My offer still stands."

CHAPTER 15

2:18 p.m.

Brad Holcomb

Telling his daughter the truth was one of the most difficult things he had ever done. He had never actually admitted it to his wife, Elizabeth. She knew. She had always known. It had come to her in a dream, but the reality was that she had known from the first day he showed up in Keotonka that he was on a mission. She didn't know what the mission was, nor did she want to know. She had been too scared, afraid what the disclosure would do to them. Jessica was the last part of Elizabeth that remained, and he had only seconds to tell her what he had done—seconds to save her and seconds to save himself.

He saw the confusion in her eyes, the disbelief, the shattering of unrealistic images, the pain of discovery. He had removed the Band-Aid all at once, and it had stung. Jessica had needed resolution. He had needed forgiveness. He was unsure if either had been achieved. Forty-six years was a long time to carry the guilt and endure the nightmares. Perhaps time would tell, heal the wounds. He had his doubts. He knew there was no future without the past and that he would never forget. Never forget the atrocities he had committed. Never forget the perfect innocence of his daughter's face as she lay sleeping as a child, her tiny features as beautiful and peaceful as nature had intended. Now, he would never forget the shock in her eyes.

He had believed forgetting would be a blessing. Now something strange was happening to him. While he could not speak of them, the memories were still there. Even in his mind the words would not come. The names were gone. All the familiar things had no names. The objects of verbs, the objects of prepositions escaped him. He could find other words that described the nouns and placed them in a different context. It was a game of charades. When speaking to people, rather than endure the frustration, he chose silence. He suspected it was something more than age-related forgetfulness. The shaking troubled him. The hallucinations, however, were downright frightening. His mind was playing tricks on him. He sometimes saw things that were not there. More frequently, he did not see things that were there, familiar things that would suddenly appear. Sometimes it was as if he existed in persistent twilight. He feared it was something more than the loss of visual acuity. He suspected dementia, maybe Parkinson's. Neither of which was as disheartening as destroying the image his daughter had of him. Perhaps the malady would finally rob him of his memory, and he could die in peace.

Ida Faye was next. He had not planned to love her. He did not mean to seek solace from her. He had deceived her, the one person who had gently allowed him to see what he had become and to let go of the past and embrace the future. Her comedic, sometimes crude examples, with her own history of injustices, were often inspirational. She kept him coming back, day after day, when he would rather crawl into a hole and wallow in self-pity. It would be unfair to include her in his unplanned life. She deserved better.

It was for her own good, he told himself as he guided the Suburban onto the highway and headed east.

⇥◉ ✖ ◉⇤

Ida Faye Mensinger

Ida Faye pried Joe's fingers from her elbow after he helped her from the floor. She brushed her uniform again, straightened her smiley face button, and scanned the cafe. The pretty woman was sitting at her table, talking to the young woman and her father. The two agents were engaged in a muffled conversation in the booth near the front door.

"Are you sure you're all right?" Joe asked, his breath sour.

"Promise me, Joe, if I ever pass out again, you won't give me mouth-to-mouth resuscitation. I'd choke to death on my own vomit."

"I won't dock you if you need to take some time off," Joe said, keeping his voice low. "You're not serious about quitting, are you?" He had a panicked look. "If that highway resurfacing project goes through, I'll need all the help I can get. We'll be rollin' in dough."

"Go ahead and dock me, Joe. Nothin' from nothin' is still nothin'. I'm out of here." She turned and scuffed across the dining room and through the kitchen door.

The relief was euphoric as she stood on the back step, surveying the cedars across the debris field. She could not help smiling, a first day at school feeling; she was young again. Deftly, she retrieved her smokes but then thought better of it. Maybe she would quit. It would be a fresh start in Montana with Brad. Besides, there was no time. Hastily, she pranced through the trailer's remains. "Brad," she called out in a whispered yell. She popped through the windbreak and stood frozen, looking down at the tire tracks leading back to the highway.

Her world suddenly closed in on her, cold and crushing. Her breath came in spasms and her hands began to shake. She wanted to drop to the ground, curl into a ball, close her eyes, and sleep. When she awakened, she would be sitting next to Brad as the green hills and snow-capped mountains of Montana streamed by the car's window. He had promised her. Deep inside her, she knew that a life with Brad was improbable, temporary at best. She had hoped beyond reason that, if given a chance, it might happen. It was her life's story of unfulfilled dreams and unrealistic expectations that never seemed to materialize. She had always blamed Darrell. Deep down she knew the fault was hers. She had made bad decisions all her life. Brad Holcomb was just another one. *Good riddance,* she thought as she pulled a cigarette from her pack and lit it with trembling hands, anger replacing despair. With a funneled lower lip, she forcefully blew smoke upward then shook her head. She would go by herself, take her chances, blow this Popsicle stand, and cast her fate to the wind. She had done it before; she could do it again. She took another drag on her cigarette. Her facial muscles rippled with fierceness and determination. The world became cloudy, blurred by emotion. She swallowed hard, desperate not to bawl like a child at the realization she had no car and no money. Ida Faye wept.

Jessica Martindale

She had confided too much in total strangers. It was time to put things in the proper perspective. Her conflicting emotions belied her professionalism. She was the vice president for domestic marketing, after all, not some weak-kneed teenager from Hicksville. Stress was part of her job. Her reputation at Pioneer was that of an iron maiden who never showed her cards, always cool under fire. Prioritize the issues, determine the solutions, develop strategies, assign responsibilities, and assess the results was her modus operandi. This was different. These were matters of the heart, and that put her on unfamiliar ground.

She had found her father. That had been her primary goal. Mission accomplished, albeit in a serendipitous manner. She would need time, lots of time, to digest the revelation of that meeting—to sort out the many ramifications of his disclosure and what they meant to any future relationship she might have with him. She had been rendered speechless. How was she supposed to process that information? How was she supposed to balance the competing emotions of a lifetime of loving her father with the knowledge of who he really was? Astonished was too simple a word to describe her mood.

Jessica reminded herself not to underestimate the federal agents. Outwardly, they appeared to be bumbling idiots who had tripped over the solution to a crime they knew nothing about. Like Laurel and Hardy playing Keystone Kops who kept bumping into each other, they suspected everyone of complicity. Eventually, they would discover the pea under the shell.

Of more immediate concern was the man standing in front of her. Her attraction to Sam was unlike anything she had ever experienced, and it was totally unprofessional. There was no plan. She was unsure of the issue and there was no strategy, only the warm security of being enveloped by someone who felt the same way. It was passion, consuming, and seemed to take precedence over all other issues. She felt vulnerable, and that frightened her. She had not meant for this to happen. All she had wanted was a photograph of her father. When she had learned of the meeting place, date, and proximity to Winston Tucker's ranch, her goals changed rapidly. The attraction to Sam was a surprise, a distraction at first. Now, a seemingly higher priority that complicated everything was foremost on her mind. The iron maiden was confused.

The bickering between Sam and Sidney Dawson, father and daughter, was a luxury they did not know they had. Jessica had gone thirteen years without speaking to her father and a lifetime of not knowing who he was. She was still unsure. Jessica would trade that uncertainty for the opportunity to argue with the man who had raised her.

"I'd really like to go now. Can we leave this place?" she heard herself say somewhat weakly.

"As I was starting to say," Sam said, "we can't go anywhere. Somebody took the rotor from my distributor."

Jessica opened her clenched hand and held out the odd-looking piece of Bakelite with a shiny spring. "Is this it?"

--=◉❈◉=--

Sidney Dawson

She knew how this would end, even though it was the beginning. She saw the ending and wished she had not. *Why?* she wanted to shout out loud. She had fallen in love before, not just schoolgirl crushes or the way you'd love a dog that had a short life. She had fallen for the ones she was convinced were walk-down-the-aisle real. The ones she wanted to curl up with under a warm quilt on a cold winter morning. They had used her, abused her, and ended up dead. Was she the black widow? She also loved Annie, and she loved her mother and she loved L2, and they were all fading memories as the cold earth gnawed at their remains and their images became cloudy. If she really liked this guy, she should tell him to take a hike, run away, git while the gittin's good. His future hung over his head like an executioner's ax. Stick with her and he would become ashes tossed out over water by his grieving mother. Sidney looked over her shoulder to see if he was watching her. He flashed a broad smile, his eyes gleaming expectantly. And she smiled back at him, a smile of unappeased desire not unlike the smile reserved for his mournful mother.

"Where did you get that?" she heard her father say. Turning back, she saw Jessica holding out the missing distributor rotor.

"My dad gave it to me just before he abandoned me again," Jessica said. "He told me he couldn't disable the Willys because it meant too much to him. I'm thinking that it meant more to him than I did. He seems to think it was his. Maybe that's the issue. I was his adopted daughter, not really his. He said it had new paint and a new engine. He had restored the wagon originally and was convinced it was his."

Sam took the rotor and brought his finger to his lips to indicate silence. "We can talk about that later. That agent over there," he said, motioning with a slight movement of his head, "wants to confiscate my ride in order to get someplace with a phone so he can call in the cavalry."

Both Jessica and Sidney looked toward the older agent, who was staring at them suspiciously.

Sidney shook her head. "He's been watching too many movies. That pretty much doesn't happen in real life. There was some ancient old-world law clear back in the twelve hundreds, I believe, that allowed that to occur in England. I'm pretty sure the Supreme Court said the danger to the public must be immediate, or impending, or imminent, or something like that. In other words, extreme, and even then the liability to the cops is off the charts. That's not going to happen, Pop. He can ask you nicely for a ride somewhere. You can say no and the courts will support you."

"There's gonna be a come-to-Jesus meeting with that guy if he doesn't stop pushing people around," Sam said.

"That's exactly why they've been advised to approach you with caution, Pop. Listen to me, you can't hit or threaten them. Do you hear me, Dad?"

"This ain't Nazi Germany, and they're not the Gestapo. This is America!" Sam declared.

"Yeah, Pop. Maybe you should read Sinclair Lewis's *It Can't Happen Here*. He wrote that book in the 1930s. You might change your opinion about the land of the free."

"Okay," Jessica said with authority, her eyes filled with tears. "Please stop your bickering and try to realize how fortunate you are to have someone to argue with." She opened her mouth to say something else, then hesitated. "Can we go now?" she said, her tone plaintive. "I want to leave this place."

"The agent will want to know how you came up with the rotor," Sidney whispered. "He'll try to arrest you as an accessory to grand theft auto."

"I'll tell him I found it," Jessica offered.

"Most likely, he'll play the suspicion card again. I have a better idea. How about you tell him the truth, and we'll offer to take the agents with us back to Cheyenne or wherever there's phone service? By the time we get there in that bucket of bolts," she said, pointing out the window toward the Willys, "your dad will be long gone."

"Bucket of bolts," Sam said with astonishment. "Need I remind you that vehicle has never failed us in well over one hundred thousand miles?"

Sidney ignored him. Instead, she looked to Jessica for a response to her proposal. The woman appeared older than she had just minutes earlier. The creases at the corners of her eyes appeared more pronounced against her sallow skin. She looked tired.

"No," Jessica said, followed by a heavy exhale, her eyes glassy with tears. "I won't help them in the least." She looked pleadingly at Sidney. "They killed my real father."

‑‑‑❦‑‑‑

Sam Dawson

In her eyes, he saw all the emotions. He had been there, too. He had experienced the helplessness of desperation, the sorrow of loss, the torment of deception, and the gnawing wrath of vengeance. When you are backed into a corner and everything you love has been taken from you, the choices are limited— fight or run like you are on fire.

When Sidney was kidnapped by a deranged killer who was protected by the government, Sam had fought bitterly. Reduced to the same level as the man he pursued, Sam had extracted information from federal agents by force. He followed up with an all-out media blitz that threatened the agency's budget. Hence the approach-with-caution label he now wore with the feds. He sensed that Jessica had leafed through the options and had chosen the opposite approach. She wanted to drive away. Perhaps it was passive aggression in that she was achieving retribution by not helping them. Whatever it was, he would help her. He liked her. He liked her a lot.

The approach-with-caution warning should be applied to her rather than him. Sidney had always accused him of giving away his heart too easily, of setting himself up for disappointment. He believed this time was different. He had not felt this type of attraction since... He thought for a moment. Since Annie, he concluded, dismissing his daughter's accusation.

"Earth to Pop," Sidney said, waving her hand in front of him. "Wipe the drool from your chin and let's go. We can be home in time for supper. I'll make spaghetti, and the two of you can have a stare contest."

Sam squinted at his daughter and gave her a tight-lipped scowl. "Don't forget the Node Cemetery. I just need ten minutes, if it's not covered with hail. And we'll need to stop in Cheyenne so Jessica can pick up a few necessities."

"If it's not too much trouble," Jessica said without taking her eyes from Sam.

"Oh, what's a little more trouble after this disastrous trip?" Sidney said and smiled politely at Jessica.

"Gather up your belongings, ladies. I'll get the Willys started," Sam said as he picked up the tabs from Jessica's table again and reached for his wallet.

"You'll need to make exact payments," the cook said. "I can't get the cash register open."

"Hold up, Dawson," the older agent barked. "Where do you think you're going?"

Sam held out the rotor in front of him and shook it. "Ms. Martindale found it out back. We're headed to Cheyenne. We would have offered you ride if you had been nicer to us."

"We'll confiscate your vehicle."

"My legal beagle says that's not going to happen." Sam smiled at him. "Don't even go down that road. She'll have your pension by the end of the day."

"Are you threatening me again?" the agent asked as he stepped toward Sam.

"No, sir. On the contrary, I'm trying to assist you by keeping you out of harm's way. From a legal standpoint," Sam added. "I've been advised that if you were to ask nicely, I could grant your request."

"I'm asking you nicely, Dawson."

Sam pretended to ponder the request for a moment. "I'm sorry, the answer is still no," he said with a smile.

"You'll force my hand, Dawson," the older agent said without moving his jaw. He looked like an amateur ventriloquist who was about to be booed off the stage. The veins in his neck bulged blue against the angry red that inflamed his cheeks. "We have a positive identification of her vehicle at the scene of a murder."

"We've already had this discussion," Sidney said, stepping between the two men. "Her car at the scene doesn't mean *she* was at the scene. Your suspicion won't get you the warrant you need. I'll have your badge if you pursue this."

"Sic 'em, Sid," Sam said, smiling.

"Hush," she said and held up a finger to silence her father. "Hear me out," she said to the agent. "I have a compromise to offer you. That Jeep," she flicked her thumb toward the Willys in the parking lot, "only has room for four. Your partner, Mark, needs medical assistance. We'll take him to the nearest hospital to get stitched up and evaluated, and he can call for your backup. The whole while, he can keep an eye on your suspect."

The agent looked at his partner, who sat smiling at Sidney. "He needs more than stitching up. He needs psychiatric help. The only thing he'll keep his eye on is you."

"Do we have a deal?" Sidney asked and stuck out her hand.

"If you screw me on this, headquarters will descend on the two of you like a swarm of locusts. If you screw him," he nodded toward Mark, "I'll have his badge and your license. Are we clear on that?"

"Are you threatening my daughter again?" Sam said, stepping around Sidney to confront the agent.

"Back off, Pop." Sidney took her father's arm.

"Yeah, back off, Pop," the agent snarled. "I'd hate to take you down in front of your little girl."

"Stop it," Sidney demanded. "You guys are like two dogs in the park, each marking territory. Grow up."

"He started it," Sam said.

"What are you, twelve?" Sidney asked with an incredulous look.

"Sorry," Sam offered.

A distant rumbling silenced everyone in the cafe. They turned their attention toward the storm-splattered window as a huge Kenworth sped eastward on the highway. A metallic purple tractor with polished chrome appointments pulling an unadorned trailer roared toward Nebraska at a speed well above the limit. The wake of displaced air caused the cafe window to shudder. Everyone in the cafe silently pondered the truck's announcement that the highway was open.

CHAPTER 16
2:23 p.m.

Brad Holcomb

Jessica would need time. She would fill in the blanks. Now, of course, he thought of all the things he should have said, how he could have rephrased the secret he had kept for nearly half a century, of how he had come to be her stepfather, her mother's husband. Elizabeth had spared him from admitting the details. She had pieced together much of it yet refused to ask him about his role. Her refusal to ask the most pertinent question had saved both of them from staining their relationship. Elizabeth did not want to know. He had not given Jessica that choice. There was no time. It came in a burst as if from the same gun he had used to kill so many people. Jessica was wounded. She would recover. The scars would remain to remind her of the imperfections of people, the hidden things that kept people apart.

A few miles west of Harrison, Nebraska, where the high plains seemed to stretch endlessly without the blight of human habitation, Brad slowly passed a homeless man pushing a shopping cart loaded with stuffed trash bags and a dog. The roadway was damp from the storm that had angled north toward Chadron. The man was unusually short, wearing soiled surplus jungle fatigues that were several sizes too large for him. Without a hat and with skin tanned like leather, the long-haired, unshaven man struggled to push the cart along the shoulder of the highway between the white stripe and borrow pit. The dog, a Siberian Husky with see-through blue eyes, rode in the folding child seat at the back of the cart and carefully watched Sam as he slowly passed by. The animal, although small for the breed, was too large for the cart. Its gray-and-white face with pointed ears loomed above the man who bent into the labor of pushing the cart with small wheels along the rough blacktop. He struggled.

Brad was struck by the unquestionable loyalty of the dog who knew no better. They were a bonded pair. The dog did not care that they had no money, no food, no home. It did not question the man's route or destination. Unaffected by the past and with no knowledge of the future, the animal lived only for the present. They met the challenges of every new day together and viewed those threats as opportunities. Brad's emotions teetered between anguish and admiration. He thought the man's misfortune was secondary, perhaps obscured by the dog's faithfulness and affection. Nothing else mattered as long as they had each other. Brad believed he had only experienced that type of devotion once. It was unplanned and accidental. He had never meant to love Elizabeth. It just happened, and it had changed his life eternally for the better. He thought it could never happen again, nor did he want it to happen, especially at his age, but it had. His hands trembled.

A few miles east, at Harrison, he pulled over and tried to catch his breath. The town had been spared both rain and hail. He swallowed the lump in his throat, flexed his shaking fingers, took a deep breath, then turned the Suburban around and again headed back to Wyoming. In his mind, he saw Ida Faye's transparent blue eyes.

Brad thought it strange that on his return trip he did not see the homeless man and dog.

⊷⊶✵⊷⊶

Ida Faye Mensinger

Tissues of smoke threaded upward from the smoldering remains of the blown-up house trailer. Debris littered the landscape behind the cafe. Tufts of insulation adorned the plump cedar trees, giving them a festive Christmas-like look that belied the depressing reality of rejection and hopelessness that Ida Faye felt. She lit another cigarette. *The mess looks like my face*, she thought. No wonder he left. She wiped her eyes and tried to take a calm breath that did not stutter in her chest. She wanted to crawl off and hide in a secret place, block out the sun, and sleep. Maybe she would never wake up, just dream pleasantly for eternity. She had that same desire many times in her life. *Maybe his leaving is for the best*, she thought. No more bad choices, no more blame assigned to others. Just disappear and don't look back. She wondered if that was possible, even if she was rich. Whoever said money couldn't buy happiness was full of baloney.

Wait, she almost said aloud. *Maybe I am wealthy. Darrell probably had money stashed someplace.* He was as bad as they come, and he was smart. He was the local kingpin of his illicit bunch of misfits. She knew there were fish bigger than him, people that he answered to. They were not divorced. She had rights to his ill-gotten estate. Brad would argue that her rights were secondary to those of the government who would confiscate everything. She didn't need to get into a tiff with the government, since she hadn't paid income tax in years. Knowing Darrell, he had money stuffed in a mattress somewhere. What about that fancy white Chevy pickup he was driving when he came to beat the stuffing out of her the other night? She had rights. When the dust settled from the storm, she would go see the sheriff. She would cooperate. She had rights to whatever they found in Darrell's motel room besides his worthless carcass. She wanted her money back; she wanted the pickup and anything else of value they discovered. It would be her nest egg for a new beginning in Montana, a man-free fresh start.

"Who needs them anyway?" she said as she ground out her cigarette and fumbled for another. "They smell like a locker room, are foul-tempered, have hair in their noses and ears, they lie and cheat, and hit people weaker than them. Who needs 'em?" she repeated.

The familiar roar of a diesel semi whooshed eastward on the highway. She watched as the huge purple rig ignored Nebraska's lower speed limit and shrank to a metallic dot in the distance. The highway was open, and with it a new beginning. She would hitch a ride west to Orin where I-25 heads north to Buffalo and joins I-90 north to Sheridan and on to Billings, Montana. She would wait at the rest stop at Orin Junction for a woman trucker and hitch north to Montana and a new life. *Horses*, she thought, she would raise performance horses and start a school for young barrel racers, girls who didn't hit or spit. "Sounds like a plan," she said and nodded approvingly. "Men, who needs 'em?"

Ida Faye carefully threaded her way back toward the cafe, hopscotching through the wreckage, mostly trash. A half bottle of ketchup from inside a missing refrigerator caught her eye. A petrified dead cat, flat like roadkill, tossed out of its final resting place from under the trailer, lay beside an unbroken coffee mug and a torn piece of paper that had served as a score sheet for something. She picked up the paper. The names Elizabeth, Eden, and Jessica were written in pencil across the top and underlined, each with a descending column of hasty additions that declared Jessica the winner. Ida Faye suspected it was the score sheet from a game of dominoes. Jessica was the pretty woman. "Eden," she whispered softly to herself. Was Eden Brad's real name? She had confided that Tammy Jo Martin was her real name, and all he had offered in return was the nickname Cowboy. And who was Elizabeth? Another daughter, perhaps, or was it his wife, maybe his sister, a friend, a neighbor? It could have been anybody, she told herself. She flicked her cigarette into the smoldering debris then shook her head slowly at the realization she knew nothing about the man she had offered herself to. She was embarrassed to be such a fool. She could care less who Elizabeth was, or Eden for that matter. She reminded herself she was done with men, all men. She stuffed the score sheet into her pocket.

Broken glass crunched under her boots as she made her way back to the cafe. She stopped, fought back her tears by taking a deep breath, and looked up at the sky as if seeking divine guidance. Billowy white clouds floated west to east without care, without purpose. She was T.J. Martin, Miss Panhandle and Boomtown Queen. She was somebody, and she was alive.

⇥◉⊱✳⊰◉⇤

Jessica Martindale

In thirteen years, she had forgotten the sound of his voice. He had come to her silently in dreams, ageless. Sometimes, in the predawn, she would find him sitting quietly in the living room. It was more a feeling of presence than actually seeing him, never her mother. The dreams were always of her father. She was always a girl, preteen, never embarrassed to hold his hand during whatever adventure he was taking her on. Often, the dreams were recurring, not exactly, but rather in a general sense. Hiking in the woods above the river, summer sounds of a tractor in the field, a whisper of wind behind her ear, the familiar trails leading to the same open meadows, laughing in the corn maze he would create at Halloween, or the overwhelming awe of a huge bookstore in Des Moines with escalators that did not end. His voice was always reassuring and confident, never harsh.

Now it was different. It was the trembling voice of an old man that sought absolution for something unforgivable. He seemed smaller than she remembered—frail and unsure of himself. He was bent at the waist and had lost weight. He seemed to have difficulty choosing his words. His hands shook, and his cloudy eyes filled with tears as he attempted to redeem himself. She did not know what to say. What was she *supposed* to say? It was too much. She was unprepared. She had stood there flat-footed, caught off-guard by the man who had taught her how to deal with conflict. Shelly Robinson, if she knew, had not prepared her for this. She needed time.

"Are you all right?" Sam's daughter asked. Her concern was evident in her voice.

Jessica attempted a smile. It was too brief. "I think so," she offered hesitantly. "This has been quite a day, hasn't it?"

"Indeed it has," Sidney said, shaking her head slightly. "Dad's getting the Jeep started. Do you have everything?"

"Just my purse. Everything else is gone. That includes my faith in humankind."

"Yours, too?" Sidney huffed through her nose. "I lost mine sometime back. I think there's something going around." She paused and smiled at Jessica. "Your eyeliner is running. Unless you want to look like the Joker in a Batman movie, you might want to touch it up. I think I've cut a deal with the agent in charge over there." She motioned with her thumb. "He won't stand in our way if we take his partner with us and get him some medical attention."

Jessica's eyes went cold as she looked around Sidney toward the younger agent who sat smiling like a Cheshire cat. "I've put up with their kind for the last thirteen years. They're like a venomous snake, always hiding and ready to strike without provocation. You and I and all the other taxpayers foot the bill for those assassins. When they're not murdering innocent people, they're protecting their own warlords like Tucker."

Surprised, Sidney jerked her head back, her eyes opened wide. "That's not a fair characterization, Jessica," she said, attempting not to show her alarm.

"Yes, it is," Jessica shot back, not waiting for Sidney to build her case. "They brought ruin to my family. They are the epitome of domestic terrorism. There's no accountability for their crimes against humanity. Congressional inquiry is a joke. The Justice Department is a political tool of the Executive Branch. Tell me how our system differs from the other totalitarian, oppressive regimes in the world."

Sidney studied Jessica's face, her eyes darting from one feature to the next. She was seeing a side of this woman she had not expected.

"Don't act so surprised," Jessica said with an ominous smile. "No wonder you fell victim to my sons' little ruse. You're easily taken in with a wink and a smile. You probably believe the people you defend."

Sidney shot a piercing glare at Jessica.

Jessica said, "You're probably thinking those boys of mine didn't fall far from the tree and that you better talk sense into your dad before he gets his heart broken."

"No, I was wondering if you'd rather stay here with Adolf than take a ride back to civilization with Benito in the car. Is that what I'm hearing? By the way, how long have you been off your meds?"

"Since my car was stolen with my luggage," Jessica said with agitation in her voice. "Look, I didn't mean to take out my frustration and anger on you. You didn't deserve that. You've been good to me. I'm sorry. It's just that right now I'm in no mood to be interrogated by either of those men."

Sidney continued to stare at her. "We'll be leaving soon. It's your choice."

"You do know," Jessica said with a sharp edge as she looked into Sidney's eyes, "that Winston Tucker got what he deserved."

⇥✖⇤

Sidney Dawson

"Where did you get that rotor?" the older agent demanded as he interrupted Sidney and Jessica.

"You don't have to answer that," Sidney quickly said to Jessica. She was uncertain if the woman had just admitted guilt to her or was simply making an observation concerning Winston Tucker's demise.

"If the person who disabled all those vehicles out there," he said with a sweeping motion toward the parking lot, "and stole our vehicle gave her that rotor, I'm pretty sure I can make the case that she's an accessory to grand theft auto in the least and possibly to murder or an accessory to murder."

"Well, if that's your claim, Agent, you need to confirm your suspicions with a judge and have them issue a warrant. In the meantime, you'd be well advised to stop harassing my client. Where did you get your law degree, anyway?"

The agent glared at her. "Yale."

"Never heard of it; are they accredited?" she asked seriously.

The agent's nostrils flared, and his lips pressed hard together. He said nothing as he continued to stare at her.

"I'm sorry," Sidney said. "That was uncalled-for. I don't see any reason why we can't be civil to one another. Somehow we got off on the wrong foot. Do you think we could start over?"

"No," the agent said. "She's a person of interest, and I'm going to continue watching her like a hawk."

"It seems to me you should have been watching Winston Tucker like a hawk. Don't you guys provide protection for former cabinet officials?"

"Not our job, Missy."

Sidney cringed at his demeaning label. "Whose job is it?" she persisted.

The agent seemed annoyed by the question. His jaw moved liked he was chewing gristle. "There's a whole array of government agencies that protect our nation's leaders from the crazies out there, everybody from the U.S. Marshals Service to the Secret Service. It depends on the position and the agency. You needn't concern yourself with things you don't understand, Missy."

Sidney's brow furrowed. She had asked him a simple question, and he had turned it into a demeaning attack. She thought him annoying to say the least.

"Tucker declined protection when he took over the helm at Quest Tek Intermodal in New Orleans," the agent droned on. "He expanded that into the south's largest trucking, hauling, containerized shipping, and warehousing company with multinational operations in Mexico and Central and South America. When he retired as CEO, he appointed himself chairman of the board of directors and pretty much controlled the company from his ranch north of here. The short answer to your question is he had his own security detail that traveled with him everywhere." He paused and attempted a smile. "There's your civics lesson for the day, Missy."

"Please don't call me that. It's degrading. Didn't the FBI teach you any manners at the Academy?"

He pondered her slight for a moment with an expression of misunderstanding. "Perhaps they would if I were an FBI agent."

⋅╾╼◉ ⚔ ◉╾╼⋅

Sam Dawson

The smell of oil and antifreeze were comforting to Sam when he raised the hood on the Willys. He had enjoyed the many hours spent working on the 1953 classic Jeep station wagon. There was a familiarity that always enveloped him when his senses came into contact with the inanimate vehicle, not unlike those of a lover. That friendship had developed from necessity. He could never afford to hire any of the work done. He did it himself, much of it through trial and error. It seemed that most everything he did was by trial and error, including his relationships with women. He replaced the rotor and distributor cap. Turning, he looked through the window of the battered cafe at the haphazard collection of people behind the glass. He was struck by the incongruity and discordance of the gathering. The conflicting elements of relationships flashed on and off like a half dozen neon lights as the people nervously waited for something or someone to provide them with answers or direction. He was no exception. Human nature, he supposed, a species with an innate desire to follow rather than lead. Sam was unsure of his role. Too often, he had followed his heart, only to be left behind, stranded in place and time. *And here I am again,* he thought. He was drawn to Jessica by an inexplicable force, a woman with more baggage than a Greyhound bus. *Run the other way,* his brain told him while his heartstrings pulled him toward the cafe and its moldering future.

Even though he made his living selling pictures of monuments of the dead, he had a knack for sorting through the tea leaves of the living and discovering the truth. When he looked through the viewfinder of his camera, he saw things others could not. He saw them clearly on the other side of the cafe glass. He could not hear them, but he read them as if they were chapters in an open book.

The cook, singular in focus, a misanthrope who saw, as Sam did, the nature of people to line up and follow like sheep. He was a man drowning in regret for his inability to conform. The cafe was his lifeline. The man awkwardly repressed his desire for the waitress. He was going nowhere, and that was fine with him. His unnamed cluster of deteriorating buildings along a ruler-straight road in a parched, unforgiving landscape was where he wanted to be. He never saw the sunlight filtering through the clouds to warm the morning dew as it released the scent of sage or heard the voice of a dove greeting the day. Sam believed Joe was pleased to labor at something he had created.

The waitress made up for her troubled past and unrealized potential with stand-up comedy, shocking her listeners with crude one-liners then scuffing offstage, leaving the audience entertained and amused. She lived in fear of her past and desperately wanted a new beginning but lacked the courage to act. Sam assumed she was protecting someone or something and would be perpetually in trouble with the law.

Jessica, the pretty woman who was stealing his heart, was looking for meaning in her interrupted life. She sought deliverance from a destroyed marriage, a stalled career, and the loss of her father. She had apparently found what she was looking for, and it was not what she expected. Sam hoped he was not merely a temporary distraction that gave her solace from a disappointing life.

The older agent, a seasoned dog that had lost its bite, was on his way out. Losing his car would be the final nail in his career's coffin. He was training his replacement and resented the assignment. He had been somebody, a force to be reckoned with in his day, and now was surrounded by an agency of people that had no institutional memory and seemed interested only in a paycheck and personal comforts. He thought himself a dangerous man with nothing to lose. He was desperate to redeem the tragedy of his failed assignment. Sam felt sorry for him. He was not sorry enough to tolerate the man's verbal abuse of Sidney or Jessica.

Mark, the younger agent, was clean-cut, smart, and in the wrong profession. There was no duty to God and country. He was killing time while he searched for his reward. He seemed to lack the ambition to make the tough decision to act on his dream and pursue a different life. Sam did not know what that dream was. He empathized with the young man, since he had been there himself. Mark's attraction to Sidney appeared to trump all else and troubled Sam. He wondered if his dependency on his daughter outweighed her happiness.

Tumbleweeds still enshrouded much of the cafe in a tangle of beige-colored skeletons. Like epithelial nerve endings that sensed pressure and vibrations, they seemed to sense the drifting nature of the souls from within the cafe. People without direction, without purpose, piled upon each other, their bones clattering in the Wyoming wind. He could have included Sidney and himself in his analysis if there had been time. Sam closed the hood and secured the latches. He wanted to be gone.

CHAPTER 17
2:30 p.m.

Brad Holcomb

There had been no plan. For years he had repeatedly tried to convince himself that he knew what was right and what had to be done. The pretense was a travesty designed to fool him into believing there was a mission. His life had been an odyssey without purpose, without an original plan. Vietnam had been someone else's plan. He had been a pawn sacrificed for political gain by a corrupt president who ordered the assassinations of American pilots to cover up his covert operations in Cambodia and Laos during the Vietnam War.

The president's henchman, General Winston Tucker, was a politically ambitious power monger who had risen meteorically in Republican politics after America's embarrassing loss in Vietnam. The president had appointed him head of the National Security Administration then later for a two-year term as secretary of defense. When the media took down the president in an unrelated scandal, Tucker disappeared into the private sector before running for the Senate on an ultraconservative platform. The Democrats had lost control of Congress while Tucker amassed a campaign war chest that allowed him to run for president and out-spend any candidate in American history. He bullied and bought his way to the top of the GOP list of nominees.

When Senate Minority Whip John Roberts, leading contender for the Democratic nomination, learned of Tucker's involvement with the disgraced president's alleged assassinations of American servicemen, the Senate Select Committee on Intelligence was convened, and Brad was subpoenaed. Brad had no intention of testifying. He would have taken his own life before exposing Elizabeth and Jessica to what he had done. When Tucker attempted to eliminate Brad as a witness and killed Elizabeth instead, everything changed. Brad knew what was right and what needed to be done. He testified. The media's feeding frenzy was almost as spectacular as when they had taken down the president. They picked the flesh from Tucker's bones and then moved on like a pack of wolves, their bloody tongues wagging, in search of other prey to consume as they competed with each other for sponsors, readers, listeners, and viewers. The Democrats had lost control of Congress and eagerly fueled the scandal. Roberts smelled political blood and positioned himself as the Democratic contender with Brad as his protected, secret witness.

Brad should have realized that Washington insiders would quietly move to protect their own. The Senate Select Committee on Intelligence adjourned without handing down a single indictment. Tucker's involvement in covering up the president's secret war in Cambodia and Laos during the Vietnam War became yesterday's news. The Republicans accused the Democrats of political sabotage, but even without an indictment the damage to Tucker's campaign was enough to destroy his bid for the presidency. Tucker quietly disappeared. Then, like the Phoenix, he arose from the ashes renewed for an equally corrupt career in the private sector. Brad had cost him the presidency and shamed him in front of the world. Tucker's political ruin had been fleeting. He emerged unaffected. Rich and powerful, he took the helm of a huge Louisiana corporation and ran it from his mega ranch in Wyoming.

Brad was left with an empty, unsatisfied feeling that gnawed at his insides day and night for the past thirteen years. The man, Brad determined, needed killing. Then maybe the nightmares, the years of deception, the guilt of his involvement, the deceitful life he had created as atonement for his crimes would disappear. He reasoned that killing Tucker was too merciful. He had planned it to be a slow, painful, figurative death followed by a *coup de grâce* delivered by his own hand, a hand that now shook uncontrollably as he lifted it from the steering wheel of the stolen Suburban.

He remembered it all vividly from beginning to end. The years of running, hiding, and stalking had come to an end. He marveled at how condensed it was, abridged from decades of an earlier life. He had to ask himself if it was worth it. The price he had paid was enormous. There was no need to rehash all the rights and wrongs. It would change nothing. The future beckoned.

--=● ✹ ●=--

Ida Faye Mensinger

"Here," Ida Faye said sharply as she approached the pretty lady. She held out the scrap of paper she had found in the debris of the ruined house trailer. "It has your name on it."

Jessica took the paper hesitantly and looked at it. She seemed unable to take her eyes from it, reading it over and over, remembering.

"It's a score sheet from a game of dominoes that I played with my mom and stepdad in a cabin somewhere in the mountains here in Wyoming." She held it as if it was something valuable, something sacred. "I can't believe he kept it all these years."

"Elizabeth is your mom's name?" Ida Faye asked.

"Yes," Jessica said with a warm smile.

"And Eden?"

"My father," Jessica said, finally looking up. "My adopted father, I should say," she paused, then added, "the only father I ever knew." She looked at Ida Faye. "Eden Cain is his name."

"Are you sure?" Ida Faye shot back. "I've known him for several years as Brad Holcomb. It seems to me he didn't want anyone to know who he really was."

"I'm quite sure," Jessica said defensively, her eyes narrowed as she studied the bruised waitress.

Ida Faye took a deep breath and exhaled it slowly. "I've known for some time that he was a man running from something. I suspected that Brad Holcomb wasn't his real name. Just like my name ain't Ida Faye Mensinger." She smiled tightly. "It's Tammy Jo Martin, and I used to be somebody."

Jessica looked at her impatiently.

"Never mind," Ida Faye said, realizing the woman was not interested in her story. "I don't know what happened between you two out there. I'm not sure I want to know. Whatever it was caused him to go back on a promise he made to me. That doesn't concern you. What I need to know is why he left me standing here like the darn fool that I am."

"What happened between my," Jessica hesitated as if searching for the appropriate word, "father," she said as if questioning her selection, "and me is not your concern. It's a long story with a surprise ending that I never saw coming; a disclosure that left me speechless. I just need time to digest it, to determine a response, and if that response is legitimate. I'm sorry if he disappointed you. Believe me, you don't know what disappointment is." She paused for a long moment. "Maybe disappointment isn't the right word. Do you think you can be disappointed if you lose something you didn't know you had?"

Ida Faye searched the woman's pretty face. Jessica's red-rimmed eyes were about to spill over with tears that had suddenly welled up. Her eyeliner had already fashioned a black tear. "Yes," she said with a smile. "Yes, I do." She turned away quickly for fear of bursting into tears herself.

"I knew you'd come back," Joe said with his approximation of a smile as Ida Faye approached him at the cash register. He put down the butter knife he had been using to pry open the cash drawer. "I had HR rewrite your job description and advertise it as entry-level. You'll have to apply along with everyone else."

"Thanks, Mister Dobransky. I won't let you down," she gushed.

"You'll be required to attend the mandatory sensitivity training during your probationary period. I'm restructuring to ensure my workforce is equitable, diverse, and inclusive."

Ida Faye wrinkled her brow and squinted. "How do you do that, Joe, when you have a workforce of one?"

"That's not your concern. Don't question my authority or I'll have to let you go. I can do that without cause during your probationary period, you know. And by the way, you just bought yourself an additional six months tacked on to the one-year probationary period."

"Before you do that, Joe, let me consult with my attorney over there." She motioned with her head toward Sidney, who was smiling with amusement at the two of them as she took in their banter. "I need to know if there is a difference between inappropriate touching and fondling."

-->==◎ ❉ ◎==<--

Jessica Martindale

The twins had been at the University of Wyoming for two years, and she had not visited them until two days ago. Jessica tried to convince herself that it was because she was disappointed with their choice of colleges. Three generations of her family had graduated from Iowa State University. She had assumed the boys would want to stay close to home. Christmas vacations and the summer after their freshman year were respites during the weaning process. It had become obvious to her that they had a greater allegiance to each other than to the mother who had raised them. When she learned of Winston

Tucker's involvement with her stepfather's disappearance, she was stunned to discover that Tucker lived just three hours from her boys.

Jessica attempted to justify her desire to confront, maybe kill Winston Tucker with the corporate mentality that had ruined her marriage, driven her children away, and taken over her life. The dog-eat-dog world of big business had immunized her to figurative death and left her capable of planning and implementing ruthless strategies in order to advance her company's cold moves on the global chessboard. She likened it to a battlefield mindset that justified her unmerciful actions. She was unsure where the line was between metaphorical and actual death. What frightened her most during her drive to Tucker's ranch was that she would discover that difference and forever regret either outcome.

The score sheet in her hand trembled. The memories it evoked were tangible. She saw her parents, heard their voices, and smelled the wood smoke from the cabin's stove. Like the thumbed pages of a favorite book, images flashed by, years reduced to seconds. By far they were happy memories of a loving childhood, a loving family in a storybook setting. But something had happened that tainted those reminiscences, something dark, something evil that lurked just under the surface of a happy life. That something was Winston Tucker. First there was sadness, followed by anger, emotions that clouded her vision. These feelings eventually gave way to resentment, the unfairness of things she could not control. The man who had destroyed her family and robbed her bank of memories was living the good life, prosperous and unmolested.

It was this unfairness that gnawed at her. It was a crawling under her skin, an itch she could not scratch. The festering irritation had to be removed.

The tidal wave of relief that Tucker's death provided had receded. In its wake was the destruction of a purpose, only to be replaced with a new dilemma. Hating Tucker was easy. Hating the man who had raised her was more difficult.

Sidney Dawson

"I don't understand," Sidney said with a perplexed look as she searched the eyes of the older agent. "Who are you?"

"There's a lot you don't understand, Missy. It's best you stand aside. Take your cretin father and skedaddle back to your hole in the ground. Your continued involvement will land you in a heap of trouble."

Sidney smiled and shook her head. "There you go insulting me again. What is wrong with you? I suspect you have an inexhaustible supply of insults, since you seem incapable of communicating civilly. It's no wonder Ms. Martindale views you as a ruffian with the manners and ethics of a grade-school bully. I'll let your rudeness slide this time because I refuse to lower myself to your level. However, I must warn you if you degrade my father again, you'll find out why you should approach him with caution. My advice to you is don't." Her icy stare told him she was not bluffing.

The nameless older agent smirked and placed his hands on his hips, pushing his coat back deliberately, revealing his handgun under his left arm.

"Put that thing away," Sidney mocked. "This isn't the Wild West. I'm not intimidated by you or your gun. Shame on you! What is wrong with you?" she demanded again. "If you don't show me some ID, I'll be forced to file my complaint with the special agent in charge of your field office."

"I don't have to show you diddlysquat, Missy. If you continue to get in my face, I'll bring the weight of the federal government down on you, the likes of which you've never seen before."

"Have it your way." Sidney forced a polite smile. "We'll take Mark to the nearest hospital, and he can call for someone to come and get you." She turned sharply, glanced out the window to check on the progress of her father, then approached Jessica.

"We're leaving as soon as Dad gets the Willys started. His invitation to you still stands. We're taking the injured agent with us. If that's unacceptable to you, stay here." She did not wait for a response. Instead, she did an about-face and walked briskly toward the booth where Mark sat, still staring at her. *No more arguing with these people*, she thought. *The last thing I need is to get caught up further in their problems.*

Mark's smile and beaming eyes caused her to smile in return. "What are you smiling at, Agent Johnson?"

"You, Ms. Dawson, you make me smile."

"That's because you have a head injury," Sidney said shyly. "I wish your partner was half as friendly as you."

"Oh, don't worry about Hal. His bite is pretty harmless."

"Hal," Sidney said with a sly grin. "That's a dog's name. Really, that's his name?"

"Harold, actually. He prefers to be called Hal. His last name is Kohler."

"Like the toilet?" Sidney asked, her eyes wide with surprise.

"He prefers Hal," Mark said, mimicking her expression.

⋅⊷═◉❊◉═⊶⋅

Sam Dawson

Sam turned the key, pressed the starter button, and the Willys growled resentfully. It did not start. He flicked on the toggle switch for the electric fuel pump he had installed in the gas line near the tank; still nothing. The smell of gas told him the carburetor was flooded. He had recently replaced the big four-barrel Holly with an even larger Edelbrock that was a bit sensitive to having the gas pedal pounded. The small block Chevy demanded the highest octane fuel he could find. It was not economical. Expensive, sensitive, and stubborn were adjectives that he believed could be applied to his automobile, but he loved that car.

Cussing beneath his breath, he jumped out of the Jeep, kicked hailstones out of his way, released the latches, raised the hood, and twirled the wing nut from the oversized, chromed air breather. He pulled out the filter and jammed his fingers into the throat of the reluctant carburetor, holding open the butterfly valve. The smell of gas was overpowering. He had meant to hook up the manual choke and override the so-called automatic choke. He wished he had taken the time. He needed a second pair of hands to turn the key and press the starter button. Turning, he saw he had an audience. Six people were standing shoulder to shoulder behind the picture window with the large block letters that spelled out *EAT HERE* over the word *OPEN* painted in bright red. Their looks were neither hopeful nor discouraging. Rather, they appeared expectant, perhaps suspenseful. They were clearly on the edge of whatever was affecting them, their individual peculiarities as different from each other as their separate personalities.

"I need your help," he mouthed silently while looking at Sidney. She immediately turned and briskly exited the cafe.

"Please tell me you can get it started," Sidney said as she approached her father.

"Not to worry, kiddo. She's had a little too much to drink, that's all. Hop in, turn the key, and press the starter button. Don't touch the foot pedal; I'll work the linkage from here."

The Willys roared to life, stretched her vocal cords a couple of times, and settled into a reassuring purr as if waking from a pleasant nap.

Turning, they saw the line of people in the cafe applauding as if it was a standing ovation. Everyone except Agent Kohler. Sidney took her father's hand, and together they bowed to the crowd.

"I'll get Jessica, you get Mark, and let's get the heck out of here," Sam said.

"I hate to be a spoiler, Pop, but your gas gauge is resting on empty."

"I bent the arm on the sending unit's float so that it would read empty when I still had three or four gallons left in the tank. Plus, we have two and a half gallons in each of the jerry cans." He pointed at the chrome gas cans on each side of the

Willys between the fenders and doors. "We've got more than enough to get us to Lusk, maybe Torrington if we have to."

"You really are a boy scout." Sidney smiled at her father's preparedness.

"I'm afraid I have to insist, Dawson," the older agent said as he approached them in the parking lot. "I'll need to borrow your vehicle." Again, he casually pulled his jacket back to expose his gun in the shoulder holster.

"I'll have your badge, Harold." Sidney smiled. "You'll have to do some serious judge shopping to find one that would dismiss the Supreme Court's view that the danger to the public must be immediate or impending for you to impose an archaic English law from the thirteenth century. Your agency's liability exposure would bankrupt a small country. And please don't show me your gun again. Do I make myself clear, Agent Kohler?"

The older agent appeared to be on the verge of combusting spontaneously, his face red and puffy. "You listen to me, Helen Keller, I'll—"

Sam's punch was quick and decisive. The agent was nearly lifted off the ground; he staggered once then fell backward, landing on his back. "Whoops! Sorry about that," Sam said, offering his hand to the prostrate agent. "I didn't see you standing there."

Again, applause erupted from inside the diner and caused both Sidney and Sam to look up. Hal shook his head slowly and struggled to his feet. The agent fumbled for his gun.

"No, you don't need that. I was just swatting at a wasp, and you stepped into it. We have a whole room full of witnesses." Sam gestured toward the cafe.

"You're under arrest, Dawson. I'll see to it that you do hard time for assaulting a federal officer." The agent succeeded in pulling his gun from the holster and was pointing it with a shaking hand at Sam as he struggled to his feet.

"A federal officer would have identified himself before attempting to confiscate a citizen's vehicle," Sidney said. "This looks to me like either a man defending himself against an armed robber or someone swatting at an insect and accidentally hitting a bystander." She lowered her voice and spoke to the agent confidentially. "Didn't I tell you not to find out why he should be approached with caution?"

"And didn't I tell you not to disrespect my daughter again?" Sam said.

"Get on your knees, Dawson. Put your hands behind your head. On your knees now," he barked. "I won't tell you again."

The unmistakable metallic sound of a slide-action shotgun being loaded and cocked oriented the three of them toward the corner of the cafe.

CHAPTER 18
2:46 p.m.

Brad Holcomb

There was no hope for the future. It would be a disappointment just like the past, Brad thought. Sometime in the future, he wished the past would turn out okay, maybe kinder than he remembered. The present always seemed to interfere with the plans the future required. He had forgotten so much. He sometimes believed he had not existed before Vietnam. When there, he had been convinced there was no tomorrow. He expected to die every day, and he accepted it without question or concern. It was his way of coping. Sometimes the memories came back to him, usually unexpected when he was doing nothing, standing, looking, not thinking, always a surprise.

Some believe that nothing is lost. It is all there stored somewhere deep in the subconscious brain. If that was true, then all the sensory experiences, all the good, all the bad, all the hope was tucked away in the folds of his now diseased mind. Everything! All the past experiences he needed in order to make decisions about the present. He only thought of the present, since he had no reason to believe the future would be any kinder than the past. He no longer brooded about killing, except for one; *now this,* he thought as he stared down the barrel of the Winchester.

His father had instilled in him the differences between right and wrong and what needed to be done to make reparations. He had spent most of his life trying to amend his sins of the past. He knew what was right and what needed to be done.

"I don't know who you are," the older agent yelled at Brad, who stood boldly at the corner of the cafe, pointing the barrel of the twelve-gauge at him. "I'm a federal agent in the process of arresting this man. You need to stand aside, lower your weapon, and identify yourself."

It all came back to him. Thirteen years dissolved into seconds. There had been no hesitation, no last-minute questions of right and wrong. The response was still there after all the years. Point and pull. Kill or be killed. The man's admission that he was a federal agent made it all the easier. Brad's finger tightened on the trigger.

The older agent had now trained his gun on Brad. "I won't tell you again. Lower your weapon."

Sam took Sidney's arm firmly at the elbow and guided her slowly toward the cafe, out of the line of fire.

"Brad," Ida Faye shouted from the front doorstep. "You came back! I thought you'd left without me. I knew you'd come back." She smiled and smoothed the front of her tattered uniform with her right hand and pushed a tuft of hair behind her ear with her left. "You're a good man, Eden Cain," she added then offered a hesitant smile. Ida Faye was oblivious to the drama before her. She seemed about to burst with unexpected hope. "We'll start over. I have plans. I'll—"

"Dad," Jessica cried as she pushed past the waitress. "I'm sorry, Dad. I didn't know what to say to you. I thought I had been lied to all these years. I realize now that you never lied because I never asked you. All I'm asking now is to know you, all of you, terrible stories included. I know that it's probably much worse than I imagined. It will be a start, though. Give me a chance." Jessica looked at Ida Faye then back to her father. "We'll start over too. Maybe—"

"Easy, Brad," the cook said, stepping out onto the crowded front step. "That guy," he said, pointing at the older agent with his spatula, "hasn't paid his bill. You can shoot him later. I want my money first. Otherwise, I'll have to take it out of your paycheck."

Agent Johnson silently appeared from behind the cafe. He held his gun at the back of Brad's head. "My head is killing me," he said to Brad in a lowered voice. "But it's nothing compared to what yours will feel like if you don't drop that shotgun."

Brad slowly lowered the Winchester, released the hammer to half-cock, and laid the gun gently on the ground.

No one said a word. Seven people seemed to collectively sigh with relief, the tension released. The silence was confusing. No one knew what to say.

Ida Faye surveyed the ridiculous gathering in front of a cafe that had once been a gas station and was now plastered with tumbleweeds. "Since we're all gathered here on the threshold of purgatory, maybe it would be appropriate if someone would say a few words."

"Amen," Sidney said with finality.

Brad took a deep breath and exhaled slowly. He had hesitated, and it would cost him. He saw the faces of the two agents he had killed thirteen years ago. There had been no hesitation, no one to offer joyous hope, no one to beg forgiveness.

⊶⊷ �֍ ⊷⊶

Ida Faye Mensinger

She eyed the older agent suspiciously as he attempted to quiet the people he had herded back into the cafe. She could care less about sorting through the facts, determining guilt, and arresting those who needed arresting. She, like everyone except Joe, wanted to be gone, away from this tangle of intersecting lives whose stories were like chewing whale blubber. The more you chewed, the bigger and harder it became to swallow. Brad and the young woman's father were placed in the second booth and handcuffed together, since the younger agent could not find the handcuffs that had been issued to him four years ago and he'd never used. Ida Faye, the pretty woman, and the lady lawyer were told to sit at the table farthest from the booth and to keep their traps shut. The lady lawyer, Sidney, challenged the older agent incessantly like a mosquito circling his head. The pretty woman stared wide-eyed at the two men in the booth. She was stuck on the lady lawyer's father like a cheap suit. Nevertheless, it was Brad who held her attention. Ida Faye sat stiffly upright as if anticipating the start of a race.

"If you don't blink once in a while, your eyeballs will dry out," Ida Faye said to the pretty lady. The afternoon sun reflected painfully from the chrome stems of the counter stools. Their vinyl seats appeared as red dots in the woman's eyes, giving her the look of a vampire or perhaps a white lab rat. She ignored Ida Faye.

The lady lawyer's eyes repeatedly returned to the cafe's door. She was obviously waiting for the young agent to return. They had heard the older agent direct him to find their Suburban and bring it around front. "A watched pot never boils," Ida Faye offered. The young woman looked at her as if she did not understand.

Together, the three women waited. Ida Faye became increasingly impatient, as was her nature. She watched Joe, who had decided to clean the grill, finally giving up opening the cash register. He occasionally shook his head as though he was arguing with himself. She had a difficult time sitting still. She had always been like that. Her first grade teacher had tied her to her desk chair with a bed sheet. She spent a lot of time in the principal's office in elementary and middle schools. By high school she had figured out how to stay just below teachers' and the school principal's radar. She had been tested repeatedly, and the diagnosis was always the same. She was dyslexic, with the added joy of attention deficit hyperactivity disorder. With an IQ of 130, she was considered moderately gifted, even though she had difficulty reading or understanding simple math. She compensated with humor and social isolation, never allowing people to get too close to her. She preferred dogs and horses.

"Listen to me, J. Edgar," Ida Faye said loudly.

"His name is Harold," Sidney said to her. "He prefers to be called Hal."

Ida Faye looked at the lady lawyer with an incredulous grin. "That's a dog's name."

Sidney smiled while shaking her head. "His last name is Kohler."

"Like a urinal? Agent Kohler," Ida Faye corrected as she called out to the older agent. "Harold," she smiled. "Or do you prefer to be called Hal? Perhaps Harry?"

The older agent glared at her menacingly.

"Oh, don't get bent out of shape, Hal. It could be worse. I had a civics teacher in high school named Mr. Head, first name Richard. He went by Richard. You can guess what we called him."

"How about I shoot you a couple of times? Will you be quiet then?" he growled.

"Look, Hal, my old pal, you don't have any right to make us sit here like we're in detention."

The agent glared at her. "Since we're on a first-name basis here, do you mind if I call you Tammy Jo? Or, would you prefer T.J., Ms. Martin?"

Joe stopped his incessant scraping on the grill and turned to face the dining area, his spatula in hand. Everyone was silent.

Ida Faye's eyes narrowed. "How do you know my name?" she said quietly.

"That's my job, T.J. I'm paid to know these things. I've got a file on you an inch thick. We've been watching you for some time. Admittedly, it's hard for us to blend in out here in the middle of Bum F ... nowhere," he corrected, "Wyoming. That truck driver, that hard-hat miner, that lost tourist were all ours. Do you remember that pleasant young woman census taker last fall? Fresh out of the Academy." He smiled.

"I don't understand. Why would you be investigating me? I've done nothing wrong." Ida Faye was clearly shaken by this revelation. Her mouth hung half open, and her hands began to shake. "Are you with the IRS?"

The older agent smiled again, this time more tightly, and shook his head. "Dobransky there," his chin pointed toward Joe, "he's paid you in cash and never filed a 1099 for you. Those number-crunching fruit loops over in Treasury don't even know you exist. As far as we're concerned, your problems with the IRS are petty. They lose a lot more money from dead people still collecting welfare and social security checks every month. Not our problem."

Joe began inching his way toward the kitchen door.

"Get back here, Dobransky," the agent barked. "You're not going anywhere. I'll deal with you in a minute."

Joe reluctantly complied. His eyes shifted back and forth. He, too, seemed startled that the agent knew his name. He looked like a man about to run.

"Be careful," Sidney said softly to the waitress. "He's baiting you."

Ida Faye looked at her with the expression of someone drowning who could not be saved. "Why have you been watching me?" she said, turning back toward the agent.

"Because you're here," he said as a matter of fact. "And, you're married to Darrell Robinson. Now deceased," he added somewhat merrily.

"I didn't kill Darrell," Ida Faye said immediately.

"We believe you, T.J. We know who did, and frankly, we don't care. Robinson needed killing. As far as I'm concerned, that's somebody else's issue. As soon as we can establish communications, we'll hand that individual over to the local authorities. We have bigger fish to fry."

Ida Faye's eyes narrowed, and she tilted her head like a robin listening for a worm. "Hand over? Who in this room should I thank?" she asked.

⇥━◉ ✠ ◉━⇤

Jessica Martindale

For the past thirteen years she had visualized him as he appeared before his disappearance. Often she saw him in her mind's eye as he was when she was young and still living at home. He had been handsome, strong, and healthy. Time and circumstances had eroded those qualities. Weathered and frail, he did not look well. White in the muzzle, sinewy, and slow, he had been gone for a dog's life. Even his eyes seemed a bit cloudy. It was cruel to chain him up.

Sam was a study in contrast. Jessica felt pangs of guilt for shamelessly staring at him. Decking the agent in the parking lot was disturbing to her. She hoped his physical violence wasn't a substitute for a lack of mental ability. Regardless, she was attracted to him in a way she had never experienced before.

"Excuse me, Agent Kohler," Jessica said politely. "Is it necessary to handcuff these men? I don't think either of them poses much of a threat to society."

"I don't give a rat's ass what you think, lady. If I had another pair of cuffs, I'd hook you up with miss smarty pants. You're both accessories as far as I'm concerned." He kept working his jaw then rubbing under his ear with his hand.

"Keep digging, Hal," Sidney cautioned. "I'll have your badge before this is over. Speaking of which, you still haven't shown me your ID."

If dirty looks could kill, Sidney is a marked woman, Jessica thought. The older agent glared at her while massaging his sore jaw. Surprisingly, he reached inside his jacket and produced a leather-bound badge and ID card with his picture. He stepped toward their table and held the identification in front of Sidney's face. Jessica leaned toward Sidney as they both stared at the small card. Large yellow letters within a blue stripe above his picture read *DEA*. Below that in smaller black type: *Harold Kohler Special Agent in Charge* above a standard-looking bar code. The badge was the typical Department of Justice shield with the eagle clutching a talon full of arrows above the large U.S. letters encircled by Drug Enforcement Agency. *Special Agent* was stamped below. "You're DEA?" Sidney said, drawing back with a surprised look.

"That's right, Missy."

"I don't understand."

"Is it because you can't see, or are you just stupid?"

Sam almost pulled the old man from the booth as he struggled to his feet and lurched toward the older agent. Salt, pepper, ketchup, hot sauce, and a napkin dispenser all fell to the floor.

"Sit down, Dawson, or I *will* shoot you this time," Special Agent Kohler ordered.

"Do as he says, Pop. He's DEA, and his badge says he's in charge," Sidney said with a smirk.

"That's right, Missy. I'm in charge. You best not forget that."
He looked at Jessica. "That's why we keep those dogs chained
up," he said, pointing at the two men handcuffed in the booth.

"You're a pathetic little man," Jessica said, squinting. "You
seem to have a total lack of understanding for other people's
feelings and a need to control and dominate people, all of
which point to low self-esteem and a sense of powerlessness
that you overcompensate for with aggression. You're a bully,
Agent Kohler."

"You go, girl," the waitress chimed in with a raised fist.

"DEA?" Sidney said again. "I don't get it. I thought you
were FBI and were looking into the murder of Winston Tucker.
What's DEA got to do with Tucker?"

The door to the cafe opened with a bang as the younger
agent scuffled with a tumbleweed that attempted to enter with
the help of a strong breeze that had come up from the west.

"Where's the Suburban?" the older agent barked. "What
took you so long?"

"The car was out back in the trees. It won't start. I called
in on the satellite phone to get an update and checked out the
old guy to see if there were any outstanding warrants. I had
dispatch contact the locals, and they're on their way."

"Did you look under the hood to see if the whatchama-
callit…" The older agent looked at Sam.

"Distributor rotor," Sam said.

"Was it missing?" Agent Kohler asked.

"It has electronic fuel injection, Hal. It has a computer that
sends fuel to the cylinders," Mark said somewhat condescend-
ingly. Sam winked at him.

The older agent seemed to ponder Mark's response for a moment then changed the subject. "What did you find out about our geriatric car thief?"

Jessica shook her head. "Isn't mandatory retirement for you guys at age fifty-seven? It looks to me like you're past due, Hal."

"Shut your pie hole, lady. I've had just about enough of your—"

"Nothing, boss," the younger agent interrupted. "Without prints, they couldn't find a thing. He's not in the system under the name Brad Holcomb."

"We'll hold him as a John Doe until we can turn him over to the locals. They'll print him and run it through the Bureau's AFIS. If that doesn't work, they can swab him and run it through CODIS."

Jessica turned to Sidney with a perplexed look.

"The FBI maintains the Automated Fingerprint Identification System. It's a biometric, digitized, computer system that law enforcement agencies use to identify people. CODIS is the Combined DNA Identification System that uses DNA profiles to identify someone," Sidney explained.

"Little Missy knows her stuff," Agent Kohler admitted with a nod. "One way or another, we'll find out who the geezer is. Frankly, I don't care who he is. As you might say up here in Wyoming, he's just a bur under my saddle. The sheriff will be here soon, and he can hold him for grand theft auto. I've . got bigger fish to fry. I do have one more question for Ms. Martindale."

Jessica looked up at him, surprised.

"Is that man your father?" he said, pointing at Brad.

"No," she said, maintaining eye contact with the agent. "My father was killed in Vietnam in 1971."

⊷⊷◉✻◉⊶⊶

Sidney Dawson

"Mark," Sidney said in a hushed voice as she looked up into his face, "if you have any thoughts of ever seeing me socially, you'll need to release my father and allow us to leave."

"Sounds like an ultimatum," he said, smiling. "I very much want to see you socially, but your dad punched a federal officer."

"Your partner had not identified himself as such and was in the act of forcefully stealing our vehicle. My father was protecting his property and preventing a crime by neutralizing a perceived threat."

"Speaking of threats, you've implied that there will be serious penalties if your terms are not met. Can you give me an example of one of those penalties?" He maintained his smile.

"You'll never see me naked," Sidney shot back immediately.

"Let me see what I can do." Mark pivoted and hurried across the room toward the older agent. A heated discussion ensued with animated gestures by both men.

Sidney wished she had not used sex as a bargaining chip. There was something about Mark that made her act like a brainless teenager, a trait she shared with her father. She approached the man who had saved her life on more than one occasion. "Well, Pop, you've done it this time." She looked out the window to see the typical afternoon storm clouds building to the west. "You've lost your light."

Both men turned to look out above the confusion of tumbleweeds at the western horizon. Their handcuffs rattled against the tabletop. "I'm Sidney Dawson," she said to the white-haired old man, who gave her a pleasant smile in return, then looked down and then back up again. He studied Sidney's face for a long moment and then said loud enough for everyone to hear, "I'm Eden Cain."

Silence descended on the dining room like a heavy fog as everyone stared at the frail old man whose head trembled.

"He's the man who adopted me when I was seven and raised me," Jessica said as she rose to her feet. "He's a war hero who deserves our respect."

"He's the man who touched my heart," the waitress said boldly. "The man who showed me how to bury the past and seek a new life." Her eyes filled with tears. "My name is Tammy Jo Martin," she added confidently.

Agent Kohler shook his head and smiled sarcastically. "You people remind of those brainless old TV game shows from the fifties and sixties like *What's My Line*, *To Tell the Truth*, and *I've Got a Secret*."

"Holy cow." Sidney laughed. "If you remember those, you're way past mandatory retirement."

"Reruns on cable, Missy. It's what agents do late at night when they can't sleep because they were being lied to all day long." He turned to Mark. "Run the old guy again under Cain, Eden," he directed. "See if we get a hit."

"Who wants pie?" Ida Faye said, wiping away tears. "I've got raisin cream, or is that custard with flies?" she said, leaning down to examine the pie in the case. "We've got one slice of apple left. It's low on apples, lots of gooey filler that looks like cow snot. What'll it be? *À la mode* comes with a free straw," she added.

"Cash only," Joe piped up from behind the counter.

"On the house," Ida Faye corrected.

Sidney discreetly flashed the ignition key for the Willys in front of Sam. She had turned off the vehicle and removed the key during the brawl in the parking lot. Sam winked at her.

Jessica, Ida Faye, and Sidney crowded toward the booth where the two men sat hobbled to each other.

"Pop," Sidney said, "I'm working on getting you released. Be patient, and no more hitting people."

"Dad," Jessica gushed, "you're the only father I've ever known. We've got a lot of catching up to do, if you'll give me a chance. The man who destroyed your life is dead. It's over, Dad. No more running, no more hiding. Let me help you move on. Okay?"

"Ditto, Brad," Ida Faye said. "The man who destroyed my life is dead. No more running, no more hiding for me either. We can move on together. I'll wait for you. When you get out of jail, I'll be there."

"And I'll be there with her," Jessica added.

"Me, too," Sam said glumly. "Let's hope we're not still shackled together."

"Hold on, folks," Sidney intervened. "Nobody is going to jail just yet. We'll get this mess sorted out." She hurriedly scanned the four people huddled in and around the booth and regretted that she had wandered into this tangled web of interconnected lives. She glanced at the playlist on the gaudy

Wall-O-Matic jukebox at the end of the table. "The Wayward Wind" by Gogi Grant caught her eye. A fitting song title for just about any place in Wyoming, even more so in this isolated remnant of the west that straddled a highway going nowhere in either direction. The restless wind and strange name of the artist seemed appropriate for the circumstances, especially her circumstances. She wished the electricity was restored so she could play the song for this band of disturbingly different people.

⊶⊷ ✦ ⊶⊷

Sam Dawson

Sam watched as the three women drifted back to their table. "This is a fine kettle of fish," Sam said, looking directly at the old man, who nodded in agreement. "I think you and I are about to have a problem."

The old man scrutinized Sam with a look that said he was not to be trifled with.

"I've had enough coffee to float a battleship," Sam admitted with a smile. "And I'm as right-handed as they come," he added, raising his cuffed right hand along with the old man's left hand from the table. "You seem like a nice guy; we've only just met and hate to drag you outside..." Sam leaned over and whispered in the old man's ear. "I have to see a man about a dog, you know, take a whiz, my back teeth are starting to float, my eyes are turning yellow. I gotta pee bad, and I'm not sure I can go chained to another guy."

The old man took a deep breath and exhaled slowly while shaking his head. "I used to have a nervous bladder. The army cured me of that. If you couldn't pee into a trough while standing shoulder-to-shoulder with a company of men and a drill sergeant screaming in your ear, you would either die of uremic poisoning or wet your pants. Soiling yourself wasn't an option in the army."

"So, you *can* speak in complete sentences," Sam said. "I was beginning to wonder." He studied the old man's face. "Thanks, by the way, for saving my hide out there. I think that guy really wanted to shoot me. Thanks, too, for letting us out of the freezer. It was a bit cramped in there. And thanks for defending us against that armed woman who stole Jessica's car. And, by the way, thanks for raising a beautiful and amazing daughter. And, most of all, thanks for not disabling my Willys and for giving back my rotor. I really do have to pee."

"Take a breath," the old man said seriously. "That's what my wife used to say to me whenever I rattled on like a physicked woodpecker. And you're welcome." He turned his head and looked out at the Willys in the parking lot. "I never thought I'd see it again. How'd you come by it?"

"It was sitting in a guy's yard in Encampment with a for sale sign in the window. He said he had found it in an abandoned mineshaft off of Battle Pass up in the Medicine Bow National Forest. There had been a forest fire that swept over the area back in 2003. Other than smelling like a campfire, it was in good shape. It had Iowa tags on it; took me a while to get a clear title. I had to stamp a new ID number on the frame. You think it was yours, huh? I really do have to pee."

Brad smiled. "I know it is. But it's yours now. I'm glad you found it and gave it a good home."

Sam could see the memories in the old man's eyes and heard the longing in his voice. "Maybe when this mess is over, you and Jessica could visit us and we'll take her for a spin, maybe a picnic, up in the mountains."

"I'd like that. Although I have a feeling this isn't going to be over with anytime soon."

Sam, bouncing his right leg up and down, suddenly turned his attention toward the older agent. "Agent Kohler," he called out. "Could I have a word, please?" He smiled pleasantly.

"Wipe that poop-eatin' grin off your face, Dawson, or I'll do it for you. What do you want?"

"I need to use the restroom."

"Not a chance, butt wipe." The older agent grinned with only one side of his mouth.

"Look, Hal, I'm sorry you got smacked out there, but this is an emergency," Sam said with a pleading look on his face.

"Your bladder can bust for all I care. It'll serve you right."

Déjà vu swept over Sam like a cold winter wind. The hair on his arms and back of his neck stood erect. He heard Hank Thompson's voice. He smelled the gasoline and felt the warmth of his own urine soaking his pants. "Suffering can be quite exhilarating," Thompson had said as he prepared to burn Sam alive. It had been more than three years since Thompson terrorized Sam and Sidney, disrupting their lives forever. The memories were still there. Both he and Sidney suffered the nightmares. He feared he always would. "Did you call me butt wipe?" Sam said suddenly.

"The old guy's clean," the younger agent called out as he entered the cafe. "We don't have a thing on him. It's as though

Eden Cain never existed. I've never seen anything like it. Not even a parking ticket. No military record. There was nothing from Social Security, Medicare, or the IRS. The guy's a ghost. When the home office contacted Langley, they were told it was above our pay grade to dig any deeper."

"Well, that's all about to change," the older agent said. "Auto theft and armed assault on a federal officer will soon be added to his resume."

"Not so fast, boss," Mark said. "We've been ordered to stand down and return to Division Headquarters."

"By who?" the older agent demanded, his eyes bulging.

"DOJ," Mark said. "It came from the AG himself. We're on forbidden ground, boss. We're to return to Fort Collins immediately."

Agent Kohler stood there, stunned, staring at Agent Johnson. "Two years," he said. "Two years we've worked this case, and now they're pulling the plug?"

"He's dead, boss," Mark said. "The order came from the top. The administration doesn't want another scandal. The public already thinks—"

"Who cares what the public thinks? We were on the verge of exposing—"

"The president cares," Mark said forcefully. "He wants another term. His party doesn't need the implication."

"What about him?" The older agent nodded toward the frail-looking old man handcuffed in the booth. "He's dirty, and you know it. Why else would they shut us down? There's a link here."

"Mark," Sam said, staring at the younger agent expectantly. "Can I have a word with you?"

"What is it, Sam?" Mark said as he approached the booth.

"I need to take a leak." Sam held up his handcuffed wrist.

"Sure thing, Sam," the younger agent said as he produced the key and proceeded to unlock the cuffs from both men. "I'm sorry about the inconvenience."

Agent Kohler drew his gun. "I'm going with you, Dawson. Don't try anything funny."

"Likewise, Hal," Sam said raising his eyebrows.

CHAPTER 19

2:56 p.m.

Eden Cain

Iimagine he was the most unpopular kid in high school," Eden said, looking up at the younger agent while rubbing his wrist.

Mark smiled and nodded in agreement. "I imagine so. In his defense—"

"There's no defense," Eden interrupted, shaking his head. "I've seen his type before. In Nam, someone would have rolled a grenade under his cot." With penetrating eyes, he looked up at the younger agent. "He shares personality traits with Winston Tucker; Machiavellian in that the end justifies the means. Tucker manipulated people for his own self-interest. He didn't care what pain and suffering he caused as long he got what he wanted."

"You don't know the half of it, Mr. Cain. We've been putting the pieces of this puzzle together for more than two years and were about to move in on him when somebody killed him. A fitting end, I might add."

"There is no end," Eden said with a sigh. "His evil will persist. Someone will take his place. Nature abhors a vacuum. Jackals have no morality. Militarily and politically, he was relentless in pursuing power and used any means to get it. He was Nixon's henchman and killed anyone and everyone who stood in the way of him gaining and keeping power." He looked into the eyes of the younger agent. "He needed killing."

Mark Johnson searched Eden's face, seemingly at a loss for words. "That may be, Mr. Cain. That's for a higher power to decide."

"If you believe in that sort of thing, then it appears that decision was made and carried out," Eden said.

"I was referring to jurisprudence. I believe the law should determine what's legal and what punishment is appropriate."

"It's that philosophy that allows people like Tucker to go unpunished."

"If you're arguing in favor of vigilantism, there's no legal authority for preventing, investigating, or punishing what you perceive as a crime. Chaos would result."

"It doesn't work," Sidney said as she approached the booth. "Sorry to interrupt. I couldn't help overhearing your discussion. Vigilante justice has never worked from a societal point of view. It has a history that goes back to the dawn of humankind. It's what gave rise to the establishment of law and order."

"Amen, sister," Mark managed as he turned to welcome Sidney with a smile.

Sidney gently adjusted the gauze wrapped around Mark's head. "You should be resting, not giving lectures on jurisprudence. And I'm not your sister. You should be thankful for that."

Eden nodded his acceptance of their arguments, then offered, "Things done outside the law are not necessarily in violation of the law. In part, that's why we have people like you."

"Point taken," Sidney said. "As such, I would strongly advise you to say no more. Otherwise, you'll have to hire a person like me to defend you against a person like him." She gestured toward Mark with her thumb.

The door to the cafe burst open as the older agent pushed Sam inside. Sidney stepped to the center of the room and held her arm out with her palm up. "Agent Kohler, since there has been no indictment issued for my client," Sidney said, motioning toward her father. "I'd like to request that he be released on personal recognizance. The defendant has given his word he'll show up in court when and if charges are brought forth."

"Personal bond; you must be joking given his criminal history."

"I'll petition for writ of habeas corpus and bring a civil action against you for unlawful detention of my client." Sidney smiled.

"You're going to challenge the application of federal laws that says he can't assault a federal officer?"

"You hadn't identified yourself as such. My client was defending himself and his property."

Heads and eyes of everyone in the cafe now shifted toward the older agent as if they were watching a tennis match.

"Look," Agent Kohler said smugly, "we can play this game all day and the result will be the same, Missy. I advise you to stand down before I charge you with obstruction."

"How many times have I asked you not to call me that?" Sidney said, thrusting her hands on her hips.

"Didn't I tell you to stop disrespecting my daughter?" Sam lowered his jaw and turned toward the agent, his eyes ablaze.

The waitress stepped in front of the older agent, holding a plate of gooey apple pie from underneath, her hand poised to throw. "Who ordered pie?"

"I did," Eden said quickly. "Thank you, Tammy."

Tammy Jo Martin

"There you go, hon. Enjoy," Tammy Jo said as she placed the pie in front of Eden, her eyes fixed on his.

Silence hung in the air of the sad cafe. The waitress and the dishwasher stared at each other.

"I think our time is running out," Eden said barely above a whisper. "It's time to get our world in order. Put the past behind us without making anymore. If you don't mind my company, Ida Faye, I mean Tammy Jo, I'd like to spend whatever future remains with you."

"I never was any good at being alone," Tammy Jo responded immediately with a catch in her voice.

"There is a nepotism clause in your contracts that clearly prevents the hiring of a close relative in order to maintain employee morale and productivity and to ensure that other employees in the cafe feel fairly treated," Joe said from behind the cash register, where he had been listening to their conversation.

"There are no other employees, Joe. And besides that, we quit," Tammy Jo said without turning to look at him.

"A two-week notice is required. Without it, I will be forced to terminate you immediately and withhold pay and benefits."

"Sounds like wrongful termination," Sidney said for everyone to hear. "It sounds retaliatory."

"You don't know what wrongful termination is," Jessica said as she stood up from across the room. "I lost my father thirteen years ago." Her eyes were glassy with tears. "It has taken me all those years to find him, and now—"

"And now you've found each other, and nothing will keep you apart," Tammy Jo said, turning toward the pretty lady. She, too, was crying. "That's a promise. I lost one daughter, and I'm not about to lose another."

"I'm tired," Eden said to Jessica. "I'm tired of running, tired of moving, of saying goodbye to people who have been good to me. I'm tired of being afraid they would find me before I had a chance to explain to you what happened and why."

"Well, now I know what happened, Dad," Jessica said, wiping tears away and stepping to the center of the room. "It doesn't matter anymore. I never met my biological father; I never knew him. When I got over the initial shock, I realized what I had done. I pushed you away, and that wasn't fair. You've been tortured most of your life. All you wanted was forgiveness, and I hesitated. I'm sorry. I don't want to lose you again."

"The audience is getting all misty-eyed," the older agent said with a sarcastic grin. He turned toward the old man in the booth and held out his hand. "Eden Cain, This Is Your Life, and I'm your host, Ralph Edwards." He shook his head. "This little retrospective of your life. Mr. Cain, is sickeningly sentimental, don't you think? The crying by the females on cue is terribly overdone."

"I think Ms. Martindale hit the nail on the head," Sam said a little too loudly. "You really are a screwed-up piece of work, a bully who somehow got through the psychological profiling at the Academy. I'd be willing to bet you kick dogs and are mean to little children."

"That's enough, Pop," Sidney cautioned.

Mark closed his eyes and held his bandaged head in his hand as if anticipating an unavoidable explosion.

Agent Kohler puffed up like a hot sausage on a grill, his face reddened, his chest about to split open.

"Somebody stick a fork in him," Tammy Jo said as she wiped a tear from her face. "I think he's done."

"Dawson—" Kohler shouted.

"Hal," Mark yelled back. "Why don't you go back to headquarters? See what we can salvage. Better yet, see if we need to cover our butts. You know Washington—if things go south, they'll throw us under the bus. I'll hitch a ride with Mr. Dawson and his daughter to the nearest hospital, get checked out, and catch up with you later in Fort Collins."

Hal studied Mark for several seconds. His eyes darted between Mark and Sidney.

"I can take you to a hospital," he said with a smile.

"Time is of the essence here, Hal. No need in both of us hanging around an emergency room for several hours. Get back to headquarters and protect our files."

"You said the Suburban won't start."

"Try putting the ground back on the negative battery terminal," Eden said with a neutral smile.

Agent Kohler glared at him. "What about Cain?" he asked with a furrowed brow.

"Boss, we'll be the laughingstock of the agency if they find out our car was stolen. He brought it back. He's as clean as a new bride. Give the old man a break."

"And Dawson, what do we do with him? The man assaulted me."

"Miss Dawson will win that one. You should have properly identified yourself. No matter. As you said, we've got bigger fish to fry. You know the FBI will try to muscle us out and take credit for everything we've done. All this," Mark said, waving his arm in an arc around the cafe, "is just static, a distraction."

The older agent seemed to ponder what the younger agent had said. He rubbed his chin, looked down at the floor, and slowly shook his head. "I'm not buying any of it," he said, looking up and directly at Mark in an attempt to take charge. "That old man," he said, gesturing toward Eden, "is dirty and you know it. For the time being, I'll put him in the custody of the waitress. It'll be like two cats in a sack. In a few hours, he'll wish for solitary confinement in a maximum-security prison. As for Dawson, I'll remand him to Ms. Doe Eyes over there," he said, pointing at Jessica. "Connubial bliss is harsher than any sentence a judge would hand down. As for you, partner, I'm putting you under the care of Meddling Missy over there." He tossed his thumb over his shoulder toward Sidney. "That leaves me and the cook, and he's just plain looney." He took a deep breath and let it out slowly as he shook his head. "You're right,

partner. This is all static." He was quiet for a long moment.
"To hell with this noise! I'll see you back at headquarters." The
older agent smiled at the speechless gathering of onlookers,
nodded his goodbye, and left the cafe.

The group silently watched as Agent Kohler connected the
battery on the Suburban. He lurched onto the highway and
disappeared to the east.

"I'll miss that man," Tammy Jo said with an air of finality.
"Just like I'd miss a boil on my butt."

⊷►═◈═◄⊶

Jessica Martindale

A light breeze tossed wisps of hair across Jessica's face as she
and her father sat together on the front step of the cafe. The
chill of melting hail caused her to embrace her arms against
her sides. Their shoes were ringed with mud and pea gravel.
The sky gave no hint of the violence it had sent down only a
couple of hours earlier. Neither of them talked. Instead, they
listened. The tumbleweeds scratched nervously against the side
of the cafe. Birds called happily as if nothing had happened. A
jet plane was a speck ahead of its contrail streaked from east to
west, a rolling thunder well behind it.

Jessica was the first to speak. "Obviously, you've been erased
from their system. I wonder when that happened."

Eden shrugged. "Maybe it's best I don't know. I knew
from the start that the only way to survive was to reject their
so-called witness protection program. I developed my own,
and it kept me alive long enough to find Tucker. These guys
were DEA. I have no idea where they are on the totem pole of

intelligence agencies and if their information is correct. Tucker had his own covert group that operated both inside and outside the spider web of government intel groups. I was one of them." He paused. "There are over fifty intelligence agencies under our government umbrella. I find it hard to believe that I have been erased from their entire system."

Jessica continued to stare into the distance. "So, you're going to continue to run?" she asked without looking at him.

"No, I'm done," he said with a tight smile. "Tucker is dead, and I found you. Mission accomplished."

"I'm glad he's dead," she said, turning to look directly at him. "He was a monster that deserved to die."

Eden nodded his acceptance and turned to face her. He studied her eyes. "I guess you know by now that I've killed a lot of men. All of them faceless, except one. Your father's face haunts me every day. I'll take that image to the grave."

"Did you know him?" Jessica asked, still looking at him.

"No. I was a door gunner in a Huey. Our job, so I thought, was to rescue downed American pilots in Laos and North Vietnam, sometimes northern Cambodia, all the places we weren't supposed to be. It seldom, if ever worked. What we really were doing was ground truthing their locations, sometimes keeping Charlie at bay until the scorched-earth brigade swooped in and did the sterilization from the coordinates we called in. All this was to protect a president who lied to Congress and the American people. He couldn't have Charlie parading a captured American pilot through the streets of Hanoi on the five o'clock news and get reelected."

Eden paused and looked toward the horizon, remembering. "In your father's case, the VC were all over him. We were ordered to do the sterilization. We were all shot to hell; half our crew was dead or wounded. Incoming was tearing us apart. We were so close, I could read the name Hallingbye on his flight suit. I see him every day of my life, reaching out to me, running for his life, mud flying from his boots, his eyes locked on mine, pleading. I see the desperation, then the shock of betrayal." He paused for a long moment then looked directly at her. "Every day of my life."

Jessica put her arm around him and pulled him against her.

"It never got better for me," he said, looking down. "Only worse; I didn't end up in Iowa by chance. Believe me, I didn't have a plan. There was no mission. I didn't know what was right and what needed to be done. I had no idea what to do. I think I wanted forgiveness and believed your mom needed resolution. We both needed closure. I found that being close to you and your mom somehow brought me relief. I didn't plan on loving her; it just happened. The memories, the visions, the guilt would disappear as long as I was close to her."

"Did she know?"

"I think she did. I suspected she knew before the explosion. She always knew, and she accepted it. She didn't hold me responsible. She loved me. She was just unsure of the details until the morning she died."

"What?" Jessica said, startled. She tipped her head sideways like a robin listening for a worm. Her brow was furrowed and her mouth appeared as if she had tasted something unpleasant.

Eden was not looking at her. He was looking down, studying his dirty running shoes. "It had been thirty-two years of nightmares, self-blame, and deception that boiled to the surface when I was summoned to testify—"

"Dad," Jessica interrupted.

Eden ignored her. "She told me she had dreamed that your father and I knew each other. She admitted that she knew I had not come to Keotonka by chance. She knew. She always knew. She didn't want the details. Your mother didn't want anything to come between us. She wanted us to grow old together. Elizabeth loved me in spite of what I had done, and she was killed instead of me." He placed his hand over his mouth and clamped his eyes shut. "Do you have any idea how that made me feel?" he said quickly, fighting back tears.

"Dad," Jessica shouted and stood up and faced him. "What are you talking about? Mom's not dead. She's getting up there in years, but she's alive and well."

Eden lifted his head and stared at his daughter. His face was blank.

"Did you hear me?" Jessica demanded. "Mom's alive. She's a little hard of hearing, having had one of her eardrums ruptured from the explosion, otherwise—"

Eden shook his head in disbelief. His eyes were glassy as tears welled up. "How?" he managed. His lower lip quivered. "Her boot." He paused. "My boot," he corrected. "I saw the smoldering irrigation boot she had been wearing lying in the gravel driveway. Flaming debris was raining down around me. I could feel the sear of the flames that swept over my body. I saw the door of my pickup smoking a few feet in front of me.

I heard the high-pitched ringing in my ears and the squeals of frightened hogs. How," he repeated, then hesitated, "could she have survived?"

"Mom had ducked into the old milking parlor to change the boots she was wearing. She was having trouble walking in your giant clodhoppers. She had just changed boots when your pickup blew up in the alleyway of the barn. She was knocked unconscious into the feed bunk in front of the stanchions. That's where Hobart Lucritz found her when the volunteer fire department arrived. Her hair was singed, and she had inhaled too much smoke. Other than that, she was okay. She refused to go to the hospital and insisted that she stay there to wait for your return. She's still there. She's still waiting. It's been thirteen years, Dad. Thirteen years to the day. You need to come home now."

"Elizabeth is alive?" he whispered.

"Yes." She said no more. Instead, she studied his face. His lips quivered, and his cloudy eyes darted spasmodically back and forth. The tears finally came, finding erratic paths downward through the white stubble on his cheeks. He made no attempt to wipe them away. The confusion of the unexpected revelation seemed to seize him by the shoulders, and he began to shake uncontrollably as he brought his hands to his face to cover his embarrassment. He shook his head rhythmically. A mixture of pain and overwhelming happiness appeared on his face. Speechless, he slumped forward with his hands cupped around his face, his chest heaving with unrestrained sobs. Jessica put her arm around him and felt her tears of sympathy running down her cheeks.

"All this time," he said, his voice muffled by his hands.

She did not know how to respond. Instead, she sat back down and pulled him tightly toward her as if she was a mother with an injured child. She could not imagine his pain.

"All this time," he repeated.

Jessica shushed him as if he were a child. She turned her head away in an attempt to calm the unease of her emotions. She tried to swallow the lump in her throat as she brushed back her tears. She handed him the tattered and burnt score sheet the waitress had given her. "I lost both of my fathers. I'll be damned if I lose you again."

Eden sat up and put his arm around her and pulled her tight against his shoulder. "I'm back, sweetie, if you'll have me?"

"Of course I will. I came here looking for you. I somehow sensed you'd be close by, given this is the anniversary of the explosion and Tucker's ranch is just north of here. I don't want anything to come between us ever again."

A comfortable silence seemed to surround them. There was no need talk or explain. The details would come later. The years needed sorting. They sat there for what seemed an eternity. Finally, Jessica cleared her throat and started, "Did you—"

"No," Eden said immediately, looking directly into her eyes. "I didn't kill Tucker. God knows I wanted to. That's why I came here. Someone else," he diverted his gaze, "saved me the trouble. Make no mistake," he said, staring back into his daughter's eyes, "I would have if given the chance. That opportunity just hadn't presented itself, and for that I'm deeply regretful. My hate for that man and my love for you have kept me going for the past thirteen years. Both of those needs satisfied in a single day. Who would have thought?" he asked somewhat nervously.

"You're wondering if I killed him," Jessica said.

"That's not a question a father asks his daughter."

"He robbed me of the only father I ever knew. My answer is the same as yours. But was I capable? I don't know. I guess we'll never know."

Jessica rested her head on his shoulder. "Now what?" she asked. "Where do we go from here?"

"Home," he said softly with assurance. Eden looked down at his shaking left hand. "Time has a way of catching up with us. Sure as we're sitting here, the sun is going to set."

She lifted her head and looked into his eyes with puzzlement.

"It always does, sweetie. We can't stop that. What we can do is grab hold of the hope that comes with each new day. Right now, I can't begin to tell you how much I'm looking forward to tomorrow."

"Me too, Dad," Jessica said softly. "Me too."

Sidney Dawson

"Meddling Missy, can you believe he called me that?" Sidney said to Mark. They stood together at the cafe window, looking out at the parking lot and the old man and his daughter who sat talking on the front step.

"Hal is a take-charge sort of guy who doesn't tolerate anyone who questions his authority," Mark said. "Once you get to know him, you discover that he really is evil, mean, and nasty inside. You just saw his soft side. When he can't win an argument, he takes command, barks out orders, and leaves. That's just his way. Most people can't stand him."

Sidney laughed. "Oh, I didn't even know him and found him difficult."

"I have to tell you, the man doesn't forget a name, a place, or a date. He was instrumental in putting the agency's case together on Tucker. We were within days of taking him and his cartel down when we heard that someone had beaten us to the punch."

"Cartel, I don't understand. Do you mean as in a drug cartel?" Sidney asked.

"He didn't make billions raising cattle." Mark reached for Sidney's arm. "Can we sit down for a minute? I'm feeling a little woozy."

"Of course we can." Sidney guided him to a table, pulled out a chair, and helped him sit down.

"Here you go, hon," the waitress said, suddenly appearing with a glass and the last of the cafe's water in a pitcher.

"Thank you, Ms. Martin," Mark said, offering a pained smile.

"You're welcome," Tammy Jo said. She leaned into Sidney and whispered, "This one's got manners, but a Bracco Italiano would be an easier keeper." She winked at Sidney before turning and scuffing her way back to the counter.

"Tucker's shipping company was huge, with tentacles into a dozen or more related industries, here, South and Central America, and in Mexico," Mark explained. "It was all a cover for one of the largest drug-smuggling rings in the country. I worked on this case in the New Orleans Division. That's where I first met Hal. New Orleans was where Tucker headquartered his business, although he ran it mostly from his ranch here in Wyoming. Long story short, the freight and hauling business was a front for one of the most elaborate drug and money-laundering schemes this country has ever seen. All the components were there: placement, layering, integration all built into a legitimate business enterprise. Dirty money found its way into the pockets of high-ranking politicos from one end of this country to the other." Mark placed the glass of water against his forehead.

"Are you all right?" Sidney asked. She pushed her glasses up on the bridge of her nose, leaned toward Mark, and stared into his eyes.

"I have the headache from hell," he said, sliding the glass of water across his forehead. "Has anyone ever told you that you have beautiful eyes?"

"Just my ophthalmologist," she said. "I'm pretty sure he tells that to all his patients," she added.

"Her husband," Mark nodded toward the waitress, "now deceased, was a courier for the cartel who got greedy. He was skimming product and had his own competing company manufacturing methamphetamine in the Texas Panhandle and was in the process of branching out into New Mexico, Oklahoma, and Colorado."

"So," Sidney said suddenly, "where's all this going?"

"Well, we were coordinating a final push to take Tucker down when we learned somebody had killed him. We needed to get on site before the cluster of federals got there and mucked up the—"

"No," Sidney said, looking into his eyes. "Where's this thing between us going?"

"Oh, I was sort of hoping that you would take me to a hospital so I could get my head examined. I'm having trouble thinking rationally."

"Get in line, buster; me, too."

"So, it's not just me?" Mark asked with a note of seriousness.

"It's not just you." She took a deep breath and swallowed hard. "There must be something in the water. I'm coming down with it too."

"Seems a little impractical, doesn't it?"

"It does."

"Is it hot in here?" Mark asked without taking his eyes from hers.

"You're not a serial killer, are you?"

"I could be if you want."

"You guys are foggin' up the windows," the waitress said as she suddenly appeared at their table. "Maybe you need to get a room."

"Get dressed, you two," Sam said from behind the waitress. "We're leaving."

Sidney gently took the glass of water from Mark's hand and leaned in to him. "I like you, Mark Johnson," she whispered, her lips sensuously brushing his ear.

⊷══◉ ✖ ◉══⊶

Sam Dawson

Sam looked around him and concluded that his life was like Wyoming weather, always extreme. It seldom just rained or just snowed. It either poured down in bucketfuls or blew a blizzard, or even a tornado. It never did anything nice and easy. He didn't just find lost cemeteries; he found killing fields, mass murderers, crazed serial killers, outlaws, and psychotic spies—nobody nice and easy. This day had been no exception. A mild, sunny summer's day; a father-daughter outing that within hours turned into the typical rip-roaring hurricane. He had come to realize that Wyoming has the lowest population density in the country for a reason. The weather is harsh. He liked it that way. Life around him was harsh. Maybe he liked it that way too.

"Excuse me," Sam said as he stepped out the door of the cafe. "Jessica, if you're ready, we're about to leave." As soon as he said it, he saw the storm clouds forming above them. Both Jessica and her father looked up at him as if he were the Grim Reaper sent to collect their souls and guide them to some afterlife. "If you're ready," he offered lamely.

"It's been thirteen years, Sam," Jessica said, her voice pleading as she looked at Sam incredulously.

Sam's eyes shifted to the old man. "You're welcome to come with us, Eden. It'll be a tight fit. I think we can squeeze you in." His lack of sincerity was obvious, and he was immediately sorry for his unenthusiastic offer. His selfish desire to have Jessica's undivided attention was obvious. "I'm serious," he added as if it were the punch line to a joke that no one understood. He was digging a hole. Sam looked to Jessica for support. He found none. She had the confused look of a person given a difficult choice.

No one spoke for a long moment. Both Jessica and Eden looked as if they had been crying. "Thank you, Sam," Eden finally said with the sincerity that Sam had omitted, his eyes glassy. "I appreciate the offer, but I just found out my wife…" He began to sob deeply. Jessica put her arm around him. "Who I thought was dead for the past thirteen years," he continued weakly, "is still alive."

Sam did not know what to say. He stood there awkwardly. *Nothing ever happens nice and easy in Wyoming,* he thought.

Eden shook his head slowly. "I have some things that need to be straightened out here before I leave, commitments I've made, and promises that have to be broken." He turned to look up at Sam. He stopped short of facing him. His attention was focused on Tammy Jo, who stood behind Sam, a look of total dejection on her face. For once, she had nothing to say. Her disheartenment caught in her throat, her mouth gravely open.

"Pop," Sidney called out as she stepped out the cafe door onto the crowded porch. "We need to go. I'm worried about Mark. I think he likes me." The breeze caught her words as the door snapped shut behind her, strands of hair stuck in the corner of her mouth. Sidney scanned the faces of the four people who looked at her as if she was a mediator sent to settle a dispute. "What?" she asked.

A chorus of sirens caused everyone to look toward the road. The red and blue flashing lights of emergency vehicles in the distance streamed toward them. They watched silently as the convoy consumed the highway that disappeared beneath their hungry grills. Gravel crunched and popped under their tires as they slid to a stop in front of the cafe. Sam sensed there was trouble ahead. Life indeed was like Wyoming weather. Nothing ever happens nice and easy.

EPILOGUE

Eden Cain

Time does not heal. Eden would never forget, never forgive. The distractions of life helped him make it through each day. Each night came abruptly and with it the horrors of a forgotten war and the aftermath of his attempted redemption. There was no absolution. Words of forgiveness were artificial and without merit, topical salve applied to mortal wounds. His hate dissolved as slowly as the corpses of those from whom he sought vengeance.

Elizabeth remained the love of his life. She had dedicated every day to finding him. She attacked each of those days with the same unyielding determination she had displayed when searching for her first husband who was lost in Vietnam—years of frustrating dead ends. Eden was thankful for her every day. She took away the regrets of his sorrowful life. Their love for each other was unmatched. They had wanted to grow old together, to bask in the comforts of each other's arms, to remember, and never to be apart again. She was destined to be on her own.

He resented the government's attempts to kill him and was embittered by the loss of so many years taken from him and Elizabeth. Most of all he resented the disease that stole what time he had left. The memories were fading. Twenty years had passed since the day he thought she was killed. Thirteen of those years were lost to fear and hate. He cherished the remaining seven years he spent with the woman he loved. The woman who had saved him when all else seemed lost. He now saw her, as she was, without age, smiling her toothy grin that took away his anger and fear. He often heard her voice on the breeze of a summer's night, as plaintive as his own, telling him to take a breath. Sometimes he wept with the realization that their time together was becoming a memory, smooth around the edges, the color washed and the sound muted. He wished he believed, as others did, that they would be reunited in an afterlife. War had stolen his religion, his politics, and his faith in man.

Shortly after being reunited with Elizabeth, he was diagnosed with late-stage Parkinson's and complicated by Lewy body dementia. His health had deteriorated rapidly. Tremors, rigidity, shuffling, stooped gait, falling, difficulty swallowing, and inability to sleep were motor dysfunctions that he tolerated. His loss of cognition was not. Dementia was frightening. Short-term memory loss was frustrating. Long-term recall was most troubling. His inability to put events into proper time frames and to recognize familiar faces made him angry. There was no cure. Eden never complained. There was no need. He accepted with stoic indignation what was to come.

Elizabeth, on the other hand, continued to fight it bitterly, always silently. She resented losing the future. The past had robbed them both of time. For years, Elizabeth hauled him to specialists in Des Moines and Iowa City, later to Rochester, and Baltimore. They tried the VA, where they were told there was no record of him ever being in the service, and they refused to see him. The neurologists at the Mayo Clinic loaded him up with L-Dopa and the latest dopamine agonists. When they saw the doctors at Johns Hopkins, they estimated his life expectancy at less than a year. Eighteen months later, Eden Cain, holding his wife's hand, simply stopped breathing and died peacefully at home in Iowa. He knew her and knew he loved her. Elizabeth wept deeply and sat with him for more than an hour as she gently traced his ruined life along the bluish veins of his hand.

Eden was buried in the family plot overlooking Keotonka and the picturesque Des Moines River valley. Elizabeth's request for a military honor guard was denied. A light breeze whispered through the leaves of the hardwoods like a wake from a passing ship, and the leaves clattered soothingly as Elizabeth stood looking down, remembering.

-»=● ✳ ●=«-

Tammy Jo Martin

The complications were many by the time Tammy Jo settled in Montana. Winter came early. The wind took her past and swirled it like snow drifting across a highway. It was the future without Eden that stung her face and melted on her tongue. She found redemption in Montana. It was her dream, and she did it on her own with determination. Down-home wisdom and unrefined humor combined with gentle persuasion were the keys to her establishment as a local personality. Money was not an issue. She had found the perfect setup in the foothills of the Bear Tooth Mountains midway between Red Lodge and Columbus. An indoor riding arena, a ranch-style home with all the amenities, productive subirrigated pastures, and a twelve-horse stable. She taught barrel racing and equitation to aspiring young women who saw the sweetness in her heart.

When Agent Kohler was attempting to take Mark to the Torrington clinic, he used the satellite phone in the Suburban to call the sheriff for an update on the Robinson murder. The sheriff informed him that the security camera footage at the Lamplighter Motel in Lusk showed Joe Dobransky, spatula in his hand, entering and leaving Darrell Robinson's room just before dawn the morning Darrell was found beaten to death with something sharp and heavy.

In a show of force, local law enforcement officials skidded into the parking lot of the cafe to arrest Joe at the moment Tammy Jo learned that Eden would not be joining her in Montana. When taken into custody, Joe began his bitter rant against modern society, repeatedly referring to people as sheep. He pleaded self-defense and claimed that Robinson had threatened him with a gun when Joe accused him of beating Ida Faye. Joe admitted he was deeply in love with Ida Faye Mensinger, a.k.a. Tammy Jo Martin, the former Tammy Jo Robinson. As he often did, Joe had followed her home on the night she was beaten. He heard the fight and saw Ida Faye, bleeding, chase a man from her rental. Joe followed the pickup with Texas plates to the Lamplighter Motel in Lusk. He told police that he didn't know what to do, so he drove to his home in Lusk. Unable to sleep, Joe went to the cafe and scraped the grill with his spatula, his anger mounting. He left the cafe shortly after 4:00 a.m. and drove back to the Lamplighter to confront the man.

Secretly, Tammy Jo was saddened by his arrest and infatuation with her. She knew that Darrell would eventually have killed her. Joe had freed her from her nightmarish past and allowed for a future without fear. The court ordered a psychiatric evaluation for the short-order cook who had been the human resources director for Black Rock Carbon, a Thunder Basin coal mine near Wright, Wyoming. He had been fired for unspecified reasons.

The gun found in Darrell's room yielded a ballistic match to the slugs dug out of Winston Tucker's body. Analysis found Darrell's fingerprints on the gun, along with the partial print of an unidentified person, most likely female based on the print's ridge density.

Tammy Jo knew Eden had been on a mission. She had always known. Tucker and his entourage of bodyguards had stopped at the cafe on several occasions over the years. Tucker was partial to vanilla malts and never tipped. When she challenged him one day, stating that it was customary for patrons to leave tips, he responded by telling her if she wanted tips she could get all she wanted at the circumcision ward at the hospital. She secretly spat in his malt.

When Tucker showed up at the cafe, Eden would become rigidly catatonic with rage, fists at his sides, face reddened, jaw set, about to explode, and uncommunicative. Tammy Jo did not know the particulars. She knew it was Tucker that elicited the anger. It was obvious to her that Eden was biding his time to square things with Tucker and that he was unavailable to her until his mission was accomplished.

Darrell's arrival was both unexpected and fortuitous. The beating she took was worth the outcome. He had always been insanely jealous when anyone showed an interest in her.

When Darrell boasted that he was on his way to meet with his business associate, Tucker, she quickly fabricated a story about Tucker's uninvited sexual advances and attempted rape. She told Darrell the gun he had found in her rental was purchased for protection against that perverted old man.

As Darrell's lawful wife and heir, Tammy Jo convinced the sheriff that Darrell's fancy pickup belonged to her. She drove nonstop to Texas and dragged out the trunks of cash Darrell kept in his secret storm shelter below an empty grain bin behind his single-wide trailer. She never bothered to count the money. There was no need. She had become a multimillionaire.

Tammy Jo's angry daughter was arrested east of Valentine, Nebraska, but not before wounding a state trooper. She would not be eligible for parole for a very long time. If Tammy Jo was still alive when that time came, she would try again.

She shared Eden's last days with his wife and daughter. Tammy Jo, Elizabeth, and Jessica loved him and were at his side when he died from aspiration pneumonia. They held each other and sobbed deeply, each embarrassed by their emotions for the man they loved. Elizabeth asked to be alone with him as she held his hand and wept. In the hallway outside his bedroom, Tammy Jo closed her eyes, pressed her lips together, and remembered.

--|==◉ ✷ ◎==|--

Jessica Martindale

At night, in Sam's log home, especially in midwinter, when the Wyoming wind moaned through the pines surrounding the house, their needles stiffened with ice; when the windows seemed to bend against a frozen sky, Jessica would awaken and listen to the voices from the past. Mostly unintelligible, they sounded like someone trying to find a station on a radio. Half asleep, she would cock her head and hold her breath as she tried to make out the words. She would hear her name. The voices were a mixture of those dead and those living. There were no condemnations, no cries for help, just snippets of familiar voices that competed with the static of crystallized snow against the window panes. She would slip quietly from bed, wrap herself in a blanket, and make her way to the kitchen, where she would stare out across the dark valley. The aspens reflected the moon's light from their bony limbs as they writhed in the wind in their attempt to hold up the darkness. She would make a cup of tea and sit at the kitchen table holding the warm cup with both hands, listening, waiting for the liquid sun to pour across the floor. Seven years, almost eight gone in an instant.

Toward the end, her father could not find the words. Eventually, the memories that made him who he was slipped away like thieves in the night. The things forgotten were no longer poised on the tip of his tongue. No more describing the nameless object or its use. No more telling who the person was related to, did for a living, or looked like. The names were just gone. Eden's world was a blank page. Death was a gift. The hurt for the living was not being remembered.

Her mother sold the farm and moved into a retirement facility within walking distance of the cemetery where Eden was buried. Jessica called her on Sunday mornings and listened. The twins would visit her on holidays and sometimes drive up to Wyoming from Boulder on weekends. Both were attorneys for the Environmental Legal Defense Fund and passionate about their work to combat climate change. She no longer argued with them. She smiled and changed the subject. Her days of kicking and scratching her way to the top were over. She had invested wisely and retired early. Jessica was happy. The past sometimes competed with the present for her favors. The choices she had made seven years ago usually won.

She had been very much in love with Sam. Sometimes, when the sun was a pink line on the horizon, she missed the corporate fray and the excitement of winning, never the resentment of losses. That longing could not compete with Sam when he would shuffle out to the kitchen with a smile and his hair mussed like a child. She would beam with excitement for the coming day. Life had been good. They talked of marriage and somehow never got around to it. They were going to be married on the deck of the log home Sam had built. The boys would give her away, and Sidney would be her maid of honor. Sam's best friend, the former sheriff, Harrison O'Malley, was to be his best man. It would be a happy occasion. It never happened. Instead, they loved each other until the love ran out. The friendship, however, was forever. She finally bought a townhouse in Fort Collins to be closer to her boys, who remained single and uniquely devoted to each other. She and Sam dated regularly and enjoyed what Cheyenne, Laramie, and Fort Collins had to offer as they slowly drifted apart. Jessica often wished for the past. Facing the future alone frightened her. She remembered.

Sidney Dawson

Sidney's maternal ancestors from central Europe and her father's people from England were the carriers. Both her mom and dad were autosomal recessives for the mutation that she had inherited. There was no cure for Usher Syndrome, the disease that caused deafness and blindness. Of the three types, she had the rarest, Type III. Fortunately, she was in the half of Type III mutants that did not have balance issues. She could manage the deafness for now. The retinitis pigmentosa, however, was more debilitating. Both conditions were progressive, and none of her doctors were willing to offer a positive prognosis.

Mark had listened patiently as Sidney explained the physical limitations of her condition. The long-term implications were obvious. He never blinked when she told him she'd had a precautionary tubal ligation in her mid-twenties. He loved her. He never told her that he would take care of her. He was too smart for that. Instead, he said he wanted to be her partner, both her life partner and in her profession. That was seven years ago, shortly after they had met at the cafe.

Sam refused to give her away. Instead, he said she was on loan to Mark. She could not be given away. There was no transfer of ownership, legally or spiritually. She was not chattel, not something possessed. Agent Harold Kohler, who had been Mark's partner and mentor for more than two years, served as best man. He repeatedly referred to Sidney as Missy and threatened Sam with arrest if he ever touched him again. Sidney saw Hal's soft side and kissed him gently on the cheek and thanked him for being there for his partner, now *her* partner. Jessica was her maid of honor. The honeymoon was perpetual. Mark left the DEA and became the junior partner in Sidney's Cheyenne-based law practice, Dawson and Johnson, Attorneys-at-Law. Sidney partially solved her future problem of not being able to drive by buying a historic Victorian building in downtown Cheyenne. Their offices were on the first floor and the upstairs was their comfortable home.

Her dad taught Mark to fly-fish, and it became a passion with Mark. The four of them enjoyed their annual breakfast in the aspens every fall. Sam would cook his traditional green chili burrito on the tailgate of the Willys in some remote area of the Medicine Bow National Forest with yellow, gold, and red aspen leaves fluttering in the background. Fishing the beaver ponds for brook trout was dessert. Sidney did not let on that she had lost most of her color vision and her peripheral vision had reduced her field of view to a tunnel. Still, she was happy and thankful she had Mark's love and support. The added bonus was that he had never tried to kill her.

Sidney continued to subsidize her independent publishing house in Denver. Book sales spiraled downward nationally. The big publishing houses continued to consolidate, integrate, and concentrate on their stable of popular authors while the public continued its downward trend of not reading books. Audio books and celebrity "kiss and tell" disclosures were read on phones and tablets, mediums not suitable for coffee table picture books of lost and forgotten cemeteries. Sam was clueless. His stunningly beautiful photography had little or no retail outlet as independent bookstores continued to disappear.

Her publisher, Pat Bateson, reluctantly sent fudged royalty checks to Sam twice a year. Jessica had been quietly skeptical. She smiled politely at Sam's amazing book sales and never questioned Sidney's business plan.

After Jessica had moved to Ft. Collins, Tammy Jo and Sidney conspired long-distance for months on dog breeds. Tammy Jo had returned to her roots with an Australian Shepherd. She continued to push for a Bracco Italiano for Sam. In the end, she agreed with Sidney that it was a hunting dog and needed to be used as such. Sidney and Mark surprised Sam with a Bloodhound puppy for Sam's birthday in February. He named the dog L3, Elle for short, since L3 sounded like Elsie pronounced with a lisp.

In spite of her physical maladies and her father's numerous faults and misadventures, she believed life was very good, and she strove constantly to present a positive outlook for the future. Sometimes at night when she removed her hearing aids and downtown traffic ceased its monotonous hum, her breath came haltingly as she fought the urge to cry in part for happiness, in part for loss of the past. She remembered.

⊷⊷�֍⊷⊷

Sam Dawson

Sam was unsure why he and Jessica never married. They were happy and in love. It seemed there was something undetermined and indescribable that surrounded them, a reversed polarity that pushed them apart. Unlike his marriage, where the reasons were stamped as irreconcilable differences, he was unable to define what separated them. He and Marcie had divorced more than three decades earlier after a brief six years of sharing their youth together. She had spent those years attempting to transform him into someone her parents would accept. In their eyes, he did not deserve a woman like Marcie. He had finally agreed.

Annie was the love of his life. He mourned the fact that it was a previous life. His missed her, and seldom a day passed without him thinking of her and the mistakes he had made in expressing his love for her. He was afraid his memories of her would fade and somehow vanish forever. He wished he would have said the things to her that he felt in his heart instead of his feeble attempts to tell her how much he loved her. She was a hero who had given him the greatest gift of all by saving his daughter's life. How could he forget her? The grief in his heart was as strong as it ever was. Remembering and imagining put breath back into her life.

All this was the past and could not be erased. His life with Jessica started as magical. It was as if they had been searching desperately for each other for a long time, a time disturbed by their past loves and lives. Seldom a cross word was spoken. They were genuinely happy, always glad to see each other. She was the farmer's granddaughter—Sam worried that she would miss her midwestern roots, although she seemed to adjust easily to her new life in the mountains of Wyoming, a place she had dreamed of most of her life. He failed to anticipate her need for the hustle and bustle of corporate leadership. Instead, Sam complicated his life by making her life simpler. He believed that might have been the underlying reason for their dissolution. While he continued to enjoy her friendship, something seemed to be missing. At night, alone, the wind pulling the fireplace flames upward and the pine boughs scraping at the windows, he wondered if the infatuation had run its course, or had she finally seen through him and discovered his private obsession with a past love and that he was not who she thought he was?

Sam suspected that Sidney was subsidizing his art. He was too embarrassed to talk with her about it. Instead, he held on to the belief that his next book would be the breakthrough bestseller that would redeem him professionally and reward her faith in him. He knew he was a hopeless dreamer and dismissed the fault by assuming it was too late in his life to change. He believed in his art.

With age, Sam seemed even more attracted to the stark beauty of lost and abandoned cemeteries in remote places. Time and nature had molded their remains into nature's canvas with all the colors of an artist's palette. Spring and summer flowers poking above the velvety moss at the base of weathered monuments promised new beginnings for the memories of those abandoned by humanity and reclaimed by nature. Beneath the ageless soil were the remains of a life once lived with all the hopes and dreams that each held while alive. Sam was partial to the epitaphs, those eroded messages to those who remained. Mostly, he liked imagining who they were, their personalities and whether they realized their dreams. He preferred the black–and–white medium that his publisher routinely rejected. Perhaps a book of both; a book that depicted the wonder of it all, life and death with every sight, sound, and smell of nature coming together in a single image. The reader would see what he saw and be overwhelmed by the fear they would be stricken blind if they put the book down. He could hear the rhythmic clicks of the camera's shutter opening and closing as if it was a respirator breathing life into the corpses beneath him. He liked spring and the hope it promised. There would be no images of snow-covered limbs and ice clogged creeks under a gray, frozen sky, the death certificates issued by an orbiting Earth. This book would redeem him in the eyes of a fickle public who had abandoned him for the tripe their phones regurgitated nonstop like a conveyor of trinkets offered to a child.

Sam had gone back only once to the cafe. It was many years later in the spring, when life had another chance. The morning air was filled with the calls of meadowlarks, the prairie bursting with new life and the pleasant smells of sage and prairie grasses. The sun's warmth felt good on the back of his neck. Life was resilient. Structures were not. Abandoned, the dilapidated structure demanded to be photographed.

The interior was gone, robbed by those who needed a table or chair. Even the booths had been ripped from the wall, along with the table-mounted jukeboxes below the broken picture window. The outlines of where the stools once sat erect on chrome pedicels below the counter were still visible. Shards of broken dishes littered the floor, hard white fragments scattered among rodent droppings. Birds had built nests in the spaces that had once held cups and saucers. A wasp climbed the wall next to the door. The broad brushstrokes that had once declared *OPEN* and *EAT HERE* were reduced to diamond-like glitter that covered the black-and-white, scuffed linoleum squares. A bulbous tan spider waited next to its orb. Bullet holes had left webs in the glass that remained. Vandals with the same intent as their ancestors, who had sacked much of Europe centuries before, reinforced the destructive and violent nature of man.

Sam saw a gathering of people brought together by chance to the Lost and Found Cafe, the name he gave to the nameless restaurant that now lay in ruin. Each soul had a story of loss; each had a story of discovery. He believed that memories were unremitting invisible clouds, sentimental keepsakes that swirled with chances in a life of chances. It all seemed so real. It all seemed so lost. Time was displaced by visions and sounds.

The photos would show what remained and more importantly what had been forgotten. He discovered that looking through the lens did not capture the human element, the fragments of souls that had dreamed of new beginnings and how lonely and desperate people can become. A portion of their lives was still there, haunting the dark recesses of the desolate structure while waiting to be released from cafe purgatory.

Unexpectedly, a pall of nostalgia spread over him with sadness. Sam lowered his camera. He left without taking a single photo.

He saw each of them clearly, heard their voices, and saw their futures. He remembered.

The End

ACKNOWLEDGMENTS

Many authors claim that writing is a lonely business. I have not found that to be the case. Getting a book out the door to the reading public is a team effort that requires a great deal of patience, creativity, skill, and hard work by a group of people whose names are not on the cover. These are the individuals behind the scenes who make it happen. I owe each of them my profound thanks for their guidance and assistance in bringing this book to fruition.

Rachel Girt, as always, knows the complexity of the communication field. She reads my drafts and tells me what the readers will see and think. I appreciate that more than she will ever know. As the book is released, Rachel goes to work getting the word out to the public through various means and tools, tasks that demand an experienced marketing and public relations expert. She is the best.

Yes, people often judge a book by its cover. Tana Stith knows that, and she never disappoints. She too reads the book then magically shows me what was in my mind's eye. She pays attention to details in the book's narrative, determines what is important, then puts it all together in covers, front and back, that say: "Choose me." Her interiors allow the reader to enjoy the comforts of a well-designed book. She is an artist.

New to our team, Allister Thompson brings years of editing experience to our crew. It's a tough job that demands skills most writers don't have. He gracefully pointed out my many assaults on the conventions of the English language and to the 18th edition of the *Chicago Manual of Style.* He is a pleasure to work with. Welcome aboard, Allister.

Vicki Forwood and Debbie O'Sullivan, both avid readers, agreed to review a first draft. Their suggestions and encouraging comments were most helpful. Writers should never underestimate the value of readers. They are the customers. Thank you.

A supportive family is important too. Daughters Tiffany, Melissa, and Amanda are always supportive and encourage me to keep writing. A father couldn't ask for better children. I am proud of them, their families, and their many accomplishments.

My loving wife, Margaret, is the omniscient overseer of the entire process. As first reader, she's my most important critic, most enthusiastic fan, and most relentless supporter. She never stops working on my behalf. My books would not happen without her.

Finally, I'd like to thank the fictitious characters of my novels. It is unlikely that most people would understand how these characters become imaginary members of my family. Writers are taught to become the person they are writing about. These alter egos can be both fun and disturbing. Many years of writing Sam Dawson mysteries have ingrained the personalities of key people (characters) in my mind. I think about them. I worry about them. When I stop writing, I will miss them. Thanks for the memories, Sam and Sidney.

ABOUT THE AUTHOR

STEVEN W. HORN is the author of the award-winning Sam Dawson mysteries. An Iowa native and decorated Vietnam veteran, Horn earned his doctorate in Colorado. After high-ranking careers in both Colorado and Wyoming, he turned to full-time fiction writing, drawing upon his diverse educational and career experiences in crafting his stories. Horn's critically acclaimed debut novel was *Another Man's Life*. *Lost & Found Cafe: A Sam Dawson Mystery* is Horn's sixth book in the mystery series. He lives in Wyoming.

www.ingramcontent.com/pod-product-compliance
Lightning Source LLC
Chambersburg PA
CBHW020951030726
47496CB00005B/1456